"Oh, did you get a haircut?"

"I wanted to look as nice as I could for you."

Last Round Arthurs

Saint Arthur & the Red Girl Knight

2

EMMA MICHELLE

A girl who learned how to fight from Rintarou before he continued to wander the world. She has a tiny crush on him, which is why she wants him to side with her for the King Arthur Succession Battle, spurring her to challenge Luna to a little contest.

"There is someone interfering with this sacred battle for succession at the moment."

VIVIAN

The head of the Dame du Lac, the collective that manages the King Arthur Succession Battle. She acts as Luna's point of contact with the organization and was the one who gave an Excalibur to the young Luna.

CONTENTS

SAINT ARTHUR
&
THE RED GIRL KNIGHT

2

Taro Hitsuji

ILLUSTRATION BY
Kiyotaka Haimura

YEN
ON

NEW YORK

LAST ROUND Arthurs

SAINT ARTHUR & THE RED GIRL KNIGHT

Taro Hitsuji   VOLUME 2

Translation by Jan Cash
Cover art by Kiyotaka Haimura

This book is a work of fiction. Names, characters, places, and incidents are the product of the author's imagination or are used fictitiously. Any resemblance to actual events, locales, or persons, living or dead, is coincidental.

LAST ROUND • ARTHURS Vol. 2 SEIJOARTHUR TO AKA NO YOUJOKISHI
©Taro Hitsuji, Kiyotaka Haimura 2018
First published in Japan in 2018 by KADOKAWA CORPORATION, Tokyo.
English translation rights arranged with KADOKAWA CORPORATION, Tokyo through
TUTTLE-MORI AGENCY, INC., Tokyo.

English translation © 2020 by Yen Press, LLC

Yen On
150 West 30th Street, 19th Floor
New York, NY 10001

Visit us at yenpress.com
facebook.com/yenpress
twitter.com/yenpress
yenpress.tumblr.com
instagram.com/yenpress

First Yen On Edition: June 2020

Yen On is an imprint of Yen Press, LLC.
The Yen On name and logo are trademarks of Yen Press, LLC.

The publisher is not responsible for websites (or their content) that are not owned by the publisher.

Library of Congress Cataloging-in-Publication Data
Names: Hitsuji, Taro, author. | Haimura, Kiyotaka, 1973– illustrator. | Cash, Jan Mitsuko, translator.
Haimura, Kiyotaka, 1973– cover artist.
Title: Last Round Arthurs / Taro Hitsuji ; illustration by Kiyotaka Haimura ; translation by Jan Cash ;
cover art by Kiyotaka Haimura.
Description: First Yen On edition. | New York, NY : Yen On, 2019. | Series: Last Round Arthurs
Identifiers: LCCN 2019015603 | ISBN 9781975357504 (v 1 : pbk.) | ISBN 9781975399276 (v 2 : pbk.)
Subjects: CYAC: Gifted children—Fiction. | Contests—Fiction. | Inheritance and succession—Fiction. |
Arthur, King—Fiction.
Classification: LCC PZ7.1.H59 Sc 2019 | DDC [Fic]—dc23
LC record available at https://lccn.loc.gov/2019015603

ISBNs: 978-1-9753-9927-6 (paperback)
978-1-9753-1288-6 (ebook)

10 9 8 7 6 5 4 3 2 1

LSC-C

Printed in the United States of America

Over there is yesterday in all its radiance. Here is today,
     faded and colorless.
And tomorrow is bound in ashes.

We reached the dismal end of the play, of our dreams.
I watched it as the cold wind blew.

Yes, he was there among the Knights of the Round Table.
Together with the one they called strong, noble—the once
     and future king.

Be that as it may, their swords etched him into stone,
     disappearing into sand and verse.
Like a dream at dusk, like a mirage of a fleeting night.

I watched everything as I slumbered.
Watched as the cold wind blew.

John Sheep
FROM *LAST ROUND ARTHUR*

On the Prowl in the Dark

New Avalon. A large artificial island off the coast of Japan.

On top of it was the up-and-coming international city of Avalonia—and there dwelled darkness.

There was another world that existed beyond the imaginations of those living ordinary lives mired in common sense.

She stood at the underbelly of that world, unknown to the residents of the bustling metropolis. It was the dark maelstrom of humanity's chaos that doggedly gnawed away at any worldly values.

"*Now, come—,*" she called out in the dead of night in an archaic Celtic language.

Looking up, she could see the outstretched skyscrapers trying to touch the sky and the deep valley between them.

Her plea echoed, rippling through the air, traveling to the far corners of the world to summon change.

"*Now, come. Thou who were born from fear, who arose from darkness, who art the subterfuge and taboo—,*" she continued, spinning her magical words together, extolling them.

This spell had been orally passed down among old Celtic druids, known as the Secret Ceremony of the Oak Tree. The source of the ceremony—the *Sefirot*—were *Keter, Chokhmah, Binah, Chesed, Gevurah, Tiferet, Netzach, Hod, Yesod,* and *Malkuth,* making ten *sefira* in total. According to esoteric Indian Buddhist yoga, they were spiritual points of the human body called chakras.

The *sefira* of the girl wielding an oak cane circulated mana, which sublimated into an aura that rose from her body. It responded to the magical words to form a circle in the shape of a triquetrum on the concrete ground.

"Ye who enlighten the ignorance of human will and drive it away into the abyss of consciousness, I command you. With the fear of the feebleminded humans who close themselves off to dreams, open thy maw of horror—"

As the magic circle formed, a black wind whipped around the hem of the black robe covering the girl from head to toe.

"Now—"

When it came time, she prodded the magic circle with her cane, and the space split open as though an enormous claw had been dragged across it. A concentrated shadow of darkness seeped out from that dark void.

That was a Rift. She had made an opening in the world.

The shadows stirred, as if a living organism, broadening the Rift before the shadows tore into shreds and small scraps.

The diminutive shadows dispersed into the streets like newly born spiders...and eventually, they disappeared into the darkness of the night.

"Hmm... Well, I guess this is all I can muster for now."

The girl grinned, chuckling quietly—like a mischievous child or even a maiden yearning for her special someone.

There was a faint purity to her, though she had evoked a strangeness that was almost putrid.

She continued snickering in the darkness. "Ha-ha, the King

Arthur Succession Battle? The Dame du Lac? ...The hell with them. I hope it's all destroyed: from that abominable Uther's bloodline to the trifling intentions of my older sisters. I hope everyone—absolutely everyone—meets their end! Now! Come dance for me, my pitiful performers! Dance on this stage of deceit, brimming with empty pageantry. I am your conductor. Everything is wrapped around my little finger. Heh-heh-heh... Ah-ha-ah-ha-ha-ha-ha-ha...!"

The girl continued to cackle to herself in the abyssal darkness unfathomable to humankind or consciousness.

Though it was well known only to a select few, her name was Tsugumi Mimori—also known as Morgan le Fay.

There, in the darkness of the international city of Avalonia, unbeknownst to the humans, the wicked witch had made her first move.

CHAPTER 1

An Ode to Scumbags

There was a conflict called the King Arthur Succession Battle. The all-out battle occurred among eleven candidates with the blood of the former hero King Arthur. It was a magical ceremony to determine who among the candidates would be the true King to rule the world.

It involved the half-fey collective—those who taught and guided King Arthur in the legendary era—called the Dame de Lac. Living quietly in the shadows of modern scientific society, those women arranged for the battle with a certain goal in mind. They manipulated governments abroad and prominent businesses from behind the scenes to create the stage—the artificial island of New Avalon—off the coast of Japan. This was where the conditions for the ley lines were the most suitable.

"The one to become King Arthur will have sovereign authority, military forces, wealth, and vassals—and the ability to indisputably rule the world in its entirety. They will receive absolute and awful power."

That legend had been passed on from generation to generation among the families of the eleven candidates for King Arthur.

The invitation from the Dame du Lac summoned the candidates to gradually gather at New Avalon Island in the present day.

And thus, fights between the candidates were already cropping up all over the artificial island.

"Let's see... We've smacked down Kujou, who was probably the strongest King in the succession battle."

The scene was the international city of Avalonia, which had been built on top of the island of New Avalon.

They were in Area Three of the island, in a deserted hallway of the main school building at Camelot International.

A fearless grin had begun creeping over Rintarou Magami's face as he spoke to himself.

He was the reincarnation of Merlin—a peerless soldier and the strongest wizard of the ancient era. He was a weirdo fighting on Luna's side as she participated in the King Arthur Succession Battle.

Several days had already passed since their battle against Souma Gloria Kujou, the King who commanded the strongest Jack, Sir Lancelot. Though they had been wounded and exhausted, they had healed to the point that they could make their next move... That was what Rintarou had planned.

But if I'm being perfectly honest...that wasn't exactly a complete victory when I'm thinking about it now...

For example, he had no idea who had used magic to control the students of the school to attack them. He had no idea who had created the parallel world of Camlann Hill to serve as their decisive battlefield.

Rintarou recalled the inexplicable events and situations that were unlikely to be the work of Kujou, who seemed magically illiterate... but thinking about it wouldn't do them any good now.

"Well, what should we do next? …Right. First, we'll prepare for the battle, which is going to get more intense going forward. There's something important we'll need to deal with first."

"Yeah. That's exactly what I was thinking, too," agreed the girl walking gallantly next to Rintarou with her brilliant-golden hair and blue eyes. She nodded.

She could almost make those around her gasp in awe at her beauty, which was in full bloom. This was Luna Artur—the King who commanded Rintarou as her vassal.

"We definitely need one of those, Rintarou!"

"Uh-huh. Yeah." Rintarou let his face soften as he responded.

In fact, this whole exchange was somewhat embarrassing for him. Until this point in time, he couldn't really say he'd had a single friend.

"Right—one of those… A base of operations while we're fighting!"

"Right—one of those! A campaign!"

But the two of them were fundamentally out of sync. Basically, everything they did together would go awry.

"That's right! It's almost time for the election for the next student president! In order to cement and sustain my authority as student president, I need to get to work sooner rather than later! Rintarou! Let's get started! We're going to scour into every personal detail of the opposing candidates' lives and make up some scandals to launch a massive smear campaign! Ah-ha-ha-ha-ha-ha-ha-ha-ha-haaaaa!"

Luna seemed incredibly gleeful and absolutely wicked as she yanked on Rintarou's hand and tried to dash away.

"That's not it!"

"AAAAAAAAAAH?!"

Rintarou had jerked his hand back from Luna and flipped around, pulling Luna on his back to throw her over.

"Are you an idiot? We're in the middle of a war! We've got no time to worry about that!"

"Hey! What's with that apathetic attitude?! I'm the king of the school! How can I focus on the candidate battle when I'm all worked up and anxious that I might lose my throne?!"

"UUUUUUGH, SERIOUSLY?! How in the world did I end up as your vassal?!"

"I am so sorry...for causing you hardship, Rintarou," murmured Sir Kay in her school uniform, trying to sympathize with Rintarou, who was howling and practically pulling out his hair.

She was Luna's Jack. Sir Kay was a bona fide knight of the famous Round Table who had been summoned by Luna, a King.

"But in the end," she continued, "you're the only person able to rein in Luna. I'm counting on you."

"And I'm just about to snap! Dammit!" Rintarou barked, then returned to his senses, turning to Luna. "Listen up, Luna! What we need is a base of operations where we can breathe easy and get ready for the battle! We've got no idea when a new King will try to fight with us... You have to understand the gravity of the situation! Hey, Luna! Where are you sleeping right now?"

"Um...the girls' dorm at Camelot International. Why?"

"You're so naive. And what's your plan if the next King is like Kujou, actively killing other Kings? What if they're a coldhearted, indiscriminate brute? What're you gonna do if they try to attack you while you're sleeping at night?"

"!" Luna finally understood what Rintarou was trying to say, opening her eyes wide and going silent.

"The succession battle happens at night. That's basically what the rules say. Even going to school is stupid...but I won't go so far as to tell you not to go. That said, you've got to at least sleep somewhere else at night. I don't really care if some stranger gets caught up in a fight and croaks, but...it bothers you, doesn't it?"

"...You're right. Every person at this school is my vassal! As their king, I can't bring harm to my precious subjects!"

As he stared blankly back at Luna and observed her natural-born cocksureness, Rintarou continued. "Okay, fine. Basically, we need a base where you can sleep safely...for the sake of those around you and us, too. We need to be working in sync whether it's night or day."

"In other words...you're inviting me to move in with you? Wooow! Bold move, Rintarou!"

"That's not what I'm doing! What the—?! No, wait... I guess you're right?! Well, whatever!"

Until that point in his life, he had been cynical, looking down on everything in the world with disdain and twisting all sorts of people around his finger...but he just couldn't take the lead over Luna—no matter what he did.

"After school today, we're going to find that base by going to a real estate agent. Got it?"

"Well, you can say that, but how're we going to get the money to buy it? Like, wouldn't it be really expensive? Of course, I've been disowned by the Artur family, so it's not like my parents will throw a penny my way."

"...Huh? What the hell did you do?"

"Nothing really. I just got mad at my dad and beat him up, chewed him out, and publicly humiliated him."

I really picked the wrong person to serve..., Rintarou thought with a straight face.

"Well, putting that aside... I'm a King... Where should I set up my castle...? Now that I'm thinking about it, this is a very important question... But we've got a money problem...," Luna muttered to herself, becoming pensive and turning serious. "Hmm. Guess we've got to get some plunder? Like from a bank? The government's finances are rightfully the King's..."

"Hey, stop that, you idiot," Rintarou snapped. He groaned and looked at Luna reproachfully before pulling something out from his breast pocket and tossing it over to her.

It was a bank deposit book. It was from the Lynette Bank in England, which was a secret establishment that gave large loans to enterprises from various countries in the international city.

"There. You can have that. It'll be our war chest for now."

"Whaaaaaaat?! What *is* this?! The number of zeros on here is making me see double!" Luna's eyes opened wide when she saw the statement in the bankbook.

"Ah! Wah! ...Gah. I couldn't even save this sum of money after a lifetime of working...!" yelped Sir Kay, who had been quietly watching over Rintarou and Luna's exchange, when she had peeked at the bankbook over Luna's shoulder. She eyed the numbers in envy and yearning.

"Hey, Rintarou...are your parents millionaires or something?"

"Don't be ridiculous. I come from a normal middle-class home."

"This isn't money that a student from a normal middle-class home would have, though."

"Did I ever tell you about my story before I came here...? I was supposed to be at school on mainland Japan, but I skipped out for a year and went wandering around the world. During that time, I used my cell phone to work the foreign exchange and saved up in my spare time," Rintarou said. Though the idea was preposterous, he acted as if it were nothing.

"In this age, you can press a couple of buttons and earn money. It's like a bad video game... The world's in easy mode."

The knowledge and wisdom Rintarou had inherited from his past life as Merlin, the oldest and greatest wizard in the world, was nothing to scoff at. Those skills were like cheat codes that made the whole world easy for him—and even made living feel boring.

For Rintarou, this stunt was a piece of cake.

"Well, I want to make sure we get a base in a good location with that money, but…I just got to this island, so I don't know what's around…"

Ah, well… What to do…? Rintarou was just thinking.

"I got it! In that case, leave it to me, Rintarou!" Luna thrust out her chest and declared to him, "I know a place that would be great for what we have in mind! There's a perfect piece of property I've had my eye on! Will you put your trust in me to secure it?!"

Luna's face was so full of self-confidence that it practically radiated. It stirred old memories in Rintarou's psyche.

In a former time, when he had been Merlin—arrogant and heretical—he had dedicated his life to one, and only one, King. And the face of King Arthur had superimposed itself over Luna's face.

"Oh? In that case, I guess I will." When Rintarou saw the traces of Arthur in Luna, he beamed.

"Yeah! You can count on me!"

Looks like I've got a weak spot for that face…, Rintarou thought. He should have been wrapping the little girl—unfamiliar with the ways of the world—around his little finger, but instead, she was having her way with him. This would have been unthinkable to him in the past, but he wasn't that unhappy about it. Had the past Merlin also been like that?

"Ha, all right then. That was just easy money that I prepped for the succession battle anyway. You can use it how you want. How about you show me what you got?"

"Yes, living up to the expectations of my subjects is just another one of my duties as King! Once I've made up my mind, I'll make it happen right away!"

"Uh! Hey?!"

"Luna?! Where do you think you're going?!"

But Rintarou's and Sir Kay's voices just rolled off her back.

Luna resolutely dashed off on her own through the hall.

"Ha-ha! When you think of a base, *this* is it! I've had my eye on it for a while! Nothing else would do!"

Luna ran through the hall as fast as the wind and went down the stairs as though she were flying, heading to the front entrance of the school.

"Well, before, I thought there was no way I could possibly get it while I was a student! But now—"

Luna hadn't even noticed she had left the others behind in her excitement. She was full of dreams as she rushed through the exit and tried to leave—when it happened.

"AHHH?!" Luna ran into someone on their way into the school through the entrance.

The two of them were thrown back in opposite directions and fell to their butts.

"Ow—ow, ow, ow! Wait—sorry! Are you okay?!" Luna had gotten up a second sooner and offered a hand to the person on the ground.

"...Oh."

Luna and another high school girl locked eyes. In a school uniform, the girl had a physique that was all around daintier and more petite than Luna's. Based on the color of the girl's badge on her lapel, she was a year younger...which would make her a first-year.

Her platinum blonde hair was plaited. Her verdure eyes seemed somewhat lacking in self-confidence.

It wasn't uncommon for students from Europe to attend school at Camelot International.

When Luna peered into her face, she could see the girl was abnormally beautiful... Well, at least, she had the potential to be beautiful, if her face wasn't half covered by her frumpy over-grown bangs, which left Luna unsure. Though it was typical for girls their age to put on a little makeup, dab on some perfume, and accessorize, this girl was obviously lacking in any on-trend items whatsoever.

To express her appearance in one word... *Plain*.

None of the male students passing by looked at the girl or even acknowledged her presence. Even though they should have zeroed in on a girl—*any* girl—the young boys in puberty didn't even give her a second thought.

Her unrefined state made her seem like a country bumpkin who had come into the city from another locale.

"I'm...sorry, too. Please accept my apology."

She took Luna's hand, appearing grateful and embarrassed, and got to her feet. In apparent sincerity, she bowed her head and tried to leave right away.

"Hey, are you a transfer?" Luna asked the girl, going off of pure instinct.

"What? I am, but...how did you know?"

"Well, uh, I know the names and faces of every student at this school."

"...Excuse me?" She blinked back in surprise. Luna had said the absurd with nonchalance, after all.

Luna went rapid-fire on her. "I'm Luna Artur! I'm the student president of this school! In other words, I'm the king of the school! What's your name?!"

"What?! You're...Luna...Artur?"

For a moment, the girl reacted strangely to Luna's introduction...

"Uh, um...well...I'm Emma...Emma Michelle..."

But she was pushed by Luna's momentum and introduced herself as well.

"Emma? Are you French, by any chance? Well, it doesn't matter! Hey, Emma, now that you're a student at this school, you're, like, basically one of my vassals! You get it, right?!"

Fat chance. Of course not. Emma blinked back in a daze.

"If you're in any trouble, don't hesitate to come to me! After all, it's the way of the world for a vassal to revere a king, but a king is only a true king if she protects her subjects, you know?!"

"R-right... Um, I don't really understand, but thank you very much... I'm sure we'll get to know each other, Luna..."

Emma gave her a flighty bow and scurried into the school.

"Heh. I keep accumulating more subjects without even lifting a finger... I'm, like, so fit to be King, it's scary." Luna planted her hands on her hip and muttered praise to herself.

"Geez...! What are you doing here? Don't run off on your own."

"Luna! You know better than that! You can't go off on your own!"

Rintarou and Sir Kay had finally managed to find her after searching for her high and low.

"...What's up with you, Luna? You're in one hell of a good mood."

"Nothing! Anyway, we've got to get going! We're going to procure our base by the end of today!"

"All right, all right."

They had transitioned right into their standard routine.

Luna pulled on Rintarou's hand and speed-walked away.

"Heh. Leave the rest to me! You guys go rest at that Skybucks or something!"

With those parting words to Rintarou and Sir Kay, Luna hurtled toward a certain real estate office.

Guess it's time to observe her skills. Well, she's not gonna be able to rent out a nice place, even with all that money. I mean, she's just a little high schooler… It'll be a good experience for her to get a taste of the real world.

In a corner of the Skybucks, Rintarou sipped his coffee with Sir Kay, selling Luna short and wondering how long it would take for her to come back with her tail between her legs—

"…"

In front of Rintarou—who was currently boggled out of his mind—was a *gigantic Western mansion complete with its own garden.*

They were on the peak of an eastern hill in Area Three. To the east, he could see the shore and sprawling ocean that faced the cliff and, to the west, the gentle slopes that housed an old-fashioned expanse of properties.

It was a slight distance from Camelot International, but if they used the bus or electric trolley, the trek to school was no problem. On top of everything, the neighboring properties were far away, which was also a plus. Even if they had a real dynamic fight, it seemed they would be able to keep the damage around them to a minimum.

"Nice! Grand enough to be fit for a King's castle!" Luna stood right in the middle of the front garden, looking up at the Western mansion in excitement.

"Indeed, Luna. If I were to be more materialistic, I would say a grand castle as big as Camelot is befitting of you, but compared to our dorms…this is a world of difference! I cannot ask for anything more!" Sir Kay was overcome with emotion, and tears of gratitude gathered at the corners of her eyes.

Once again, Rintarou gazed up at the mansion.

It really was a magnificent manor. Though it was on the smaller side, the estate had been built in the style of English baroque and beheld the beauty of an aristocrat's country home.

"What do you think? Isn't it amazing, Rintarou?! I mean, this piece of property was so great that the real estate office wasn't even willing to show it to me! I had to work so hard to get it! And that is a true testimony of the King who you serve!" Luna was basically radiating self-confidence, sticking out her chest in pride. Her entire body practically begged Rintarou to praise her.

"...Yeah, it is a great place," Rintarou muttered. "I haven't got anything to complain about battle-wise. In terms of location, it'll be easy to protect. It's good as far as ley lines, so it'll be easy to set it up magically... To be honest, I haven't got anything bad to say about it as a base."

"Uh-huh! Right?!"

"But..." Rintarou was shaking, gripping the deposit bankbook.

He looked down at it...perfectly whittled down to a zero-yen statement.

"Are you an idioooot?! What kind of person *buys* a place this expensiiiiive?!"

"Aaaaah?! YOW! OW-OW-OW-OW!"

Rintarou had grappled with Luna and put her in a cobra twist.

As her rib cage and arm creaked in pain, Luna started screaming as tears formed in her eyes.

"I had fifty million yen in there! Fifty *frigging* million! How did you drain it all?! And perfectly down to zero without a single cent left to spare! I mean, a normal person would *rent* a place like this! Why'd you *buy* a whole house?! Are you an idiot?! Hey! Answer me, my King!"

"Whaaat?! But you said I could use it the way I wanted!"

"There are limits, restrictions, terms and conditions!"

Blat! Luna sprung out from between Rintarou's joints.

"Wait—wait a sec! Do you think you're the only one with an emptied wallet?"

"...Aren't I?"

"Of course not! I'm sure you know that subjects' possessions are the King's, and the King's possessions are the King's! But it is my kingly duty to share the troubles of her subjects, too! Look!"

With a smarmy grin, Luna tugged something out of her pocket.

That was her bankbook, marvelously at a balance of zero.

"Ha-ha, in order to buy this house, I took out my four hundred thousand in savings, too."

"Are you an imbeciiiiiile?!" Rintarou pincered Luna's head between his hands and violently swung her like a metronome.

"What do you think you're gonna do without a single cent to your name?! You've put your livelihood in jeopardy even before the succession battle has finished! And stop smiling! All you've done is contribute chump change to cover taxes!"

"I'm sorry! I'm sorry-sorry-sorry! But, you're, like, a miracle worker, Rintarou! I mean, you did that whole 'foreign exchange' thing, didn't you? Can't you just save up again?!"

"Fine! I'm sorry, okay? I may have exaggerated a little! It's not every day that you get a chance to rake in money! And you need seed money to make even more! I'm *so* sorry for being a useless vassal!"

After giving Luna's head a good rattle, Rintarou threw her aside and grabbed the deed to the mansion, stood up, and started to leave.

"Well, anyway, we need to cool our heads, you dunce! We're reselling this place!"

"Whaaaaaat?! No! Nooo! No! No!" Luna latched onto Rintarou's feet.

As Rintarou walked, he dragged Luna behind him.

"I want this house! I wanna live here! I don't want another one!" Luna threw a childish tantrum.

Rintarou sighed. "Complaining isn't going to get you anywhere! What are we going to do without any cash?"

He kept ignoring her and trudged forward.

"Hmph! You big meanie! If that's how it's going to be, then I've got my own bright idea!"

"Yeah? Tell me, right now! I'll have you know that half-assed threats won't—"

"I'll step down from the King Arthur Succession Battle!"

"Not that! I'm begging youuu!" All Rintarou could do was cry.

"Heh-heh-heh… I remember, Rintarou…that you told me 'I'll make sure you win' and 'Anyone with me as their ally is basically the victor.' How can you let things end after you're the one who told me these cringey things? …Would your pride let you walk away? Mwa-ha-ha-ha!"

"You're…the worst…!"

She was taking advantage of him… Well, not exactly.

The present Rintarou wanted to see Luna win the succession battle. At first, he had wanted to use Luna for his own amusement until he was done with her, but now he really did want to see Luna become the true King Arthur.

Rintarou wasn't a match for Luna thanks to his desire to see her become King, even though he was arrogant, insolent, unparalleled in his mercilessness as he roamed the lands, and generally acknowledged to be a heretic.

"Ha-ha! Are you still going to sell back this mansion, Rintarou?! If you can, I'd like to see you try! Ah-ha-ha-ha-ha!"

"Argh..."

"Uh...Lunaaa... You're starting to seem more and more like Arthur every day..."

Rintarou lifted both his arms as though he had given up, and Sir Kay breathed a sigh as tears mixed into her eyes.

That was how they found their base in one day, defying all expectations.

With a nauseating grin, Luna christened the mansion as Logres Manor. Which was incredibly embarrassing and cringey.

It would be Luna's domain during the war.

Incidentally, the everyday expenses were made up later by Sir Kay, who began working at a place with some nonsensical name: *P-Please Just Kill Me! The Lady Knight Café.*

Luna was blissfully unaware of the tears that Sir Kay spilled in secret.

"But whew! I guess this place is impressive..." Rintarou had thrown himself down on a sofa in the living room of Logres Manor, grumbling to himself.

In that living room was a somewhat dated television that had been set up when they got there.

Rintarou held the remote as he absentmindedly watched the news.

"*Next up on the news, we cover a recent burglary incident at the Monstre headquarters. The company is owned by the large, multinational corporation.*

"*According to the newest report from the city police, the burglar destroyed the building with what appeared to be a pair of swords, one red and one white. Then, the man managed to steal a precious antique sword in the safekeeping of the company.*

"*For unknown reasons, the burglar was not caught on surveil-*

lance cameras. In an abrupt scuffle with the culprit, members of the company's staff and private security were injured, but luckily, there were no casualties.

"Mr. Spencer Warwick of Monstre Corp. has been quoted with the following bizarre testimony.

"'That boy was a monster. He made copies of himself, unleashing fire and beams from his hands. Our company troops were useless against him.'

"The city police are fast-tracking their investigation, searching for clues about the culprit and Mr. Warwick's mental state. Furthermore, in the past, Monstre Corp. has been involved in illegal operations and illicit smuggling, suspected of underhanded business deals, and—"

Click.

"Aaaaah..." Rintarou flipped the television off after watching the news for a while. He must have gotten fed up, tossing aside the remote as he looked up at the chandelier on the ceiling and yawned.

The Logres Manor that Luna had acquired was a two-story establishment. The first floor had an entrance hall, a living room, a salon, a drawing room, a dining room, a kitchen, a bathroom, and a laundry room. It had both the communal living spaces and functional spaces.

The second floor had recreational areas—including a lounge and a playroom—and living spaces for the inhabitants... They had a number of individual rooms and a somewhat out-of-place room that appeared to be a fully equipped office.

"On top of that, there's even a wine cellar in the basement. It leaves nothing to be desired, huh." Bored, Rintarou left the living room and investigated the mansion.

Naturally, it had lights, gas, and water. But it also had several furniture fixtures and electrical appliances that had been left behind in addition to the television in the living room. They had a fridge in the kitchen, along with a microwave, and the washing machine for the laundry room. Though the appliances were older models, they were all there. There were even two computers set up in the second-floor office. Even though they were two or three generations past their prime, it was obvious the computers were functional, and on top of that, they had already been connected to the Internet.

And even the underground cellar was stocked—not just with wine, but with alcohol preserved from all time periods and all reaches of the world. There was even sake from famous brands that would have made collectors water at the mouth if they set them up for auction.

"This place is in a convenient location with a big lot of land. And it's really high class... On top of that, it has the option to be completely furnished...which is a little over-the-top. This place is obviously worth more than fifty million yen. I mean, there has to be another decimal missing in the price tag. I bet it could go for five *hundred* million."

Based on this guesstimate, he could piece together that this mansion had previously been the aristocratic estate of some real billionaire.

"How did...Luna drop fifty million to get this place?"

On top of that, it was perfect for them to use as a military base in the succession battle. When he saw the favorable conditions of this mansion, he just couldn't bring himself to be angry at Luna—even if he wanted her to incur his wrath.

"What is this? It feels like someone had been living here until recently... But wasn't this an empty house?"

There was one thing that still troubled him.

"Something about this place...makes me think that the original resident...went up and missing one day..." Rintarou spoke his doubts as he investigated the mansion and walked along the carpeted second-floor hallway...

On a whim, he opened the door of the room next to him when he saw it.

Creak... The oak door groaned as it opened up to a library.

All four walls were crammed with bookshelves and lined with expensive-looking foreign tomes.

In the back of the room, there was a mahogany desk on standby that looked like it had belonged to the previous owner of the mansion.

And...in the center of the library's floor were the traces of a faint chalk line.

"......" Rintarou went silent. He had frozen in place.

The white line seemed to be tracing around something—something that had once been contained inside it—and it appeared to be in the shape of a *human body.*

"But, Miss Luna... Are you sure that you're fine with this house? We have explained this to you several times, but the previous owner of the house had it in their family for generations..."

All of a sudden, Rintarou recalled...when the real estate agent had brought them over to the mansion in a car, scowling strangely with those disquieting words.

"...Aaaaand I'm gonna pretend I didn't see that."

Clunk... Rintarou gently closed the library door.

"A-anyway! Th-this isn't bad for a base of operations! Right?!"

Rintarou tried to convince himself, quickly putting the library behind him. "Trying to maintain this whole place will be hard, but... Well, I guess we could summon a broonie later."

A broonie was a residential fairy of Scottish lore that could sneakily clean up a house while everyone was fast asleep. They were an incredibly useful and admirable fey to have around.

"Oh, and order an exorcism—stat! Sounds like a plan!"

There were the two others who were utterly unaware of Rintarou's worries...

"Here, Sir Kay! Make sure you keep a firm hold on that end! And *that's* a royal order!"

"Eep?! Wait! I can't! That's impossible—AAAH?!"

He could hear Luna and Sir Kay making a commotion far off in the mansion.

Luna had taken up base in the biggest and best room. She was in the middle of a giant remodeling job.

Only one more day remained until the weekend, so they would have a break from school. They had tons of time to settle in.

I wonder which room I should take...? Well, definitely the one farthest from the library... Rintarou was deep in thought.

Ding-dong. The sound of the doorbell echoed throughout the mansion.

"...A visitor? Who the hell could that be...?" Rintarou headed to the entrance hall, feeling a bit peeved.

He had just put up a defense barrier around the plot of land, and it hadn't reacted to any hostility, so it didn't seem they had enemies nearby...

Ding-dong. Ding-dong. Ding-dong-ding-dong-ding-don—

"Ugh! Stop! That's so annoying! Stop ringing it! Okay! Okay! I'm coming to open it now! Dammit!"

He clucked his tongue at the dismal visitor and roughly opened the door.

"Oh-ho-ho-ho! Hope we're not intruding!"

"Heh. We meet again, Rintarou Magami!"

He recognized the two faces. They were lugging around unsophisticated bundles wrapped in cloth.

The visitors were a girl about Luna's age with silver hair in pigtails and a muscular blond man: Felicia Ferald and Sir Gawain, a knight of the Round Table. Like Luna, they were a King and her Jack aiming for the seat of King Arthur in the succession battle.

"Ha-ho! This house isn't too shabby! For the Artur family. I mean, you lack the prestige of the Ferald family, but I'll praise it as a worthy abode!"

"Hmph. Just thinking of my liege staying in this seedy place... Well, it doesn't matter. Rintarou Magami, prepare the most luxurious guest room in this estate! Got that?!"

Click. Rintarou quietly closed the door and locked it...firmly.

"Hey! Wait?! Pleeeease open the door!"

"Wh-why would you close the door on us?! Let us in, Rintarou Magamiiiiii!"

BAM-BAM-BAM-BAM-BAM!

DING-DONG-DING-DONG-DING-DONG-DING-DONG!

"You're *such* a pain in the ass!"

When Rintarou slammed open the front door again, he thrust his left hand out and shot a magical *Fireball* at them.

Fiery spitballs rained down at Felicia's and Sir Gawain's feet and enveloped them in raging flames.

"AH! GAAAH?!"

The impact rocketed both of them into the air.

"You two have a lot of nerve walking up here in the first place!

Even with a truce and alliance, we're still enemies!" Rintarou threatened, drawing his swords. "Oh, I see. You wanna break the alliance and settle this early?! Fine by me! Try me! I can more than handle you nobodies all by myself—"

"Wait! Please! Please wait a second! And please put away your sword!"

"Rintarou Magami?! Didn't you hear from Luna?!"

Covered head to toe in soot, Felicia and Sir Gawain turned blue and backed away, voices cracking.

"What? Luna? What was she supposed to tell me? What's going on?"

Speak of the devil...

"Oh, Felicia, you're here! That was quick!"

Luna and Sir Kay appeared at the front entrance.

"Geez," Luna continued, "the two of you had it rough until now, but never fear! You can stay as guests in my castle as long as you want! Heh-heh! Accepting guests of honor is just another duty of—," Luna babbled, sticking out her chest.

Rintarou grabbed the hair at the back of her head. "Hey, Luna? Earth to Luna. What the hell's going on here?"

Yank! Yank-yank-yank! Rintarou pulled on her hair as though she were a puppet.

"Yow! Ouchie! That hurt! Seriously, dude? You're supposed to be my vassal! What do you think you're doing?! Do you have a death wish? I'll kill you with my bare hands for disrespecting me!"

"Answer the question! Why are these two staying at our base of operations?!" Rintarou questioned, radiating a demonic aura as Luna held her head with tears in her eyes and objected.

Felicia proudly butted in. "Why, that's because our mansion-slash-base was just attacked when we broke our alliance with Lord Gloria, and it's been destroyed to smithereens!"

"Actually! Felicia's parents—the Feralds—are destitute and suffering from financial strife despite their lineage and high status! Which is why Felicia is having trouble finding a place to live—and even getting a bite to eat! Don't you feel pity for my liege?! Don't you feel bad for her?!"

"Yo... It seems like you spilled some low-key heartbreaking secrets... You sure that's okay? You've just made your precious master cry." Rintarou glanced at Felicia, who was smiling brightly as tears flowed in wide rivers down her face behind Sir Gawain. Rintarou sighed.

"See? That's the situation. Felicia called me on her phone a moment ago, crying that she couldn't stand living in a cardboard box in front of the station anymore... Hence, why I invited her over," Luna added.

"...This is way too sad," Rintarou lamented into her ear.

"Hey, you're okay with this, right? Is it okay if we let Felicia stay at our place?"

"But, Luna, they're enemies. We have a truce right now, but the fight is gonna keep getting more intense, and we'll need to settle things eventually..."

"Please..." Luna looked intently at Rintarou, who showed his displeasure and disapproval.

He'd seen that look before—not in his current life, but in his past one. He was remembering the former great king of Britain, who had unilaterally defeated his enemies. He was thinking about Arthur.

Even if the enemy bared their teeth at him, Arthur rarely let go of them, and they had joined his following after their defeat.

In the war to unite Britain, the eleven kings had joined together to stand against King Arthur (except King Lot, who had died in battle), and then they mostly became Arthur's followers after the war—and Arthur had unfortunately accepted them.

In the past, Merlin had told Arthur to quickly behead the enemy, but...

"Please, Merlin..."

When she implored him, he could see a strong resemblance to the expression Arthur had turned to Merlin. From that somewhat scummy, constantly congenial, people-pleaser boy king...

"Tch... Fine."

He couldn't say no. Rintarou scratched his head as he turned away.

"Hey, you two. If either of you try anything funny anywhere around this place, I'll kill you instantly!"

"Yay! Thank you, Rintarou!" Luna said, giddy. And when she was as happy as the boy in his memories, Rintarou just couldn't find it in himself to be angry.

"Oh-ho-ho-ho! Well, I offer you my deepest gratitude!"

It all got to Felicia's head. "Lead me to my room right away! Well, I *am* a real aristocrat and know my manners! I will allow you to give me the *second* largest room in this mansion! Now, Mr. Magami! Please take my things!"

Rintarou looked at her with unimpressed eyes as he pointed to the corner of the front garden. "Well...your room's over there."

...He was pointing at a small and shabby storeroom.

"...Say what?"

"It's over there," Rintarou emphasized with a straight face and turned his back right on Felicia and her knight as they stared at him with boggled eyes.

"Wait! Y-y-you've got to be kidding, right?! Mr. Magami! Y-you're forcing a fragile maiden of the aristocracy to live in a miserable shack?!"

"P-please wait! I don't mind if you put me in a doghouse, but at least put her—," stuttered Sir Gawain.

"Shut it. You're so annoying." Rintarou ignored them, and turning away, he went back into the house.

Felicia and her knight clung to him with tears in their eyes.

The commotion at the front door had devolved into earsplitting chaos.

"Um... It's nice to see so much energy, but...are you almost done?"

An outsider's humble voice addressed all of them.

"...Tch. Guess we couldn't hide this place completely." Rintarou sharply glanced at the girl standing beside Felicia and Sir Gawain.

She was a young woman with a strange atmosphere around her—an extraordinary beauty wearing a light–blue dress that wrapped around her like a robe. Her fascinating face was beyond human, and she couldn't be described as anything but devilish or bewitching.

"R-right! I forgot all about it!" Felicia said, though she was already late. "We came for the living arrangements, but there was something even more important to talk about! We brought her here to..."

The woman stopped Felicia with her hand and stepped forward.

"No, I'll speak for myself." She gracefully bowed to Rintarou, Luna, and Sir Kay. "It's been some time, Luna... We might not have met since I transferred your Excalibur to you when you were young... Because I was your supervisor."

"...What?! You—" Luna blinked as though she had remembered something.

"Hmph." Rintarou snorted crudely and cast a sharp glare at the woman.

But his insolent attitude didn't seem to affect her. "Then I will once again introduce myself as a manager of the Dame du Lac, Vivian. That's right...I'm on the management side of the King Arthur Succession Battle."

When the woman—Vivian—introduced herself, Rintarou eyed her with even more hostility, glaring bitterly at her.

Soon after they had led Vivian, Felicia, and Sir Gawain into the drawing room...

"Wow! You gave the former King Arthur his second Excalibur?!"

"Yes. That child was a real rascal. He didn't think twice about breaking his precious sword... He was a handful."

"If I may interject with a word, Lady Vivian... That only occurred because of King Pellinore's brute strength. Though Arthur was at fault for trying to hit King Pellinore from behind in a surprise attack," Sir Kay added.

They surrounded a table to have tea with Vivian at the center of their conversation.

"But I couldn't have guessed that I would have my head suddenly cut off by that barbarian as I went to get our gift for giving him the second Excalibur."

"Ah, Sir Balin... He was the source of trouble for us during that time."

"Y-your head?! Are you okay?!" Felicia yelped.

"Yes, I'm fine, Felicia. We, the Dame du Lac, are part fey... As the organization's head, I lean more on the fairy side. I wouldn't die from a beheading," Vivian replied with a chuckle.

As all of them were enjoying their idle chat...

"..."

...Rintarou was the only one who had become silent as he hatefully glared at Vivian with his feet on the table.

"What's gotten into you, Rintarou? Why are you in such a bad mood?" Luna asked.

"Leave me alone. I just hate the Dame du Lac."

When Luna gave him a dubious look, Rintarou snorted and turned away. As soon as he did, their happy banter stopped.

Without a word, Vivian peered deep into Rintarou.

"And? The manager of the Dame du Lac, gracing us with her presence, huh," Rintarou commented. "I'm sure you wouldn't come out of your way just for...some conversation and tea, right?"

When Rintarou coldly looked at her, Vivian answered with a settled expression. "Yes, I get it. Let's get to the subject at hand immediately."

Vivian falteringly started her explanation. "There is someone interfering with this sacred battle for succession at the moment," she admitted with an earnest expression.

Everyone spoke at once.

"Oh, you mean Rintarou."

"It's gotta be Rintarou."

"You're talking about Mr. Magami."

"Who could it be other than Rintarou Magami?"

The eyes of Luna, Sir Kay, Felicia, and Sir Gawain all collectively went distant. They spoke with extreme certainty.

"Hey! Hey?!" Rintarou howled at the four, who had finally agreed on something for the first time in their lives.

"Rintarou, I'm sorry! It's been a short time, but I won't forget you as my subject—for at least a minute!"

"Drop dead!" barked Rintarou.

Vivian smiled wryly as she calmed Rintarou and Luna down.

"No. It's certainly true that Rintarou Magami...that the reincarnation of Merlin has participated in the succession battle. That is a situation that no one at the Dame du Lac could have anticipated...even though we are the ones who serve the three goddesses of fate..."

"...Hmm? You didn't anticipate me getting involved?" Rintarou raised his eyebrows.

"...Is there something wrong, Rintarou Magami?"

"......"

The Dame du Lac managed the succession battle. They should have known everything that happened in the battle between the Kings on New Avalon Island. Of course they would have known that he was Merlin.

But what did she mean that they hadn't been able to *anticipate* him?

What about the girl in black claiming to be from the Dame de Lac and telling him about the existence of the succession battle? Who had she been? At the time, he had been wandering the world after skipping out on school in mainland Japan.

"...Uh-huh, it's nothing. And? Keep going."

"Yes. It is certainly true that you are irregular and one we call a Joker, but that itself is not an issue. It doesn't change the fact that each King must use their social status, influence, and help from the real world in order to fight. The point is, if they aim to become King Arthur and win over everyone, it's fine with us."

"Hmm? In other words, the outsider isn't entering this King Arthur Succession Battle on a whim or for show. Are they actually causing a disturbance?"

"It's nice that you've been quick to grasp the situation quickly. That's basically the gist of it." Vivian nodded and continued. "We've found Rifts all over New Avalon Island with each passing day."

"...Rifts?"

"There's the illusory world on the other side, where fairies and apparitions and all types of gods live. And then, there's the real world, where humans reside. These two are firmly divided by the Curtain of Consciousness, which acts as a boundary between worlds. I'm sure you know about that."

When Luna tilted her head, Vivian provided an additional explanation. "Because we have this Curtain of Consciousness, humans are able to live in this real world—free of the control of the gods and fear from fairies. They can live peacefully inside the realms of 'common sense.' A Rift is a hole in that Curtain of Consciousness."

"Wait, does that mean...?!" Luna gaped.

"Yes, if this is true, this could become a serious issue. If we don't do anything, the apparitions of the illusory world could come through the hole, traveling to this side as they please." Felicia nodded.

Vivian confirmed that everyone was on the same page before continuing.

"Let's start with apparitions... At their source, they are born from the natural disasters outside of humanity's control—plagues, droughts, famines, storms, lightning, earthquakes, and wildfires. Or they come from negative emotions—betrayal, envy, lust, jealousy, and recklessness... They are beings that became tied to a culture or faith, given shape by the many things that humanity spurned and feared. They are born because humans wished for them to be."

"Because they were originally born from concepts humans had no control over, they can't be handled by people, right?"

"That's it. The Rifts that we have seen so far are still small. Meaning apparitions that could cause great harm won't be able to come through them. However, it seems as though the holes have gotten increasingly larger as more have appeared. If we let things continue, one strong enough to threaten humans may invade this side."

"I suppose that if there are strong apparitions wandering

around the streets, we wouldn't be worried about the succession battle."

"Yes. And these openings did not come about themselves. They are artificially being opened by some kind of magic. They began appearing around the streets in various areas around the same time as when we started the King Arthur Succession Battle... It is now clear that there is an outsider attempting to interfere with the battle. So we have a request for all the Kings who are part of the battle." Vivian turned to face Rintarou and the others and lowered her head. "Would you take on our request...to defeat the person responsible for these Rifts?"

"—?!" Rintarou narrowed his eyes sharply.

"The Dame du Lac are giving official notification for this request to all the Kings who have gathered on this island right now. This is an official mission request from the Dame du Lac as managers of the King Arthur Succession Battle. You may answer the request—or not... What will *you* do?"

"Heh, don't mess with me, idiot."

As expected, the edge of Rintarou's mouth went up to reject her.

"That's awful presumptuous of you to think we won't be concerned about the succession battle with this in the background. I mean, as the managers of this whole thing, shouldn't *you* be cleaning this up? That's absurd of you to think you could just borrow our help," Rintarou spat.

"...You're right. I have nothing I can say in return." Vivian could only apologetically lower her eyes.

"Anyway, we're turning down that task! Try somebody else! Who cares if some strong apparition appears or some commoners might end up victims to it? Hmph. As if I'd care about a couple damn humans dying. Actually, in order to make sure the battle doesn't end up being delayed because of that stuff, you should—"

Rintarou had gone off on a tirade, saying anything and getting everything off his chest.

"Rintarou." Luna stood up with a sincere expression...and stopped him with her hand.

"Hey, Luna...you couldn't...?" With dubious eyes, Rintarou stared up at her.

As if she knew not to let him down, she nodded and looked straight at Vivian.

"...How much'll you give us for it?"

"I knew it!" Rintarou thumped his forehead on the table. "Well, that's way better than getting involved in a fight out of a sense of righteousness, I guess!"

"Wh-what are you talking about?! I'm taking on this request because my passionate soul burns bright with justice! Obviously, that's why!" Luna chided Rintarou. "You got that? I'm the one who's going to eventually succeed King Arthur and become the ruler of the world! In other words, all of the people in the world are my subjects! In that case, I'll work myself to the bone for the sake of every single person in this world since I have the duty to protect them! That's a King's duty!"

"Hey..."

"Well, to accomplish that duty...I need all kinds of provisions beforehand, right?"

In front of Rintarou, Luna put on an obscene smile as she stealthily sidled over to Vivian...and put her arm around the woman's shoulder, brought her face to her, and whispered in her ear.

"It's not like I'm fighting *just* for money, okay? If you dress it up a little with a small reward, I'll feel a little more motivated or whatever, right? You get that, right? Miss Vivian?"

"Hey, I could hear all of that, King Airhead. At least put some effort into hiding it," Rintarou sneered.

"Heh-heh. Thank you, Luna." Vivian grinned and pulled a check from her pocket. "This is a formal request from the Dame du Lac. Of course we will pay recompense… Yes, this is the advance… and if you're successful…"

In order to show it to Luna only, Vivian smoothly wrote something on the check.

From next to her, Luna opened her eyes wide for a moment. She turned an unusually earnest expression to Rintarou and looked straight at him.

"We're doing it, Rintarou. I'm protecting these streets."

"Hey, her check is hanging out of your pocket. At least try to hide it, dude."

He was tired. He was genuinely exhausted. When he thought about it, he felt he remembered Arthur being a moneygrubbing guy, too. The stories passed down in the world that he was a knight king motivated by the ideals of honesty and purity were all lies.

In one way or another, Luna was similar to the former King Arthur.

Had the former Merlin felt this way, too?

Well, it's fine. We might get info about the other Kings trying to bring down the culprit… It's not like it'll be entirely useless. It might even help me regain my powers from my previous life, too.

After he had been instructed to participate, Rintarou forced himself to agree.

"O-of course, we will also accept your request!" shouted Felicia.

"Yes, this is great, my liege! We won't have to worry about our livelihood for a while!"

Of course, Felicia and Sir Gawain answered that they would be accepting the offer, too.

And just like that, Rintarou and the others had signed up to find the culprit responsible for summoning the apparitions.

CHAPTER 2

The Saint of Salvation & the Red Knight

After Vivian left, the sun sank below the horizon, beckoning night.

In twilight, the world seemed completely severed from daily life. Those of the illusory world acted behind the scenes, and night had manifested itself.

"But...I can't believe we'll be taking down the outsider interfering with the succession battle... The future is looking bleak."

Walking along the deserted city streets, Luna looked up at the night sky, obscured by silhouettes of skyscrapers, and sighed.

At that moment, Rintarou, Luna, and Sir Kay, along with Felicia and Sir Gawain, were in the middle of wandering the streets at night with no destination in mind.

Luna and Felicia were armed with their Excaliburs, and Rintarou held his familiar long sword and hidden sword cane. Sir Kay and Sir Gawain were wearing their knight equipment that had been woven with their auras.

Without a moment to waste, they had started their search for the one who was creating these Rifts.

"This might be one of the few situations where I agree with Luna," Felicia replied, nodding.

"In these circumstances, when will we actually start the quest for the four treasures that make up the crux of this fight?"

Oddly enough, the conditions for victory in the King Arthur Succession Battle were not an unconditional win in a battle royale. Instead, the rules stated that the one to obtain all four treasures hidden on the artificial island would be the victor. Fighting wasn't their only means of achieving that goal.

"...It's been several days since the battle started. The administration hasn't shown any intention of starting the great treasure quest at all, plus...we haven't come across any Queens. I'm starting to feel nervous," Felicia mumbled with a sigh.

"Hmph. Just give it time. They probably have specific *conditions* for starting the treasure quests," Rintarou snapped back from the very end of their procession.

"...Conditions?"

"Yeah. Once those are fulfilled, they'll officially announce the treasure search... I'm willing to bet that's the rule. Those smarmy Dame du Lac love shit like that." His tone was prickly.

Rintarou had been in a foul mood ever since their talk with Vivian in the afternoon.

"Anyway, it's too early to start thinking about treasure now. Just worry about what the other Kings are doing. Hmph... That's simple enough for you to understand, right?"

"Seriously... How much longer are you going to be mad, Rintarou?" Luna objected, observing his annoyance. "...For real, though. Why are you hating on Vivian?"

When she hit straight at the crux of the issue, Rintarou went quiet. For a while, they remained in silence...until he finally opened his mouth as though he had thought of something.

"...No reason. It's not Vivian so much as the Dame du Lac that peeves me." Rintarou unsteadily started his explanation despite spitting out his words.

"The Dame du Lac is an organization that's set out to separate this world from the illusory one by expelling the apparitions and gods, thereby making this place into a world only for humans... That's the objective of these half-fey creatures."

"But it doesn't sound like they're doing anything bad? If we had apparitions and gods strutting around this world, humans wouldn't be able to build a peaceful society or live their lives."

"I'll acknowledge that they have their merits. This world exists because of their extensive work anyway. All the rumors say that they were the ones who wove the Curtain of Consciousness, too."

"...Then why do you hate them?"

"Like I said, they just rub me the wrong way," Rintarou grumbled. "They act like they supervise all humans. Since they're half fey and the ones who warded off illusions using the Curtain of Consciousness, they can intervene all they want in this real world. In other words, they're the most powerful organization right now. They're taking advantage of powers that originated from the illusory world to their fullest extent. They've burrowed their way into the upper echelons of every country to influence politics. The reason this artificial island got to be created in eastern waters was because they've been pulling strings behind the scenes. They're nothing but some damn nobodies, but they've pushed aside the ones with actual power. They act all smug and pretend they're in charge of this world... I can't stand their arrogance."

"Ha-ha-ha... You're such a grouch, Rintarou." Luna smiled wryly.

"On top of it all...they thought of Arthur as nothing but another one of their tools in the end," he added, unusually solemn.

Luna opened her eyes slightly wider.

Her intuition told her this was actually bothering Rintarou.

"To make a world where the humans could be free of the reign of apparitions and old gods...they chose Arthur and used him as the leader of humankind. They pushed him around until they had no use for him. They're the ones who forced him into Camlann Hill. They're so full of it."

"..."

"After they had their way with him, I tried to help Arthur; they... *Those bastards...!*"

Suddenly, Merlin's memories in Rintarou came back to life—of a smiling girl from the Dame du Lac, facing him, Merlin. It was a dreadful memory: betrayed by someone he had believed from the bottom of his heart... It was bittersweet.

"Anyway! I can't trust the Dame du Lac! I despise them!"

"Seriously, dude? How can you say that when you're a part of the succession battle organized by them...?"

"Like I said! I'm gonna turn the tables on them and mess with them good!" Rintarou whined, childlike. At the same time, he knew things rarely went according to plan.

I'm most worried about that girl *who leaked the succession battle info to me...*

Rintarou recalled that certain someone.

He hadn't known her identity as she had clothed herself entirely in black to hide her face and whole body with a hood and robe. She was the person who had told Rintarou about the succession battle and Luna. The girl had introduced herself as being part of the Dame du Lac, but...if that was the case, why hadn't Vivian caught on?

And then, there was the outsider interference that had started alongside the succession battle. A foreign element that was not originally part of the sacred magical ceremony had come into the mix.

It was obvious that the outsider had come in from the start and made calculations of unknown depths behind the scenes. Rintarou was starting to feel that this succession battle wouldn't simply stop at deciding the next King Arthur.

But Rintarou grinned and chuckled to himself.

Well, I guess that's fun, too... I don't care as long as the battle is entertaining for me. Who cares about her identity and motives? Who gives a shit what that intruder is planning? If they try plotting some-thing to stand in my way, I'll stomp all over their little plans, Rintarou thought arrogantly.

"Geez... Your previous memories have a stronger influence on you than I expected." Luna shrugged as though she was exasperated at that point before she beamed at him, radiating self-confidence.

"But I'm fine! I won't end up like my ancestor! That's because I'm the person who's meant to become the true King who rules this world! And more than anything, I've got you!"

"!" Despite himself, Rintarou blinked several times and watched Luna.

"You're gonna protect me, right? And you're gonna make me King, right?"

She looked straight at Rintarou, holding trust of unknown ori-gins in him.

Her gaze was somehow nostalgic...

"...*Tch*. You annoy me." Rintarou clucked his tongue and turned away from her.

Well, it's not like I'm going to stop having fun with this fight...

Propping up King Airhead to become King Arthur would just help him add to his fun.

Luna continued watching Rintarou with a grin as he was lost in thought.

"...Rintarou, over here... Here it is," Sir Kay called, and Rin-tarou came to the forefront.

They were in Area Two, where Rifts had apparently been found frequently as of late. This was the business district.

Between the standing skyscrapers in a claustrophobic corner of an alleyway was a shadowy void. It was as if it had been formed by a giant claw tearing a hole through the ground. It was most certainly an opening, gouged into the world by something.

The people of the real world, who were imprisoned by their common sense, would never be able to recognize the schism. At first glance, it would have certainly looked like a physical hole, but in actuality, it wasn't. The thing was a hole that had opened in humankind's consciousness itself.

"Huh. It really is a Rift… And it's probably been a while since it opened, too."

"Urp… Then, does that mean apparitions from the illusory world have already invaded ours?" Luna asked.

Ignoring her, Rintarou scraped *vanish* in old Celtic Ogham letters over the Rift using the tip of his sword. He was *Breaking the Curse*.

"Nah. At least, not any apparitions that we should be worried about. I mean, it's a scrawny hole. Well, there *will* probably be some mischief. You know, machines moving of their own accord, chores being magically finished at night, talking cats. All that jazz."

Once he finished carving in the Ogham letters that looked like Nordic runes, they glowed for a moment. Then, the opening closed as though it had never existed.

"But I don't think the future gaps will be this small," he added.

"Right. That's already the third one on the first night."

That was right.

For some reason, it was almost as though Rifts had been forming ahead of Rintarou and the others even as they wandered aimlessly around.

"…But what's this culprit really trying to do? These gaps are obvious and conspicuous. They're obviously going to be closed back up."

"Yes, their intentions are cryptic. It seems all we can do is directly capture the culprit," Sir Kay replied to Rintarou's suspicions.

"Mr. Magami!"

A small fairy girl was floating above Rintarou's head, flapping her wings. It was a Messenger Pixie that Felicia had employed with magic.

"Over here! This way! I've found another opening! Heh-heh! See what happens when you rely on me?"

"Yeah, yeah. I got it. Great job." Rintarou sighed as he stood up and swept up his bare sword, then sheathed it. "...All right. Luna, Sir Kay, we're on to the next one."

Like that, Rintarou dragged along Luna and Sir Kay to head to the next one.

But around this time, he had started to feel a sense of unease wash over him.

...I dunno why... But the Rifts that we've found tonight are arranged in a way that feels...somehow off. It's almost like they're leading us somewhere... It feels...intentional, he thought.

But they didn't have any other choice but to follow the trail.

They went around the streets searching for the holes that continued to crop up, seemingly leading Rintarou's crew somewhere.

As they continued to follow the openings, they finally came upon a park.

There was a jungle gym, a seesaw, a sandbox... And in the middle of all that play equipment—

"...And that makes seven. It looks new, too." At the tip of Luna's pointed finger was another Rift.

"How much time do they have on their hands? Seriously... If we don't find the person doing this and crush them, we're just going to be playing catch-up," Rintarou bemoaned, fed up. He started *Breaking the Curse.*

All they had been doing was closing up these fissures. There hadn't been a single change or development in their situation.

Felicia and Luna were losing interest in the identical tasks. But in the unchanging developments, it seemed their vibe was less tense until…

"—Ngh?!"

Out of the blue, it felt as if an ice blade had been mercilessly gouged into their backs. A sharp chill ran down the spines of all those gathered there. They sensed bloodlust—thick and deadly, like the delight of a feral predator that had found its prey.

Something was watching them. Rintarou drew his swords and looked around his surroundings cautiously.

"Heh… Found ya. ♪"

The voice of a young girl came from above their heads. It was almost pure and innocent, like a child enjoying a game of hide-and-seek.

"Oh, my Lord. Our Father in heaven, I am grateful you have led us to this meeting. Amen."

"—Hnh?!" Rintarou quickly looked above his head.

A girl was on top of one of the rows of lights in the park. She swung her legs under her as she sat on the T-shaped light. She drew a cross on herself with her right hand as she looked down on Rintarou and the others.

What the—? When did that kid get up there?! I didn't notice her at all!

He felt a shiver… A faintly chilling shudder ran up his spine.

Rintarou gazed at the girl, who resembled a monster more than a shadow in the light of the lamp.

She was slender, petite, young. She couldn't have been older than ten. In fact, she wasn't so much a girl as a child.

Even in that shadowy night, her hair glowed brilliant crimson. The long strands flowed freely, fanned up in the night's wind, undulating like it housed a roaring fire.

As she looked down on Rintarou, her large, sharp eyes glistened like droplets of blood. They were opened wide, glinting ominously like rubies in the darkness.

Her youthful face was constructed like a porcelain doll, and she wore an innocent smile, but…beneath that purity was unconcealable venom and cruelty.

That girl wore scarlet knight's armor and looked straight down at Rintarou and his companions.

Of course, she wasn't anyone to trifle with. Radiating from her every cell, her aura simply wasn't normal. Sir Kay and Sir Gawain were no match for her. To put it humbly, she might have been a formidable opponent even for Sir Lancelot of the Round Table, and on top of that—

It need not be repeated that she was not an ordinary person.

She was a Jack.

"*Tch*, you're—"

"Y-you—"

"Wh-wh-why you?!"

Rintarou, Sir Kay, and Sir Gawain instantly recognized the girl.

She looked down on the three, who were filled with dismay and distress, and flashed a lopsided grin… Just one corner of her mouth went up.

She spoke as though she were reciting a love poem.

"Oh, Merlin. How I longed to see you. With the passing of time, your physique may have changed, but the light of your soul is unforgettable—immutable. Oh, I have yearned to see you—"

In that moment, the girl made her move—launched herself with a quiet flip into the air. She had used the springs in her body to move quickly.

She *ran down* the light pole in a split second and rushed at a right angle all at once.

"*Cantate et exsultate et psallite*— Sing and revel and frolic... Ah-ha! Ah-ha-ha-ha-ha-ha!" She recited a psalm, cackling like a foul fowl as she ran at full speed.

The girl bent forward as she dashed toward them, low enough to be crawling along the ground.

She wielded a cruciform claymore with her thin arms. Like the white teeth of a predator hunting its prey, her frosty blade reflected the moonlight.

They were faced with the girl pursuing them so fast that she didn't even leave an afterimage—

"Ah—?!"

"Tch—?!"

In positions closest to the incoming girl, Sir Kay and Sir Gawain faced against her, weapons raised.

Her sword flashed a single time—carving through the air in the shape of an ominous crescent moon that sliced the night in half. There was a roar from the impact.

The girl had swung her sword too quickly to be perceived by the human eye and sent Sir Kay and Sir Gawain flying.

"Aaah?! Why does this always happen to me?!"

"Whoaaa?!" boomed Sir Gawain.

As if struck by a bullet, Sir Kay and Sir Gawain were sent flying horizontally. Sir Kay was sent to the bounds of the park, where she scraped the ground as she skidded. Sir Gawain crashed into the jungle gym, which crumpled upon impact, leaving it unrecognizable and unsalvageable.

"Keep back, you lackeys!"

Though the two Jacks had been forced away from the fight, the girl did not stop her full-speed pursuit. She charged at them, aiming at Rintarou and the others. With another reckless burst of acceleration, she resolutely came after them.

Heh, I've got no clue what's going on, but—

Rintarou took his beloved pair of swords—his red long sword on the right and his white one on the left—readied them, and eyed the approaching girl. When their eyes locked, Rintarou was certain: *I'm the one she's after!*

That moment, Rintarou took a step forward. "Luna! Get back—"

The girl closed the ten yards between them, clashing with Rintarou. Her claymore struck down like lightning, meeting his crossed swords.

The sound of metal rang out as sparks flared up into the air. Upon impact, the force from the blades swept a storm, blasting aside Luna and Felicia, who were overcome in shock.

Rintarou was on the receiving end of the girl's terrific attack, holding her back with his crossed blades. She ostentatiously pushed him back, subduing him. On the defensive, the soles of Rintarou's shoes scraped against the ground, pushing up a mound of dirt as he began to slide back.

His surroundings started to whizz past him.

Even if he tried to persevere through it, her power and the intensity of her pursuit could be compared to the likes of a steam engine.

"You can put up a fight, Merlin... But you're missing some of your intensity, no?"

"Gah—?!"

With the momentum of her charge, she mercilessly shoved Rintarou back.

"When it comes to the man of her affections, a girl wants to be pursued, not be in pursuit... You know."

"Oh, shut up!" Rintarou hated shoving matches. He flipped around the weapon with his hands, parrying the almost transcendental force with which the girl came at him with her claymore, and deftly moved to go past her.

"RAAAH!"

"Ha! Fine, come at me!" she snickered.

The two of them instantaneously took different positions, turning back to each other—and struck.

Rintarou's two swords danced through the air, as though they were striking lightning. Like a violent storm, her claymore wailed.

They clashed time and again, facing each other directly. They exchanged blows. They parried.

Her claymore tore through the air, slicing and running through the space between them.

Rintarou jumped away to avoid her sword sweeping from the side.

Her strikes pressed at him. She continued to bring down her weapon to strike him as he used his dual swords to block her.

When her sword flashed, he narrowly managed to meet her blade and swipe it to the side. The pommel of her sword aimed to strike at his chest as she pounced on him, and he stopped it with the bottom of his feet.

He turned away her sword when she jabbed at him like a high-power laser. The flickering sparks blinded his eyes.

Their sword dance was one-sided. Her claymore had completely overpowered him. The weight of her attacks was an order of magnitude different from his strikes. When their weapons met, even the atmosphere quaked. Rintarou couldn't help but waver from the sword's impact.

As Rintarou tottered, she assailed him, coming at him with less mercy and more severity each time. He didn't even have a moment to breathe.

The blows had to be strong enough to collapse a building with a single stroke, and they continuously assailed Rintarou.

"Hmm? Is that all you can do with a sword? You think you can satisfy a woman with that little thing?"

"—Hgh!"

"Now, Merlin! Deeper! Oh, ravish me! Harder!" She provoked Rintarou, who was nothing but on the defensive. As though she were intoxicated and just straight out of her mind, she continued to assail him with her sword.

Rintarou gritted his teeth as he continued to meet the blows.

Slowly, the claymore's tip grazed Rintarou and scraped him. It cut him.

And when Rintarou eventually missed the girl's claymore, he lost his balance.

"—Rrk?! No—"

"Amen!"

Like a thunderbolt, the claymore flashed, bisecting Rintarou and severing his body down the middle—

—or at least, it tried to.

"Haaaaaaaaaaaaaaah!"

With desperate resolve and determination, Luna intervened between them in that moment. She held her Excalibur diagonally over her head, meeting this lightning bolt of a weapon, and parried it.

Jshhh! groaned the weapons, as if a gnashing sound of an industrial grinder. Sparks came from the Excalibur Luna held, bursting forth as they burned and cut through the shadows of the night.

The blow sent Luna flying.

However, the claymore the girl brought down on Rintarou just barely missed him, grandly passing by his side.

"Rintarou! Now—," yelled Luna, even as she rolled along the ground.

In that moment, her claymore was more than half buried in the ground, and she was rendered immobile.

His liege had given him the opportunity of a lifetime by putting herself on the line.

"AAAAAH! DROP DEAAAD!"

This time, Rintarou swung his swords, aiming to send her head flying. The girl had been completely taken by surprise, and she couldn't intervene on the attack—

—or she shouldn't have been able to.

"—?!"

Everyone expected her arteries to spray blood through the air as though blooming red flowers. But instead, she unleashed a spark that pierced with whiteness through their vision. It was completely unexpected. It was the tip of his own sword being sent aside.

When he looked, he saw three red heater shields that had been deployed at some point to each float in the air to the right, left, and behind the girl. One among those shields had stopped Rintarou's swords.

She chuckled as she calmly yanked out her claymore and swung it at Rintarou.

Rintarou jumped away—two, three times before fully escaping.

They reached an intermission in their sword fight and stared at each other with several yards between them.

Rintarou breathed roughly with his shoulders. Sweat trickled down from his whole body. He felt dead as lead.

On the other hand, his opponent had shed not a drop of sweat, and she looked invigorated.

"Oh, Merlin. Though boorish liaisons do exist…that was something, huh?" She readied her sword again and lavished him with praise. "I know I was going easy on you, but I never would have imagined you'd make me use the Rothschild..."

Shivers went down his spine. His opponent licked her lips in ecstasy, gazing at Rintarou as though she had finally found her long-lost love.

That heater shield had easily fended off Rintarou's lethal attack. The shields were still floating to the right, left, and back of the girl with no supports.

"I feel as though the very core of my body burns with passion. I wonder how long it's been since my body was overcome in pleasure before this night? Ha-ha-ha. Hee-hee-hee... Now, Merlin, if you would be so kind... Can you satiate this excitement of mine... with your sturdy sword?"

The girl laughed with dubious charm and lavished him with allure at odds with her youthful features. She swiped off Rintarou's blood from her claymore with her plump fingertips... A sliver of tongue peeked out from between her lips, licking his blood, as she watched him.

"Tch... You little pervert!"

Putting aside her incredibly weird actions and behavior for now, he didn't have a doubt in his mind, piecing together her overwhelming valor and—more than anything—that Rothschild...

He knew her identity.

"Fine! I'll shove this sword in your pathetic little body and make you gasp and pant—Lamorak of Gales!"

She was the fourth seat of the Round Table, Sir Lamorak of Gales.

A knight rivaling the strongest of the Round Table—Sir Lancelot and Sir Tristan—stood before them.

Answering Rintarou's will to fight, Sir Lamorak grinned and slowly readied her claymore.

"Nice, Merlin. You make my heart soar. The night is still young. Hee-hee... How about we savor the moment together? Oh, and also..." Sir Lamorak glanced at Luna and spat out unpleasantly, "You there... I'll only allow one affair. You were brave enough to jump into the carnage at risk of your own life. I spared you out of respect, but...next time, if you try that again...you'll die."

"Urp..." Luna gulped, intimidated by Sir Lamorak's dreadful gaze.

Sir Lamorak wasn't bluffing. At least, that was what Rintarou had gathered from his intuition.

In that last bout, Luna would have become two lumps of meat if Sir Lamorak had decided to end her on a whim. And that was a testament of her terrific power.

She took no notice of anyone but Rintarou. That was their only saving grace.

Let me observe this current battlefield... I've got no clue about the statuses of Sir Gawain and Sir Kay, and this is completely out of Luna and Felicia's league.

He looked over at the two Jacks who were in a terrible state, beaten and lying facedown on the ground, and then at Luna and Felicia, who were so lacking in combat ability that they could only be paralyzed from shock.

I don't know why, but I'm her target. Rintarou looked at Sir Lamorak once again and stuck his right sword into the ground.

Trying to retreat from her won't work.

He grabbed his left sword with his right hand and gave himself a shallow cut, then on the backs of both his hands, he drew an evil eye.

And...I can't die. I said I'd make her...make Luna into the King... Heh... Which means I can't die here. In that case—

A black aura swelled from Rintarou's whole body as he invoked his *Fomorian Transformation.*

His eyes glittered gold. His hair grew long and white like one of the Two Lions from a famous Kabuki play. His black battle robes billowed.

In that instant, Rintarou controlled an immense power and skill incomparable to his abilities until that point.

"...Hmm?" Sir Lamorak's eyes glittered with glee as she watched.

"Rintarou?! Y-you can't use that power—" Luna winced as though she were in pain.

He knew that even without her input.

Originally, this *Fomorian Transformation* had been Rintarou's last and greatest trump card.

According to Ireland's myths from the Irish *Lebor Gabála Érenn* mythology, there was an evil Danann of darkness—the Fomorian line. This power temporarily brought back the Fomorian ancestral line of Merlin, and it was a serious burden that would impose reactionary damage to Rintarou's body and soul, as he was nothing more than a modern human.

On top of that, he had used the transformation in their fight against Kujou just a few days prior. He still hadn't finished healing from that refractory damage. Even maintaining his *Fomorian Transformation* greatly strained his whole body. It seemed to scream from its own destruction, and he felt as though he was going to faint.

But—I've got to try!

As far as Rintarou understood it, Sir Lamorak was an equal to Sir Lancelot, praised to be the strongest of the Round Table. Perhaps she was even better. In that case, there was no other means to beating her except the *Fomorian Transformation*.

Rintarou readied himself and prepared his swords.

However, even though Rintarou was releasing all the intensity that his aura could muster, Sir Lamorak didn't seem eager to fight at all, grinning in glee.

"How wonderful. It seems my eyes did not deceive me. I had the faintest thought that it wasn't Sir Lancelot or Sir Tristan who was the strongest of the Round Table...but you, Merlin."

"...?"

"You have still a way to go before getting back to your former strength...but, eventually, I'm sure you will regain your power. Yes, when I defeat you, I will show that I am the strongest...and prove God's love for me."

With a bloodcurdling laugh, Sir Lamorak readied her claymore once again.

The three shields that had formed around her released a crimson glitter as they cut through the night.

"Now, let us begin. Under the name of the Father, the Son, and the Holy Spirit... We shall see who has received the love of God—you or me. Let us ask what his divine will is with our swords... Now," Sir Lamorak declared.

In that moment—there was silence.

The world was in stagnation. The air froze in place. All sounds were extinguished. Time stopped ticking.

And after that—

"AAAAAAH!"

"HYAAAAH!"

Rintarou and Sir Lamorak kicked at the ground, whizzing toward each other. They ran so fast they seemed to almost disappear. Their spirits had been strained to their limits and even made time go awry. A moment stretched into eternity, and Rintarou and Sir Lamorak both slowly closed in on each other.

It took forever for the two of them to be lured into their deadly meeting point.

Rintarou's pair of swords and Sir Lamorak's claymore sluggishly closed the distance on each other.

The space between Rintarou and Sir Lamorak became shorter and shorter and shorter.

Finally, the two of them made contact—and it happened in just that moment.

"That's enough," called out a clear voice, deescalating the situation.

"—Ngh?!" A sword pommel had stuck out right in front of Rintarou's nose.

"Wha—?!" A sword tip had been thrust in between Sir Lamorak's eyes.

In the moment before they crashed into each other, they stopped and froze—or rather, they had been forced to freeze.

A flag billowed in jerky movements.

The flow of time went back to normal, and color returned to the world.

When they realized it, there was a girl standing between Rintarou and Sir Lamorak.

"Please lay down your swords."

At first glance, the girl between them seemed plain with her heavy, unkempt bangs and her plaited platinum blonde hair.

On the whole, she was slender and petite, and her torso seemed oddly muscular. She stood up straight, and she didn't give off any sense of being unreliable at all. The demure curve of her body seemed proof of her purity and impeccability rather than her fragility.

There was a certain dignity about her. Something about her that made her appear as collected as a saint who had gained enlightenment. When paired with the untarnished and pure religious robes she solemnly wore, she could be described in one word as a *saint*.

On her slim waist, she wore a dangling talisman engraved with *IV*. In her willowy hand, she held a peculiar sword.

Its handle and blade were equal in length. The guard of the cruciform sword had a majestic battle flag furnished on it, which was fluttering in the night's wind. It was more like a flag on a javelin that would be held over one's head to rally one's allies on the battlefield than a sword.

But the sword released a strange glint. It had to be forged from some precious metal that was neither gold nor silver. It had to be an Excalibur. There was no doubt about it.

She had stopped Rintarou and Sir Lamorak right before they clashed with that flag-javelin of an Excalibur.

Is this girl a new King?! Rintarou's eyes peeled open. He couldn't believe it.

Standing with her back facing Rintarou, that mysterious girl was not at all stronger in comparison to Rintarou and Sir Lamorak. There was just no way.

If things had gone awry as she stepped between the two of them, she would have become mincemeat.

Regardless of that, she had intervened. Her skill at wielding her sword might have been beyond the average, and yet, she was proof that it was better to bend than break.

Rintarou was overcome by his surprise as he watched that girl's aloof back.

"Oh? What? You're already here? ...That's not what I was promised... What a killjoy," Sir Lamorak muttered cryptically to herself.

"Sir Lamorak, I don't think these people are responsible for the Rifts...," the girl started. "I think they might be Kings who received the same request as we did from the Dame du Lac. Just look at the Excaliburs of those two girls," she urged in a cool voice.

"...Oh my! They *do* have Excaliburs. I didn't notice in the slightest." Playing dumb, Sir Lamorak glanced at Luna and Felicia.

The girl started an insistent sermon. "Sir Lamorak! If they are fellow Kings, you first ask for their version of justice. And then you can tell them about your own ideals. You must have a fair battle and ask God: Who is in the right? Our battle is a holy inquiry to God of whether we have the capacity to be King!"

"Ha-ha... I see you're perfectly fine. Well, I just thought these guys could have been the culprits responsible for those openings. I mean, the two of us were separated by some strange magic earlier. I thought it might have been because of these guys, you see?" Sir Lamorak transparently vaunted.

Sir Lamorak's passionate will to fight and cold-blooded ferocity had all but disappeared. She grinned, abandoning her preparation for war, and put away her claymore. Following suit, the Rothschild—her three red shields invoked around her—also turned transparent until they disappeared.

The heightened tension had been strained to its limits and broke all at once. Luna wiped sweat from her forehead as she breathed out, and Felicia sat right down where she had been standing.

"I did this just to save you even a moment sooner... Is that so hard to understand?" the girl implored.

"Really now...? I'm fine, as you can see."

Then, the girl turned gracefully to face Rintarou and the others. That was the first time the girl's face became clear to Rintarou in front of him.

"To the two Kings, I would like to issue an apology. My Jack was out of line. I—" She was about to politely lower her head.

"You're...?" gasped Luna.

"H-hold up...?!" stammered Rintarou.

"No way...," blubbered Felicia.

All three of their eyes opened wide at the girl.

"Aren't you Emma? You're that transfer student I met at lunch! You're a King, too?!" Luna shouted.

"You're Emma Michelle?! Aren't you the prized pupil at the Religious Order of Saint Joan...?!" Felicia yelled.

Ignoring Luna's and Felicia's outbursts, the girl—Emma—looked straight at Rintarou.

"Master?!" she yelped.

In the same moment, Rintarou's face soured, and he turned away.

"Master! It's been so long! It's me! Emma!"

Without minding his reaction, Emma ran to Rintarou like a puppy and grabbed his hands as she smiled.

The stern vibe around Emma disappeared. In that instant, she was like an innocent girl, fitting for her age.

"I can't believe I'm meeting you here! It's a dream come true! Have you been doing well?!" Emma grinned at Rintarou, overflowing with fondness and doing a complete one-eighty from her hard expression from before.

"...More or less."

In contrast, Rintarou's attitude was blunt and half-hearted.

"What's the meaning..."

"...of this?"

Luna and Felicia looked at them with unimpressed eyes and tilted heads, finishing each other's sentence.

"Ugh... S-someone, please treat us soon... Gah..."

"Urgh... All the bones in our bodies have been pulverized, if you wouldn't mind..."

From far off, Sir Kay and Sir Gawain were in tatters, groaning with tears in their eyes.

"Oh dear. You knew each other? ...This might make things complicated," Sir Lamorak remarked, smiling coldly and bewitchingly as she watched Emma cling to Rintarou happily. "...Now, how will things go from here?"

Sir Lamorak had a smile that didn't reveal any of her thoughts as she continued to observe Emma with Rintarou.

For the time being, Rintarou undid his *Fomorian Transformation*.

They healed Sir Kay and Sir Gawain, who were nearing death, with *Healing* magic.

They introduced themselves to one another and began to explain the situation.

"Oh, but…it's been so long, Sir Gawain. I just noticed you now. It's not as though a dragon pays any mind to the ants that crawl beneath its feet… I'm sorry about that." Sir Lamorak approached Sir Gawain with the creepiest smile.

In the same moment, Sir Gawain turned blue, and his back started shaking uncontrollably.

"Heh-heh… But I'm so happy that you've decided to participate in this battle… If anything, there are many things I need to *pay you back* for… Right?"

"EEEEEEEK!" Sir Gawain was acting like a frog that had been eyed by a snake, but that was beside the point.

Rintarou ignored Sir Gawain and the rest of them as he continued to indifferently explain the situation.

"So that's that. There was a period in my life when I skipped school on the mainland and wandered the world aimlessly for a year, right…"

"…I've asked this before, but what the heck were you even doing?" As usual, Luna stuck her nose in dutifully at his flighty behavior.

"I was bored out of my mind at school… Well, I met her while I was wandering around Orleans in France."

"Yes, I learned so much from you during that time, master!" Emma's spine was stick straight as she saluted Rintarou.

"I've been wondering: Why do you keep calling him master?" Luna scowled at Emma.

"Well, that's because as a representative of the Religious Order of Saint Joan, which will bring salvation to the world, I was chosen to fight as a King in the King Arthur Succession Battle. While I was under the guidance of the priests in the order, I spent my days going through religious training to learn the ways of magic and the sword... Back then, I was in a rut." Emma turned to Rintarou with an expression full of confidence. "That was when my master appeared before me. My master only taught me the ways of the sword for a very brief time, but...because of him, I improved tremendously."

"Ha... It was a mistake having those nobodies teach you in the first place, Emma, when you've got your wit and mana. Would an ant teach a young dragon how to fight?" Rintarou snorted as though it were nothing.

"I—I guess we should've expected that from Merlin's reincarnation... He *was* the master who taught King Arthur the sword and magic after all...," murmured Luna.

"He was an arrogant man who followed the doctrines of the Spartans, but he's unexpectedly good at teaching others." Sir Kay nodded in agreement.

"...Well, you've done more than enough, Mr. Magami," Felicia interjected with a sigh. "The Michelle family is one of the family lines that King Arthur's blood has continued to run through in modern times. The Religious Order of Saint Joan has protected the Michelle line for generations. They uphold order and herald world salvation. At face value, it appears to be a group that has dedicated their lives to church work, but underneath, they're grooming a powerful King to prepare for the eventual King Arthur Succession Battle and the Catastrophe... That's the gist of it."

"Are they really?! I had no idea!" Luna marveled.

"Hold up! How do you not know? You're not an outsider like me!" Rintarou interjected.

"And taking on the duties for the present-day Michelle family... Emma's outstanding bravery as King is compared to that of the former hero of France, Joan of Arc. She is called La Pucelle, the Saint of Salvation. Alongside that Kujou and me—Felicia Ferald—she is counted as one of the first-choice champion candidates for the King Arthur Succession Battle!"

"It's not like you're actually a first-choice champion," Rintarou said with unimpressed eyes as he waved his hand at Felicia's smug face.

"Ah...but what can I say? She's an underclassman *and* a King... And Mr. Kujou was a King, too... I wonder if the world is smaller than expected when it comes to this line of work?" Luna muttered to herself.

"But you were so mean to me, master...," Emma said, sulking as she completely ignored Luna. "One day, you suddenly left me after *saying those words*. I can't believe you just went off somewhere..."

For a moment, Rintarou seemed to be at a loss for words.

"...Sorry...about that," he eventually muttered.

"You could have at least let me say good-bye... I was planning on opening up to you about the King Arthur Succession Battle to ask whether you would join me..."

"Huh... Back then, I didn't even have an inkling that there was a battle as interesting as this one being planned behind the scenes..."

"Oh, master. But I don't mind. That's just me being greedy." Emma laughed surreptitiously and looked straight at Rintarou. "Hey, master. I'm able to fight as a King, and I attribute it all to your teachings. This is all thanks to you, master. Thank you so much for everything!"

"...But this isn't the reason I taught you," he muttered with a peculiar expression.

"Hmm? Did you say something, master?"

"...Nothing." Rintarou turned away with a sigh.

"Hrrm..." From the side, Luna glared at them in an incredibly ornery mood.

She pouted like a child. In fact, she didn't find this amusing at all. Not one bit!

Rintarou did seem cold when it came to Emma, but...ever since Emma had reunited with him, she'd been smiling happily at Rintarou, blushing softly. With slightly misty eyes, she was glancing at Rintarou and gauging his mood almost as though she were a girl in love.

"Whaaat, master? Are you a student at Camelot International High School, too?!"

"Basically. But I just transferred the other day."

"Oh, your uniform... Wow, I'm so happy. We're going to the same school!"

It was so obvious that Emma had special feelings for Rintarou.

To Luna, it was as if Emma was making a pass at her belongings, and that didn't sit well with her in the slightest.

On top of that, something else also grated on Luna's nerves...

"...Hmm? Were they friends in their past lives? Why does he remember her even though she's been wiped from his memory? *Hrng... Hrm...*"

"Uh. Um...Luna? H-how about we just cool our heads a bit...?" Sir Kay called out to her lord, who was maximally unhappy, as though trying to console her.

"Wh-who cares if Rintarou has feelings for another girl?! As a sisterly figure, I would rather have a rotten heretic find some other girl. That would take care of him! It would be a blessing for the sake of your future, Luna—"

Thud!

"—You know what? Just ignore me!" When Excalibur was thrust into the ground at her feet, Sir Kay dejectedly recanted.

Next to Luna and Sir Kay's little exchange, there was another conversation happening at the same time.

"Um... Master... There's something I wanted to ask you..." Emma seemed to struggle to broach the topic.

"What is it?" Rintarou asked.

"Well... If you're here, it must mean that...you're also part of the succession battle, right?"

"Yeah, that's right. I've got my reasons."

Then...

"Hey-yo, Emma! It's been so long! I haven't seen you since the afternoon! It seems you've really helped out *my vassal*, Rintarou... You know. My. Vassal. Rintarou." Luna placed extra emphasis as she swooped in.

"Luna..." Emma looked at her coldly and spoke to Rintarou with great misery. "I thought that was the case based on the situation, but...it seems you are on Luna's side."

"Well, that's right... But I've been thinking lately that I might've made a grave mistake."

"Well, well, well! I wouldn't have guessed someone who transferred today could have been a King participating in the succession battle! No, sirree! Not even in my wildest dreams!"

Everyone watched Luna as she brought out a giant thumbtack from out of nowhere and taped it to the palm of her left hand with cellophane tape.

"It must be fate that we've found out about each other at an early stage! Nice to meet you, Emma!" Luna offered her hand to Emma for a handshake, looking absolutely breezy. The needle of the thumbtack was in line with her left hand...

"What are you, a kid?!"

"GAAAAH?!" Luna nearly fainted in agony as Rintarou immediately locked her in a cobra twist. "Y-you cretin! How *dare* you attempt that on a King! A crime of this nature calls for the death penal—"

"Oh? And how would a corpse execute the death penalty? Ah, hey!"

"Owwie! Yow! Wait—stop! I'm sorry! AAAH!"

Like a married couple in a familiar comedy skit, the two of them exchanged barbs.

Emma stared intently at them…seemingly unsatisfied as she gloomily narrowed her eyes. "…Why would my master like *her*?"

"…Ha-ha." Taking notice of her lord's behavior, Sir Lamorak secretly grinned.

"Well… Nice to meet you… *Cough!* Gah!" Luna had somehow escaped from Rintarou's grip and once again came to stand in front of Emma. She hadn't taken notice of Emma's or Sir Lamorak's behavior. "Well, we're both trying to become King Arthur, so let's fight fair and square moving forward—"

This time, Luna offered her right hand for a handshake…

Slap! Emma unexpectedly hit Luna's hand aside.

"—Huh?!"

Everyone on Rintarou's side was perplexed as Emma looked at Luna with cold eyes.

"…I am not convinced."

"Say what?" Luna blinked at Emma's denunciation.

"For you—of all people—to make *my* master into *your* vassal… I just can't accept that. You're Luna Artur, the 'weakest candidate in the King Arthur Succession Battle.' Yes, I know you. You're infamous."

"!"

"He is…an amazing person. I think that the only person my master should serve as a vassal…would be the 'true King' who will rule over the world."

"Wh-what are you trying to say?!"

"Luna, I'm trying to become King in order to save the world. The destruction of the Curtain of Consciousness will eventually come...which will bring on the Catastrophe. I'm fighting in this succession battle with the aim of becoming King Arthur so I can save the world on the verge of ruin when it comes to it."

Emma flipped her battle flag spryly and pointed the tip of the sword at Luna. "...And why do you seek to be King, Luna?"

"*What?!* Isn't that obvious?!" Luna screeched, thrusting out her chest to give a majestic declaration. "To become King of the world and brag and boast and live large! *Duh!*"

"Oh, come on! Why can't you at least say something better for show?!" Rintarou howled, turning to the skies.

"What? But it's the truth."

"I saaaid! There's this thing called 'saving face'! Keep your real thoughts to yourself! That's what normal people do!"

With the two of them having that exchange in front of her, Emma gripped her sword tighter. "I knew it, Luna. You aren't right for my master," Emma said in a voice thick with enmity. The tension returned.

Sir Kay unsheathed her sword, and Sir Gawain protected Felicia behind his back.

"Hmph... What're you trying to say?"

At the premonition of something lethal coming, Luna narrowed her eyes and put her hand on the hilt of Excalibur at her hip.

"The King of salvation needs the best vassal possible. But you're a big doozy! You don't need a superior vassal like my master. It would be better if he was at my side..." Emma glared intensely at Luna, and then as though she were holding her breath, she whipped around to face Rintarou.

"Master! I beg you! Please do not join forces with that girl!

Instead, lend me your strength! Just like the good old days when you taught me!"

"—Ngh?!" At Emma's sudden entreaty, Rintarou could only blink.

"I know! I was immature and uncertain about my own strength back then! I know that's why you got fed up with me and left! Am I wrong?!"

"Well..."

"But I'm strong now! I followed your teachings and became powerful! I could be a great King now! I am a fitting King for you to serve! Please lend your strength to me—not Luna! I *need* you...!" Emma implored.

Rintarou was left speechless.

"Okay. If that's what you want, my beloved liege, then leave it to me. ♪"

No one could react in time.

In a split second, Sir Lamorak had come to a suitable distance and swung down at Luna's neck.

Not Luna, Felicia, Sir Kay, Sir Gawain, or even Emma—not a single one of them could react to Sir Lamorak's sharp movements.

Well, all except Rintarou.

"WHY YOUUU—!"

"AHHH!"

Rintarou had quickly moved in front of Luna to cover her, stopping the claymore that Sir Lamorak swung with his pair of swords.

If Rintarou hadn't jumped in, Luna's head really would have been sent flying.

The impact of the interlocking blades swept through the area around them, sending Luna, Sir Kay, Felicia, and Emma away like leaves scattered in the wind.

In a moment, the tension in the battlefield had been heightened to its max.

"Wha...? Sir Lamorak...?" Emma hadn't been able to process any of this as she watched in a stupor.

"I'll kill Luna and steal Rintarou for you. That's God's will." With an expression that was a mix between delight and madness, Sir Lamorak glared at Rintarou passionately over the interlocked swords.

"*O res mirabilis! Manducat Dominum pauper, servus et humilis.* Oh, what wonder! Heaven hath provided a master as provisions for which to feed the vulgar and lowly servants... Amen." In hushed tones, Sir Lamorak almost sang that psalm in Latin before smiling sinisterly.

"Merlin... For the sake of my King, I've decided to kill yours. If you're opposed, why don't you fight me for her? With your whole soul... If you don't, I'll kill her."

"You're not making any sense... Are you serious...?!"

"Why, of course. Though if you ask me whether I'm sane, I may have trouble answering." Sir Lamorak returned her blazing-crimson gaze to Rintarou.

For some reason..., Rintarou thought, *Lamorak wants a match to the death against me... Looks like I really can't avoid a fight with her...!*

"See! Look! Hurry and bring it out! Bring out that black power from earlier! If you don't, we'll keep this going without it!"

"You...don't have to tell me...!"

He had already drawn the seal of the evil-eye pattern on the backs of his hands.

It didn't matter that his entire body had been ravished from the short period of time that he had activated his *Fomorian Transformation* earlier. He couldn't be swayed by that.

Without hesitation, Rintarou once again invoked his *Fomorian Transformation*.

"W-wait! Please wait, Sir Lamorak! I—"

Emma was about to say something.

"I know, Emma! How much will you pay to buy Rintarou's freedom?!"

Luna had shouted. Their faces scrunched up in confusion—and time locked in place.

"Excuse me?"

"Geez! We can't fight that strong and scary Jack head-on! If you want Rintarou, then take him! As his owner, I will allow it!"

"Hey... Hey? ...You serious?" Rintarou's face was strained, and he was at a loss.

"...Are you...sure...?" Even Sir Lamorak's pupils had constricted, and she froze.

"Emma, don't you want Rintarou?! And you know what? He's on sale for a limited time! Let's say...four hundred thousand yen! And then we can pretend this never happened! How's that? Tee-hee!" Luna sported a foolish grin as she attempted to curry favor with Emma.

"......L-Luna?" Rintarou opened and closed his mouth as he gawked at her.

"Ah-ha! Ah-ha-ha-ha-ha-ha! Luna Artur! That was a good one! *I see! That's your angle, eh?!* You really had me there!" Sir Lamorak started laughing loudly as though she couldn't stand it anymore...

"Everyone, please get back to your senses!" Finally, Emma had collected herself. She looked exhausted. "Sir Lamorak, please lay down your sword! I have told you this multiple times, but our battle is—"

"Riiight! It was a joke. I'm reflecting over my bad behavior." Sir Lamorak easily drew her sword away, turned her back to them, and moved away from Rintarou.

"You're always—*always*—going too far with your jokes!" Emma turned to Luna next. "And you, Luna! What in the world do you think you're doing?!"

"What did I do?"

"You don't have the confidence to rule the world or the drive or the sense of justice! I mean, you just tried to sell my master for money to save your own neck!"

Emma stood before Luna and sharply stared at her.

"But it's totally Rintarou's fault that we've been targeted by this scaaary knight. This seems like the best choice. Plus, we'd get some money out of it." With a shameless attitude, Luna continued to brush aside Emma's disapproving stare.

"So? What'll you do? Are you going to buy Rintarou or not?"

"As if I would be able to accept that offer?! Do you take me for an idiot?!" On Emma's forehead were twitching blue veins as she seethed. Pure, unbridled rage flashed over her face.

"Did you hear that, master?! This is the true face of your King! Why do you serve her?!"

"Shut up! Rintarou is mine! The way I treat my belongings shouldn't concern you."

".........Ha-ha-ha."

On the other side of things, Rintarou's face was strained, and he seemed troubled as he looked between Luna and Emma.

For a while, Luna and Emma continued their argument like fighting children...

"Fine! In that case, I've got an idea, too!"

Finally, Emma took her sword—her Excalibur—and pointed its tip at Luna as she declared, "We'll have a contest for my master, Luna!"

"—Kh?!"

As they all stared at Emma in astonishment, Emma informed them dispassionately.

"You received the Dame du Lac's request today, too, I imagine. In that case, someone is making holes around this island to interfere in our succession battle and to harm civilians... And we'll need to handle the culprit when we find them. We'll have my master judge our capacity as Kings as we try to complete this objective. According to those results, we'll have my master choose... whether he wants to be with me or you, Luna."

"Uh-huh?" Luna must have been expecting Emma's response because she broke out in a fearless smile.

"I'm sorry, master... I made you the prize for a bet without asking...but please let us do this! Please give me a chance!" Emma ignored Luna and turned back to Rintarou as she lowered her head to him. "I...just want you by my side! I'll prove myself! I'm different from before! I would be a suitable lord for you now! So—" Emma desperately implored him, not caring how she looked.

"...Hey, hey. What the heck do you think you're saying...?" Rintarou shrugged as though he had given up...when Luna butted in.

"...Okay, fine! I'll take you on that challenge!" Luna beamed, puffing out her chest.

"...Ha-ha. What the hell is happening?" At that point, all Rintarou could do was smile dryly as his face twitched.

"Wha...?! Luna?! Are you in your right mind?!"

Felicia, Sir Kay, and Sir Gawain were in shock.

"A battle to prove our quality as Kings? Ha-ha, I'm down for that. It's not as though I'd lose to you. I mean, Rintarou will choose me, no matter what. I don't think this will be a real battle, but I'll take you on! I'll show you what it means to be on a whole other level!"

"What arrogance! What conceit... I knew you weren't suitable for my master... I'll prove that my abilities as King greatly surpass yours."

Everyone anxiously watched Luna and Emma staring each other down.

Then, Luna gloated as though victory was hers.

"Are we set? Until we conclude this battle, we'll say that our sides are at a truce. How does that sound? We won't interfere with each other... Are you okay with that?"

"Yes, that's fine by me, Luna... I'll give Sir Lamorak strict orders, too."

"Ha-ha! Don't come crying to me later!"

"That's what I should be saying to you!"

They glared at each other in this cat fight.

"This is getting..."

"...weird..."

Felicia and Sir Kay finished each other's sentence as they anxiously watched the developments.

"...Oh... We'll go without fighting each other for now... Thank God..." Secretly, Sir Gawain breathed out a sigh of relief.

"Oh, right, right! Sir Gawain?" Sir Lamorak turned to him. "As soon as this armistice ends...I'll make sure to thoroughly kill you straight away... Just you wait."

"EEEEEK?! I knew this would happen!"

For some reason, Sir Lamorak had been glaring at Sir Gawain with maximum hostility from the outset. Sir Gawain cowered.

"Hmm...but...," Sir Lamorak mused, putting aside the cowed knight for now to look at Luna, Emma, and Rintarou.

"This...has gotten...messy," she cheerfully muttered, unbeknownst to the others, placing her pointer finger to her chin. "...Maybe I'll talk to *her* later?"

After all of that had happened, they ended up splitting up there, dealing with all kinds of premonitions of trouble.

Things had gone awry ever since they accepted the request from the Dame du Lac.

Rintarou and the others had separated from Emma and Sir Lamorak, carrying their fatigue with them as they headed home.

"...Luna! What in the world did you think you were doing?!" Sir Kay flew at the girl to scold her.

Luna whistled, showing no concern at all.

"I can't believe you'd try to sell Rintarou to tide things over! And why would you accept her challenge?!" Sir Kay turned around and pointed at Rintarou, who walked at the rear end of their group. "Just look at him! He looks so pitiful and dejected!"

When Luna obeyed, she saw that Rintarou was actually trudging behind them with his shoulders slumped, facing down. His sighs had become more frequent. It seemed he was terribly depressed.

"Geez! I'll have you know, Merlin can be sensitive! Sure, he's outrageous, arrogant, and an insolent outsider, but have you already forgotten the great debt of gratitude you owe him?!" Sir Kay was genuinely upset.

"But...if I didn't...," Luna mumbled with a semi-gloomy expression as she tried to make an excuse for herself to Sir Kay.

However, in the next moment, she changed her tune.

"But it's fine! Because Rintarou is mine! A King can do whatever she wants with her vassal!"

Heh! Luna crossed her arms and turned away as she spurned the lecture.

"I mean, to start, what was up with you, Rintarou?! Just because she's kind of cute and offered you a place with her doesn't mean you can go philandering! Friends from your past lives?! *Master?!* That's so stupid!"

As steam sputtered from her ears, she started to turn the blame on Rintarou.

"Making puppy dog eyes at another King while he's serving

me is plain disrespectful! And that's that! He doesn't have a sensitive bone in his body! You can treat others the way they treat you!"

"You really aren't cute. When was I allegedly 'philandering' with Emma?" Rintarou muttered, breaking his silence.

Luna's words had really hit home.

"We haven't chosen the victor yet. Maybe I should jump ship to Emma?"

"Wha...?!" Luna seemed startled, as though she hadn't expected that.

"What's wrong? You got something to complain about?"

"Wh-what's with you?!"

The two of them glared at each other...

"Th-this isn't the time to be fighting, Luna!" quipped Felicia.

"R-r-right!"

Oddly at their wit's end, Felicia and Sir Gawain intervened.

"After this truce ends, we will end up in an actual battle with Emma and Sir Lamorak! If that happens, my life would be in serious danger! Sir Lamorak is out to get me!" Sir Gawain yelped.

"If Sir Gawain is killed, my life would be on the line, too!"

"Seriously, you two..." Rintarou breathed out as though absolutely exasperated.

"A-anyway! I think we need to talk more about that Sir Lamorak! Emma is a threat, but the gravest danger is Sir Lamorak! We need to take countermeasures against her while we have a truce!"

Felicia must have been trying to subtly dispel the bad air between Luna and Rintarou. She ended their argument and forcibly changed the topic. She could be rather overbearing, but there was an unexpectedly attentive and considerate side to her.

Whether she was aware of Felicia's motives or not, Luna pulled herself together and cast some doubt.

"Hey, is Sir Lamorak really that strong? I mean, well, I already know she is, but I haven't really heard much about her as a knight of the Round Table..."

Sir Kay dispassionately replied, "Sir Lamorak, along with Sir Lancelot, and Sir Tristan, were of the strongest among the Round Table. Because she left the picture rather early, she's not that famous in the modern day, but...in the legendary era she was called Lamorak of the Red Shield or Lamorak of the Rothschild."

"The Rothschild...?"

"Yes. The origin of her name is her Rothschild—named *Gunimo*, for action; *Philiotaio*, for resistance; and *Ramheid*, for balance. They are the three shields, artifacts of her illusory armor. Those shields can automatically protect her from enemy attacks with the equivalence of her own skill in close combat. In other words, when you battle Sir Lamorak, you're going against her *and* her three shields, which are essentially three more of her."

She was already a difficult enemy, but to handle three additional selves?

"Wh-what kind of hack is that...? Isn't that stupid?" Luna's face twitched.

"Even without that Rothschild, Sir Lamorak's valor by itself... There's a story that goes like this," Sir Kay told Luna gently. "In the past, in the age when we were alive, the admired path of the knight was divided among the Round Table. Basically, 'Sir Lancelot's road lived of loyalty,' 'Sir Tristan's road lived of love,' 'Sir Lamorak's road lived of valor'—"

"And for me, 'Sir Gawain's road lived of justice.'"

"You're not included in this one," Rintarou snapped, interjecting.

"Urgh?!"

Rintarou had kicked over Sir Gawain, who had nonchalantly inserted himself into the story.

"What's with you guys? I swear, it's like you just don't feel at home without showing off to everyone?" Rintarou complained.

"Ow?! Sorry! Don't step on me, Rintarou Magamiiiiiiii!" Sir Gawain shrieked pitifully as Rintarou stomped all over him.

"A-anyway, Sir Lamorak's valor is real! In which case, she might be an even stronger enemy than Sir Lancelot... You must center yourself, Luna. Please."

"B-but there's something else I want to ask about Sir Lamorak... She was kind of looking at Sir Gawain funny... Why?" Luna uttered in suspicion.

"Oh... *That*..." With disgust, Rintarou looked down at Sir Gawain squished under his heel. "It was back in the age of legends. There was a tournament at Surluse. This idiot waited until Lamorak was dead tired after winning multiple rounds. While Lamorak was on the way home, he tried to launch a four-person surprise attack on her along with Gaheris, Agravain, and Mordred. They essentially mobbed her and ended up beating her to death..."

At the same moment, Luna and Felicia froze.

"...Uh, for real?" Luna asked, turning her eyes to Sir Kay.

"...Unfortunately, yes. At the time, it was a serious matter," Sir Kay awkwardly replied, turning her eyes away from Sir Gawain.

"Wow, you're the worst..." Felicia looked down on Sir Gawain, who was under Rintarou's heel, as though she were looking at grime...

"Y-you've got it all wrong! Please listen to me! I had my reasons! Do you know what that perverted slut of a little girl did to my mother...? Ah! Felicia! Please don't forsake me! Please don't abandon meee!" Sir Gawain's eyes were filled with tears as he clung to Felicia's feet.

"So about Sir Gawain...," Luna started. "Was he this hopeless in the past?"

"Yes, incredibly. He was King Arthur's nephew, so that really might have gotten to his head." Sir Kay let out a sigh.

"Huh? But...about that..."

"Is something the matter, Luna?"

"Yeah... It's about Sir Gawain and the others... About how Sir Lamorak was killed being mobbed by four people... Something about that bothers me...? I wonder what it is...?" She tilted her head quizzically, clearly lost in thought.

Sir Gawain was continuing to desperately make excuses for himself to Felicia.

At the sideline of all the commotion, Rintarou was looking up at the night sky.

"Well, regardless of that... Emma, huh? I can't believe that little chickling would end up being a King...," Rintarou muttered to no one in particular, then sighed.

"Well, anyway, Rintarou!" Luna had made a beeline for Rintarou when her conversation wrapped up.

"...What?"

"We ended up changing the topic, but...you know what I'm thinking, right?" Luna seemed somewhat hesitant...

"Rintarou... Y-you'll pick me, regardless of the results of our little contest, right? You won't actually ever leave me in the dust, right?"

"Who knows? I wonder what I'll do." Rintarou laced his hands behind his head and sarcastically curled up the corners of his mouth. He didn't even turn to Luna as he spoke.

"It's not like you've appointed me to an important position or anything. You might even end up coming across another King who'll buy me for a really high price... It all depends on the circumstances, I guess."

"Whaaaat?! Y-you're kidding, right...?" Luna exclaimed, but Rintarou had only a faint grin. He neither confirmed nor denied her question. It seemed that he actually was sulking.

"Wh-wh-what is wrong with you? To have an insolent attitude toward your King! That's disrespect!"

"Hmph!"

Luna and Rintarou's argument had once again come to a boil.

I beg you two to please make up soon... In her heart, Felicia prayed. But all she could do was sigh.

On the other side of things—

"I'm sorry for making a rash decision, Sir Lamorak."

After they had broken away from Rintarou's group, Emma apologized to Sir Lamorak next to her on their way home.

"I agree with you that the most efficient way to win the succession battle is...to systematically battle the other Kings until they're all eliminated... I know that way is better, but I..." Emma was filled with distress.

Sir Lamorak grinned. "It's fine. That's fine for you, Emma."

Her demented behavior from the battle had disappeared.

Sir Lamorak carefully handled Emma. There was deep love and affection in her every expression.

"All you should do is go down the road that you believe is just for a King. At times, you'll be troubled. I know times will be trying...but regardless, you need to abandon your life to your faith and take the path of thorns... That path is incredibly sacred and holy. Like Jesus Christ, who took the burden of all humankind's original sin upon himself as he endured the sufferings of the cross, and Joan of Arc, who sacrificed herself until the very last at the stake... I responded to your call and decided to serve you because you are noble like those saints... Amen."

Sir Lamorak drew a cross on herself with her right hand and offered her prayers.

"Sir Lamorak... Thank you so much! I'm so happy you'll be

with me!" Emma's face suddenly became bright as she smiled happily at Sir Lamorak.

To Emma, Sir Lamorak was certainly a reckless, problematic knight, but…she was also the greatest and most trustworthy Jack that Emma could ever ask for.

As long as she was with Sir Lamorak, Emma knew she could get through the battle until the very end.

And if my master also joins me…then I'll…, Emma thought absentmindedly.

"Hey, Emma, my King," Sir Lamorak said, sounding as though she was poking fun at Emma. "Because we've finally come upon this opportunity…you should make sure you make a good catch."

"Catch… What? What am I supposed to catch…?"

"Why, that's obvious. Merlin… Rintarou Magami."

"…Huh?"

"Is it that hard to understand? While we can't have a direct battle in this truce, this is your chance. It doesn't matter where this battle goes. Shouldn't you recruit him as your ally?"

"Er. Um… Sir Lamorak? J-just what are you trying to say…?"

"Listen, Emma…"

As Emma continued to be perplexed, Sir Lamorak gently stretched and brought her mouth up to Emma… She breathed into Emma's ear and whispered as though playfully nibbling on it. "When it comes to men… If you do it with him once, he's all yours."

"Whaaat?!" Emma's face turned bright red from this ridiculous advice.

Sir Lamorak chuckled at Emma's naive reaction. "Well, that was half a joke. In the end, he's choosing the King he will serve himself, right?"

"—Ngh?!"

"In other words, you merely need him to choose you. Don't use all your energy on this challenge or whatever. It would be faster for you to get him to like you. For boys and girls alike, I know people would want to be by the side of the person of their affections, right?"

"A-affections?! N-no, it's not like I was trying to— It's just that I can't stand having my master accompanying that scummy girl!"

"Be honest with yourself, Emma," Sir Lamorak said, as though admonishing her beloved child. "You like him, don't you? Merlin... Rintarou Magami."

"Uh!"

"Though you are naturally docile and gentle, you were upset... Isn't that right?"

When that was pointed out to her, Emma's face turned redder. She opened and closed her mouth.

Eventually, she gathered her courage with resolve.

"Y-yes... I...do like...my master... And I-I've always liked him...!"

"Oh, how cute. It's so nice being young."

"I—I have everything that I have now...because of my master. I want him by my side. I want him to look at me as though I were the only girl for him... I want him to always guide me..." Emma smiled—euphorically and yearningly—and looked into the distance.

Sir Lamorak watched Emma and let a smile play across her lips, too. She continued to smile, filled with affection and joy.

"Ah, well. It's for the sake of my revered lord, after all. I suppose I will help."

"Th-thank you so much, Sir Lamorak!"

"Ha-ha, *petite et dabitur*—ask and you shall receive... This is all also God's will. Put your best foot forward, my King."

As Emma turned a pure smile to her, Sir Lamorak grinned back—eerily and more luridly than anything else...

CHAPTER 3

𝕷𝖚𝖓𝖆 𝖛𝖘. 𝕰𝖒𝖒𝖆

The week of the challenge between Luna and Emma had started. Their prize was Rintarou.

The classroom at Camelot International High School for Class 2-C of the second-year students was unusually astir.

"Wh-what the heck…is going on with those two?"

They were in a break between classes. From a distance, the students watched Luna, at her window-side seat in the back, and Rintarou, who sat immediately behind her.

"Hmph…" Luna was usually in a stupidly sunny mood, but on this day, she was clearly pouting. She propped her cheek in her hand and, feeling on edge, tapped on her desk. Occasionally, she would check how Rintarou was doing in the seat behind her.

"……"

On the other hand, Rintarou was being his usual self, completely ignoring Luna's piercing gaze. He put his hands together behind his head and threw his legs onto his desk, feigning ignorance as he looked out the window.

"Hmmmmph!" Luna had tried to make a point of her

unhappiness, but when it was ineffective on Rintarou, she continued to sulk even more.

"H-hey... What's up with those two?"

"They were, like, best friends before the weekend started..."

"Right? They beat Mr. Sudou and sold bread and stuff together."

The students whispered to one another.

There was a girl with long black hair who was watching over Rintarou and Luna with concern. That was Nayuki Fuyuse, who was sitting politely, dressed in her school uniform.

"Hey, Kay," she started, "do you think something happened between those two during the weekend?"

"Lady Fuyuse... Um, well... It's complicated. This situation came to be from an accumulation of factors... I don't think I should be the one to explain it..."

It wasn't as though Sir Kay could explain the succession battle, so she tried to lead Nayuki off the scent by being vague.

"Ah-ha-ha, we're not in the greatest place. I mean, Mr. Kujou's taken a leave of absence because he's sick, and the vibe of our classroom has been in the gutter... Even Luna is in a bad mood..."

"...You're right..."

Sir Kay remembered their earlier homeroom when it had been announced they would have a temporary substitute as their homeroom teacher. They had been informed the homeroom teacher would be taking a sick leave and that the other class's teachers would be taking turns as their homeroom teacher for a while.

However, all of those arrangements had been made officially for show for the students.

Underneath it all, the city police of Avalonia had to be secretly investigating Kujou's whereabouts as a missing person case—and the loose ends of that investigation would probably never be cleanly tied up.

The students around them were talking about rumors: "Wonder who the next homeroom teacher's going to be?" and "Maybe Luna and Magami aren't getting along because they're in love?" Nayuki continued to watch Luna and Rintarou with nervous eyes.

"I think that…as long as it's those two, they should be fine."

"Gosh… I hope."

In the eddy of noise from the class, Sir Kay's sigh dissipated into nothing.

"Hey, was there something you wanted to ask me, Rintarou?"

It would have appeared that Luna couldn't stand this mini Cold War anymore. With her head propped up in her hand, she was still pouting in annoyance as she spoke to Rintarou behind her.

With his eyebrows raised, he looked at the back of Luna's head.

"What? …Nothing really," he replied.

"Liar. I know you do." Luna became more worked up. "For example, don't you want to ask about why I tried to sell you to Emma or something…?"

"……" Rintarou narrowed his eyes slightly and remained silent.

"With everything going on, I missed my chance to apologize, and I want to start by saying sorry… I did something terrible without asking. I'm a failure of a King for making light of my vassal… I think."

She must have been uncomfortable or embarrassed or frustrated because Luna looked into the distance as she wrapped her long hair around her pointer finger. With some hesitation, she started to incoherently mumble again.

"But…about that… You *know*. I'm sure that you've got the wrong idea or something. Well, I guess you couldn't help but get the wrong idea? Um… It's like that… You get it, right?"

Her eyes flicked to him again. Then again.

There was something about her eyes. With every glance, Luna seemed to be imploring Rintarou from over her shoulder.

"And for that battle... I'd really like you to choose me... I'm sure you can understand."

There were no traces of her usual arrogance and self-confidence. It was almost as though she were a kitten that had lost sight of its mother.

"No idea," Rintarou snapped with disgust in his eyes, thoroughly rejecting Luna's desperate plea.

"Aaah! Are you for real?! You're seriously the densest!" Luna clutched her skull and ruffled up her hair. "Fine! I'm not good at being subtle. In that case, I'll just tell you straight out!"

She kicked over her chair and stood up and turned to Rintarou.

"The reason I tried to sell you to Emma and took on that challenge was because—"

But she wasn't able to finish her sentence.

"Excuse me. Is my mast—er, I mean, is Rintarou here?"

The classroom door opened with a clatter, allowing entry to a petite girl.

The students who had been anxiously watching the developments between Luna and Rintarou all turned their attention to the unexpected visitor.

When she stepped foot in the classroom, it was as though their monochromatic lives had turned into technicolor, glittering like an opera stage flooded with light.

That was because the girl who had appeared was that glamourous and cute.

Her eyes were a brilliant green. Her features were dashing. Her platinum blonde hair flowed loose and soft, cut and permed in a way that accentuated her features. She had on a hint of makeup that was barely detectable. It didn't obscure her natural naïveté and purity, but they were emphasized with grace.

She had a ribbon adorning her with a silver cruciform pendant... Even the accessories were unobtrusive. She wore her uniform on her small frame in a refined way without deviating from the norms. It enhanced her understated fashion choices and transcendent beauty.

As she passed by the other students, lightly fragrant perfume tickled their noses.

She was the perfect specimen of a natural beauty putting in some effort.

It was almost as though an idol had transferred over to their school, bringing radiance to their drab and humdrum classroom.

"H-hey, who is that?! Looks like she's an underclassman?!"

"Did we always have this knockout cutie at our school?!"

The classroom was in an uproar.

Who is that? Rintarou's and Luna's expressions practically said. Based on their confused faces, they clearly had no clue.

As she was showered by the stares of the class, her eyes scoured the classroom.

"Oh." Eventually, she caught sight of Rintarou and let a grin escape. "Maste... I mean, Rintarou! Hello!"

She lightly waved her hand at Rintarou as she trotted over to him.

"Hold up... Emma?!"

"Whaaaaaaaaaat?!" Luna shrieked in hysterics when Rintarou finally made the realization and blinked.

"Wait! A! Second! No way?! I'm sorry. *What?!* Where's that untrendy and unkempt country bumpkin...? *Excuse me?!*" Luna sputtered, unbelievably rudely.

Ignoring Luna, Emma gleefully stood in front of Rintarou.

"Hmm? Oh, did you get a haircut? It's like you transformed overnight. What the heck happened?"

"Oh, ah-ha-ha... Um, well... Sir Lamorak showed me how to do this... I-I'm not really good at this stuff or that interested in it, but...I wanted to look as nice as I could for you, and I tried my best..."

Emma seemed embarrassed, turning red and looking down.

"I—I guess it doesn't look good on me at all... I am an oaf, after all... Even if I dress up, I..." Emma kept her face hidden and insecurely shied away.

"You can't be serious! You've never looked better," Rintarou praised, softening his face. "I didn't recognize you at first. You never dressed up before... But wow. This is miles better than before. This is definitely how you should dress from now on. Got it?"

"Um? Ah! Okay! Thank you so much!" Emma smiled happily. Her blushing face and her misty eyes were cute enough to even make a girl's heart flutter.

"Wh-wh-wha...?!"

Luna, who had secretly prided herself in her looks—and won over Emma in that department before—grimaced and broke out into a cold sweat.

Crap! She's on par with me! You know...some people might even prefer Emma over me! Luna thought as Rintarou and Emma's conversation continued.

"I knew you transferred to this school, but I didn't think you'd come and find me... What's up? Did something happen?"

"No... Well...there wasn't any specific reason... I just wanted to talk to you."

"Talk? To me?"

"Yes. Well, maste... I mean, Rintarou. Since we haven't seen each other in a year, I thought we could catch up... Oh, I guess we're enemies right now. Is that a problem for you?"

"Not really. I couldn't care less. I'm good at separating business and pleasure. When I'm living my own life, I can even share a drink with a foe, my mortal enemies, and even a serial killer."

"...What a relief! Thank you so much, Rintarou!"

Rintarou and Emma were in their own little world and completely ignored Luna.

"*Grrrrr...!* What's with this?! All she did was dress up! *Cough! Cough!*" Luna began to hack up a lung—intentionally—as she continued to be left out. She glanced behind her, purposefully trying to draw Rintarou's attention as he chatted.

Those who would have noticed would have already seen the difference: Luna had changed out her ribbon from the day before.

"*Cough! Koff!* Aaah! *Hack-hack!*" Luna continued her attempt to blatantly appeal to Rintarou.

"...Are you feeling sick? You should go home." Rintarou gave her a disaffected response.

"AAAAH! GEEEZ!" she wailed.

Bam! Bam-bam! Luna violently hit her own desk with her notebooks.

Even as Luna acted so strangely along the sidelines, Rintarou and Emma continued to chat.

Eventually, time passed, and they were nearing the end of the break...

"...Oh, it's time for our next class," Emma muttered with reluctance and a pointed look at the clock.

"Right. Okay, hurry and get back," Rintarou urged.

As if her mind had settled on something, Emma spun around to Rintarou.

"U-um... Rintarou... Would it be okay to keep visiting you?"

"...? ...*Me?*"

"Um... I still want to talk to you about some stuff... But... Of course... I don't want to annoy you..."

"Welp, you're already too late for that! You've already annoyed the crap out of both of us! Don't ever show yourself in front of me or Rintarou again! *Shoo! Shoo! Shoo!*"

Luna shoved her hand into a bag of Takata Salt—from god-knows-where—and started sprinkling it all around.

"You know what? Why not? I'll keep talking to you until you've had enough." Rintarou had readily consented...

"Aaaah! How couuuuld you?!"

Fwump! Luna roughly hurled her bag of salt onto her own desk.

"See you, Rintarou! Excuse me!" Emma saluted Rintarou with a cheerful smile as she said good-bye.

The students in the classroom watched her in awe as though they were in a dream as Emma trotted away from their classroom in her squirrel-ish way.

That was how a girl named Emma entered Rintarou's and Luna's school life.

During their short hour-long breaks, Emma would frequently come and chat with Rintarou about anything and everything, then would reluctantly leave when classes resumed.

Emma was starting to act like a puppy pining for her owner.

When it had just started, their peers couldn't hide their bewilderment...

"Oh, Emma's here!"

"Yo! Rintarou! Your cute little long-distance wife's here for you!"

"W-wife?! H-hold on!"

"Ah-ha-ha... Don't worry about it. All right, come on."

…But the students got used to it over time.

During breaks, it became normal for Emma to make the trip to their classroom, though she was from a different grade.

"P-pardon me."

"Ah-ha-ha, good luck, Emma!"

Emma was honest, courteous, and diligent. On top of that, her affection for Rintarou was obvious from her behavior. It was clear that she had no ulterior motives. She was completely different from Luna, who was twisted to her very core.

Furthermore—

"Oh, Rintarou! Your uniform cuff…is frayed and coming undone."

"Hmm? Huh. You're right."

"Ha-ha, just hold still for a bit. I have a sewing kit with me."

"Oh… That's what I'd expect from a girl."

"……Hmm. There we go. What do you think?"

"Wow, it's as good as new. Thanks, Emma."

"No worries."

Emma was apparently the devoted type, incredibly gallant and admirable when it came to Rintarou.

She was happy to do anything when she could… It was just in her nature.

That was why everyone wanted to cheer Emma on.

"Oooh! *Damn!* I'm so jealous of Rintarou!"

"Seriously! I can't believe he's got a nice cutie fawning over him! Damn!"

"I hope things work out for Emma."

The students chatted among themselves as usual as they watched Emma come to Rintarou.

"But I don't think anything will come of her feelings anytime soon..."

"Yeah... Plus, Rintarou's got Luna, and she's his childhood friend, too..."

"But Luna and Rintarou are obviously in a huge fight right now."

"Which means...this might be Emma's only chance?!"

"Emma or Luna... Who will win?! This is a must-see!"

After everything, they were still young boys at that age.

It was incredibly entertaining to observe other people's love lives.

It had been three days.

They were approaching the routine time for Emma to come to the classroom.

During the break, Luna went to freshen up. When she came back, a conversation was already in progress.

"Hey, where did the two of you meet?"

"Oh, I wanna know, too!"

"C'mon! Rintarou, hurry up and spit it out!"

Emma was perched on Luna's seat in front of Rintarou. A small cluster of their classmates was surrounding the two, merrily asking them questions.

"Uh. Um... Erm, Rintarou and I... Well... Ha-ha-ha..." Emma started to blush, looking down...

"Yeah. I met her briefly on a trip and helped her out... She was so clumsy that I couldn't just stand by." Rintarou was laid-back, his hands behind his head and his legs tossed over the top of his desk.

"Uh... You're so mean, Rintarou...but I'm really grateful..."

"Wow... I can't believe you would try to pick up a girl on a trip..."

"Rintarou, I never would have pinned you as the romantic type..."

"And? And then what? How did you help her? What happened?"

That corner of the room began to buzz with excitement, as though they were actually talking about a budding romance.

"......Why...! Why you...!" Luna scowled as veins popped out of her forehead. She looked at them with unimpressed eyes.

Like, it was as if her place had been taken! She didn't even have a place where she belonged anymore!

To add insult to injury...

"I'm so sorry for this last-minute invitation."

"No worries, it's cool. We're only really busy at night anyway."

It was after school. Rintarou and Emma were walking side by side on a large street heading toward the area near the station. There were all kinds of stores and types of entertainment for students.

".............."

"...Uh, um. Luna?"

Several yards behind the two was Luna with strangely steady eyes and a dark aura rising off her. She walked along with Sir Kay, who was loitering with her master.

Emma hadn't noticed the dark vibe that consumed Luna, talking blissfully with Rintarou.

The two were oddly close together. Slowly, it seemed that Emma was closing the distance between her and Rintarou. At some point, they were no longer "walking together" so much as "leaning into each other."

But the thing that grated on Luna's nerves the most was Rintarou's attitude that suggested he couldn't help but oblige. He didn't seem that annoyed by Emma.

"It's a really cute place. I'd be happy if you liked it, too, Rintarou."

"Yeah? I'm picky about my coffee."

"Urp... Now I'm getting nervous... But I'll try my hardest!"

"Ha-ha-ha, you're not the one who needs to try."

The two of them already seemed like occupants of their own little world.

"*Grrr...!* I-is this the rumored Curtain of Consciousness...?!"

"Oh, I see! In other words, we're the illusory beings that have been forgotten and left behind, right?! Good one, Luna! Gotta hand it to you— *Yow!* That hurt! Sorry!"

Luna put Sir Kay in a headlock, and her knight was in tears as she apologized.

Even as Luna and Sir Kay were causing a ruckus, Rintarou and Emma had eyes only for each other.

They were supposed to be going to this café together, but Luna and Sir Kay had been fated to be third wheels from the outset.

For a while, Luna stared at the backs of the two as though she were a shadow girl.

"Waaah! S-Sir Kaaay?!" she cried out as though she had finally reached her limit.

"Huh? Luna... Aaah?!"

Luna had grabbed Sir Kay's collar, practically dragging her knight as she madly dashed away and jumped into a nearby alley.

"Wh-wh-what is going on there?! What is that?! What is this?!" Luna interrogated.

As Sir Kay coughed and sputtered, she was pushed into the wall.

"Wh...? What's *what* now...?"

"Th-the whole mood between those two changed over the course of a few days. They're basically clinging to each other, *and* it's like they're a step away from getting to something, *and* everyone is rooting for them, *and* the entire situation is just too much!"

It seemed Luna had gotten a sense of the imminent danger. She had turned blue and lost all composure.

"I-isn't Rintarou my vassal?! He's cast me aside and…now he's with that girl—that's unbelievable, right?!"

"Please calm down, Luna. You're not making any sense." Sir Kay sighed and soothed Luna. "…In any case, this must be Sir Lamorak's doing."

"Sir Lamorak…?"

When Luna tilted her head, Sir Kay dispassionately explained her theory.

"Yes. Sir Lamorak is trying to find the best way to bring Rintarou to Emma's side regardless of who Rintarou chooses as the better King after the challenge."

"Y-you don't mean…?"

"Yes, I do. Frankly speaking, the fastest way to achieve this role is to make this about a romantic relationship." Sir Kay shrugged and continued.

"On the outside, she's just joking around. But the method is unexpectedly logical. Judging by her actions from our first encounter, it's clear that Emma is attached to Rintarou… From ancient times to modern day, men want to stand next to the woman of their affections. It doesn't matter if it isn't completely logical… Or so I've heard."

"Wh-wh-wh-what a coward! I can't believe she's using psychological warfare to give her an edge…?!"

Hmmmph! Her face turning bright red, Luna stomped her feet.

"Wh-which explains why Emma has been dressing up and coming by to see Rintarou! She got the whole class on her side for this…?!"

"Yes, this is Sir Lamorak's wiles... I'm willing to bet Emma is closely following her detailed directions. She probably doesn't even know what she is doing herself." Sir Kay sighed. "Sir Lamorak is an expert when it comes to love. Because of some tonic that she took when she was young, Sir Lamorak remains in the form of a child, as you can see. Even though she has this disadvantage, Sir Lamorak is a veteran of romance. She's been with countless lovers as the result of her hard work and research."

"...Meaning she doesn't depend on her looks to attract people... That must mean she mastered the inner workings of men and women!"

"Yes. It doesn't matter if her potential partner is in a relationship—or even married. When Sir Lamorak feels like it, she has a one hundred percent success rate, whether it be man or woman. Plus, she's a beast in the sheets, and all the people that she's been with have fallen head over heels for her."

"...What? Wait a second! W-women...? You just said women, didn't you?" Luna's face froze when she caught that bit.

"Yes, she's bisexual."

"She's so indulgent! That little tramp!" Luna's head was starting to pound. "I guess that's what I'd expected for an era that just did people in and *did* people... What was that about chivalry? I can't believe Sir Lamorak would be allowed to claim that she was part of the Round Table."

"She was simply that valiant and loyal to her King... And that's that," Sir Kay said sternly, and Luna went silent. "Emma has Sir Lamorak on her side. You would do well not to underestimate her methods of psychological warfare."

"B-but..."

"Naturally, Emma isn't Sir Lamorak. Emma can't do what Sir

Lamorak does. But...if this continues, there's a chance Rintarou might turn to Emma's side."

...*Though I wouldn't mind that*, Sir Kay would have grumbled.

"Th-that's stupid! Th-there's no way that Rintarou would abandon—"

Luna was obviously upset. Her eyes were swimming as she refuted Sir Kay.

"Yes, it's true that Merlin would never abandon King Arthur—even if hell froze over. But...right now, he's 'Rintarou Magami' and you're 'Luna Artur.' You're not Merlin and King Arthur."

"...Gh?!" At Sir Kay's dispassionate words, Luna could only go silent.

Eventually, Luna continued. "Ha-ha-ha-ha... Fine... I got it... If that's how it is...!" She smiled ominously, full of passion now, even though it was the dark kind.

She pulled a magazine from her bag.

"I thought this might happen... Now I know buying this was the right decision!"

"Um...Luna... What *is* that book?" Sir Kay glanced at it without interest.

SHOW HIM THE GODDESS INSIDE! KILLER MOVES FROM KIRARA HIMEBOSHI ★ screamed the garish cover. SWEET TECHNIQUES TO MAKE HIM MELT! MAKE THE GUY OF YOUR DREAMS CRAZY ABOUT YOU ♥

"It's not okay for a King to flirt with her vassal! And it's not like I see Rintarou like *that*! But as a woman, I can't stand anyone thinking I'm any less than Emma! Just watch... I'll use the techniques in this book and...! Heh-heh-heh...!"

"Um, Luna? I think someone as pretty as you could get by without relying on that odd book... You should pursue him as you normally would... But as your pseudo-sister, I object to pursuing him, regardless of the chosen method."

"It'll be fine! I'm going to try this out! As a King and as a woman, I outclass Emma, and I'll prove it! Prepare yourself, Rintarouuu!" Luna gave herself a little pep talk before resolutely dashing away from that place.

"......" Sir Kay watched her master's back with half-open eyes... and eventually, an idea come to her.

Ah, I can already tell this isn't gonna work out. Sir Kay's sigh echoed through the now abandoned alleyway.

It was the following day.

Their morning classes passed without a hitch, and it was now time for lunch.

As Camelot International students, they had several ways to spend the break.

First, they could go to the cafeteria.

Second, they would buy bread or boxed lunches at the school cafeteria.

Last, they could leave campus to eat.

Because this was an international school with many students from abroad, the administration was generally lax. As long as they did it during lunch break, the students could leave the school grounds. Because of this policy, the hungry students would go their separate ways, procuring their lunches through their own methods.

In that daily shuffle, Emma headed to the classroom of second-years, wading through the students.

Her goal was, of course, to see Rintarou.

...Hmm... Maybe I'm being too persistent? I've been trying to be with my master at every available opportunity... I wonder if he thinks I'm annoying...?

Though she was anxious, she didn't stop.

It's fine... At least, it should be fine. I'm doing exactly what Sir Lamorak told me, after all...

As she rebuked herself, Emma recalled Sir Lamorak's lecture.

...

"*—Do you get it now? Do you understand the importance of presentation and style?*" Sir Lamorak had proudly thrust out her chest and explained as Emma sat in front of her and nodded, a pen and pad of paper in hand.

"*You need to make yourself look cute, pretty, and cool to your target. If you have childish features, you make yourself more mature. If you look old, you make yourself look young. If you're fat, get skinny. At the very least, fix yourself up to the point where you're not unsightly. This isn't even about love as the basic foundations that make up interpersonal relationships.*

"*Even gender knows no bounds when it comes to this. The losers of the world who complain about their undesirability have already failed this step. They all have uncool haircuts, frumpy clothes, and flabby bodies. There's just no effort at all.*

"*I mean, even the ugliest person in the world could look halfway decent with some serious effort.*

"*Basically, all those people ranting about how we shouldn't 'judge a book by its cover' are fools. I'll tell you this: Fixing yourself up is basically social charity. Someone who can't even do that couldn't have anything on the inside, right? To start out, you spruce yourself up. That's the first step to mastering love.*"

"*Y-yes! I'll take that to heart!*" Emma was incredibly sincere and nodded in a way that satisfied Sir Lamorak.

"*Good. Then let's review. 'Make yourself look as stylish as possible.' But the caveat is—?*"

"To keep it natural! We're being considerate to society when we look better!"

"Bene est! Good! There's no need for you to go over-the-top. You shouldn't wear unbecoming brand-name items or dress up for sex appeal. The only ones who get caught up by that are himbos anyway."

"H-himbos...?!" Emma's face turned bright red beside her.

Sir Lamorak continued dispassionately. "Okay, next! Let's go over how you'll approach him. We need to make you a persona."

"A—a persona...?" When Emma heard she would be acting, she showed her slight disapproval. "Um... I'm not sure about pretending... Wouldn't it be better if I acted like my natural self?"

"Unfortunately, you need to make up a persona to a certain extent when it comes to love. Don't overdo it, but if you're naturally moody or shy—or have an ugly personality—you can't help it, right? Plus, there are popular and unpopular types of personalities. Well, just think of it as your little act of social charity."

"Y-yes... Charity... Right!"

"But...when it comes to you, I guess there really isn't much of an issue? We can work with your natural personality. If anything, a twisted guy like Merli... I mean, like Rintarou, might react better to your normal self."

"Oh? Y-you think so...?"

"Yes. But to make up for that, I'll let you know something that you absolutely can't do when it comes to a persona. You can't pretend to be a good girl. Trying to act innocent or dumb also won't work—especially with someone as shrewd as Rintarou. He'll see through the thoughts behind your thoughts. He'd hate you even if you only did it once."

"Even after only doing it once...? O-okay...got it..."

"Also! I forgot to tell you the most important thing! You can do *things for your crush, or devote yourself to them in some way, or make sure they're enjoying themselves... This is a basic skill when you're dealing with someone indifferent to you, but you absolutely cannot think they owe you for their actions!"*

"What...?"

"Humans are often the type to fall for that kind of idea. Like, thinking the other person owes you, because you've done all this stuff for them. But you're actually just trying to sell yourself with your kindness and goodwill... And that's a trap.

"I mean, you have no idea if your actions can make them happy. They might not even give it a second thought. You might end up causing trouble for them. You might end up seeming annoying. You always need to keep that in mind whenever you do things for anyone.

"And these actions might even bring on pain. If you end up being rejected, then you'll end up embarrassed.

"Though it's sad to say, you just won't be able to get the person to look at you if you don't do something. I'm sure you've heard about people with enough charm and kindness to attract people. But that only happens in stories. You got that?"

"I—I understand, Professor Lamorak!"

"Good. Then, I'll be your love professor and teach you practical strategies from here on."

...

...Yeah, it'll be fine. I'm following Sir Lamorak's teachings! And she said...that master was lonely all the time, and his type wouldn't hate someone just for hanging around him all the time...

Okay. Emma regained her motivation and hastened her feet as she headed to his classroom.

Emma Michelle...was serious.

She was serious, and she was in love with a boy named Rintarou Magami. She wanted him to see her and only her. She wanted him to come to her. She wanted him to be by her side...

I mean...! I finally...finally found him...!

She remembered the days she had spent with Rintarou in the past.

While Emma had spent her days in rigorous religious training to become a King in the remote French countryside, Rintarou Magami had appeared in front of her one day aimlessly carrying a duffel bag.

Even though Rintarou had taught her the bare minimum about swordsmanship and magic, she had gotten a grasp on it very quickly. At the time, her lack of training and sluggish progress had exasperated her.

In just a short time, she had grown enough to be considered among the upper crust of the candidates in the succession battle.

Right... Everything I have now is thanks to my master... Thanks to Rintarou...

If only she could be with him—she had been thinking that was what she wanted. It didn't take long for Emma to be drawn in by Rintarou.

But one day, Rintarou had abruptly disappeared from Emma's side.

And he had left her with those *brutal words.*

I...hate this. I hate being left by someone I treasured...

By the time she realized it, Emma had clenched her hand into a fist.

We're finally together again! It was a miracle...! If I let him get away again, I'll regret it for the rest of my life...! Please Jesus, Lord in heaven... Give me strength... Give me the courage of a lifetime...

She closed her eyes tight as she put her hands to her chest as if in prayer.

Eventually, Emma opened her eyes, and she stepped forward with an expression full of determination.

"...So. It's fine that we left the classroom...but what are we doing now?" Rintarou asked Emma, who walked next to him.

Emma had successfully gotten to his classroom and invited Rintarou to lunch.

When she had invited him out, she had been so embarrassed and nervous that she had been belligerent, but the other students around her cheering her on had been her saving grace.

If Luna had been there, they would have ended up in a fight, but...luckily, she wasn't anywhere to be seen.

Emma had invited Rintarou out. She had been real smooth.

"Want to go to the cafeteria? Or we could just buy bread at the school store?" Rintarou suggested. "Well, it's been a while since I've had a meal with you... It's a special occasion. How about we grab a bite to eat off campus?"

"Uh! Um...!" She had to admit she was charmed, but Emma already had her own plans.

Their personalities were different, and they couldn't do anything about that, but if Emma was careless, she would immediately get swept up by Rintarou. Emma took a deep breath and resisted.

"A-actually, I—I made lunch for us today! Would you eat together with me?!"

...It was a completely corny and classic move.

However, according to Sir Lamorak, Emma could use this cliché move to show her affections—and it was a way of obtaining information necessary for her next strategy.

Naturally, it was *a lot* for someone to make lunch for another person without advance notice. Like really intense.

Would they eat it? Would they reject it? If so, how would they say no? If he ate it, what would he look like?

At the present moment, it would gauge his affections for her—and apparently give her an idea about their next steps.

"Of...of course, I didn't ask if you wanted this. If it's inconvenient, then..."

Sir Lamorak had said she didn't need to worry whatsoever about the outcome. Even if Emma were rejected, there were apparently all kinds of ways to deal with it. (Sir Lamorak was a veteran of love, after all.)

The most important thing was to determine his reaction.

But Emma was a young woman. It was scary to be rejected.

Emma's face turned red, and her heart thumped as she waited for Rintarou's decision...

"Oh? You serious? Is it homemade?" Rintarou didn't look all too displeased as he grinned. "You know, I've been eating out a lot lately. I haven't had anything but meals from convenience stores! I'd be happy to eat your lunch."

"Y-you would?! Th-thank you so much!" Emma let her lips spread into a smile.

"...Hey, hey, why are you thanking me? I should be the one thanking you."

"B-but I'm happy!"

They were in the middle of this exchange when *stuff* happened.

"Wait right there, you glamourous duo!" shouted a voice from behind.

What's going on...? Rintarou and Emma both turned around.

"Heh-heh-heh!"

Behind them was a girl with a smarmy grin who thrust her chest forward and posed in an alluring—albeit forced—way.

Her blond hair had been set into huuuge ringlets. Along with the overpowdered and ghoulishly white face, she wore a surplus of eye shadow and false lashes. Her red lipstick was sickeningly sticky. From all limbs dripped accessories of gold, silver, and precious stones—jangling and gaudy. The pungent perfume made its way to them even from a distance...

It was Luna—after going about some dizzying transfiguration.

"".. Holy...,"" groaned Rintarou and Emma in synchrony as they looked at her with unwelcoming eyes.

"Heh-heh! What do you think, Rintarou?! You almost didn't recognize me, huh?!"

"...Yup. You got that right," Rintarou said for the time being.

"Heh-heh. See? This is what happens when I actually try to look cool!"

"Uh. Um... Luna? I think coolness comes from a more natural look... And this is very unnatural..."

"Whaaat? You haven't got a clue! You're a little oaf that just couldn't understand my dignified style. Wah-wah! How *pw*athetic!"

Who's the pathetic one? Rintarou and Emma couldn't help but want to retort.

"And get a look at this. See these brand-name accessories? Aren't they wonderful?!"

Luna had mistakenly assumed they had been overwhelmed by her beauty and jangled her jewels as she showed them her head-to-toe accessories.

They had no idea how she had procured them, but she had necklaces, bracelets, earrings, and a tiara all made from precious metals and stones. She had stacked two rings on each of her fingers.

The sparkle was blinding. Just looking at her directly made their eyes hurt.

…*Oh, this has got to mean that all the front money from the Dame du Lac's request is down the drain.* Rintarou was exasperated with her.

"A high-class girl has got to have the accessories to match, right? What? Are you upset, Emma? Are you crying over my accessories?! All you've got is that shabby cross pendant!"

"…Um, Luna… Those high-end brands are really overdoing it…"

"Jealous, huh!" Luna smiled as though she had triumphed, continuing with her deplorable attacks… "It sure is balmy today."

Gazing into the distance, she purposefully fanned at her chest and hiked up the end of her skirt.

She opened her shirt wide at her chest, scandalously shortened her skirt, and rolled up her sleeves as far as they would go. Her shirt was short enough already, and her stomach and belly button were laid bare for the world to see.

Basically, she had gone overboard. Luna was trying to explicitly appeal to Rintarou with an excessive amount of exposed skin.

I mean, all boys are perverts. You should be practically drooling. Go on, she seemed to say.

"…Uh. Um…Luna… I think you should stop trying to expose yourself…"

Emma was good-natured enough to even help her enemies, but it still didn't register to Luna.

"Hey, Rintarou! Yoo-hoo! I made you lunch, too! Hee-hee, this is the first time ever in my whole life that I've made lunch. ♪ I worked hard to make it for you, and I'd be so happy if you ate it!"

"…I think you should also stop acting cutesy…," Emma added.

"Emma, don't waste your breath."

Rintarou and Emma were expressionless in the face of Luna, who was all enthusiasm.

They were swept up by the sheer force of Luna's appearance.

Rintarou, Emma, and Luna ended up laying their lunches out in the courtyard at school. Basically, they were having somewhat of a battle between Emma's and Luna's homemade lunches.

In the courtyard, there was a little corner with an outdoor terrace with parasols, tables, and chairs. Luna and Emma sat at the table to the left and right of Rintarou, sandwiching him as they started their luncheon.

"I realized this yesterday while I was cooking, but...it turns out you can't just microwave eggs. ★ Hee-hee. ♪ I had absolutely no idea. Tee-hee. ★ Oopsie! I'm recording that bit of information into the hard disk in my little heart. ♪ Inputting data! Loading! And saved! ♪"

Rintarou had no idea what Luna was trying to even appeal to him with anymore.

"...Luna, you probably shouldn't act dumb or oblivious..."

"...You're a good person, Emma." Rintarou smiled lukewarmly at the entirely admirable Emma.

With Luna beside them, Emma started setting up her lunch on the table.

"Umm, so...master. This isn't much, but..."

Emma had made sandwiches for lunch—egg sandwiches, ham sandwiches, tomato-and-cheese sandwiches, the whole nine yards... She hadn't pulled any fancy tricks or brought anything out of the ordinary. They were just plain old sandwiches.

Emma had really wanted to make Rintarou a more elaborate meal, but Sir Lamorak advised otherwise: "An elaborate meal takes too much effort, and you'll be *too much* for him." She had decided to follow Sir Lamorak's advice, even though it was hard to swallow.

And it seemed she had made the right choice.

"Wow, looks good! This is the perfect amount of food for lunch!"

Because it was so simple, no one would put up any resistance to accepting it. Rintarou didn't hesitate to pick one up and start eating.

"Yeah, this is great. Thanks, Emma."

"M-master... It's really not anything special!" Emma happily let her face break into a smile.

Then, Luna shoved aside the box of Emma's homemade sandwiches to the corner of the table, throwing down an impossibly large basket with a resounding *thump!*

"Um...Rintarou, I made a little something, too."

"Hmm. Come to think of it, what *did* you make, Luna?" Emma asked.

Luna opened the basket eagerly and started putting out her lunch.

"It's stargazy pie and jellied eels."

""Geez, this is a *lot!*"" Rintarou and Emma said at the same time.

Thump! The bona fide feast that suddenly materialized out of the basket made Rintarou's and Emma's eyes peel open.

As an aside, stargazy pie got its name because it involved several Pacific herrings stuck in the pie and positioned to gaze up into the sky. Jellied eels were thick slices of eel hardened into semitranslucent jelly.

"Hee-hee. ♪ Just some local fare from my prided hometown in England! (But it's the first time I've made either of them)."

"W-well...I knew that, but..."

To the English's credit, stargazy pie and jellied eels weren't half bad at all. If anything, they were delicacies when made right.

But...these...looked absolutely terrible. They were plain grotesque. Unfortunately, when it came to Japanese sensibilities, they would be classified as a bizarre combination in the way a foreigner would view Japanese natto, fermented soybeans, squid, or octopus.

"Uh... Luna? Don't you think...this is overkill...?"

"I made it all for Rintarou. ♪ Now, eat up! All! Of! It!" Luna ignored Emma and shoved the food toward Rintarou.

The fish that faced the sky met Rintarou's eyes with their white, cloudy ones. They looked unbelievably foul.

"Uh... Ugh... Are you for real...?"

Rintarou started eating the pie and jelly with tears in his eyes. They were good. They were really good, but...

"This is a lot... In a variety of different meanings...!"

"Oh, Rintarou, are those happy tears?! I knew my meals would be leagues better than the meager little sandwiches, huh?!"

Their chaotic lunch eventually ended.

"...URP."

"A-are you okay, master?!"

After having been coerced into forcing down every bit of that "incredible" meal, Rintarou stopped himself from barfing, and Emma devotedly nursed him to health.

"Hah... I couldn't expect less from the teacher of my heart, the love-meister Kirara Himeboshi... It was perfect. It was moving. Now, then... I guess we can settle this once and for all." Luna stood, full of confidence.

"Now, Rintarou! It seems like the results are finally in! Is it me or Emma? Which of us is the better woman? Make your declaration here! That's a royal order!"

Fwoosh! Luna pointed right at Rintarou...

"...The winner is Emma."

"Oh, ah-ha-ha..."

Rintarou didn't hesitate, and Emma could only laugh evasively as Rintarou held her arm up in the air.

"Wh-why?!"

"Well, you're a great girl, for sure... If I close my eyes and ignore that you're a girl." Rintarou spoke as though he had never been this exasperated.

Luna opened her eyes from shock "Wh-what?! Rintarou! You idiot! I did so much for you! You could've at least swooned a little or something! You oaf!"

"Uh, um...Luna...you shouldn't expect him to owe you for..."

Luna gave off the air that she might have done all of this on purpose, anticipating a reward. As Luna did everything Sir Lamorak had said was taboo when it came to romance, to the point she was obstinately trampling her own path through things, Emma felt a little pity for her.

"Ahhh, I guess I feel something? Maybe I'm starting to feel like becoming Emma's ally without even waiting for the results of your battle? Plus, you're insensitive and undisciplined, but Emma is principled, honest, and just a good girl. Maybe I'll actually take this as an opportunity to switch sides?"

"*Grrrrr...!*" Luna's face was bright red as she glared at Rintarou with rage for a while... "Waaaaaah! Rintarou! You big dummy!"

She turned her back on him and ran away.

"Sir Kay! Sir Kaaay! You know what Rintarou did? Listen to this!"

Then, she went crying to Sir Kay, who seemed to have been watching from the shadows.

"There, there, Luna. He was mean to you... Let's start by working on your femininity and common sense..."

With an indescribable expression, Sir Kay soothed her own lord.

As he watched that from the side of his eye, Rintarou sighed. There was nothing else he could do.

CHAPTER 4

The Qualities of a King

Their school day was a whirlwind. Time flew until the sun sank and brought night upon them.

It was time for the humans to ease into sleep, entering the tranquility of night. It was time when human consciousness was at peace.

But when most humans were sound asleep, the Curtain of Consciousness—the foundation of collective unconsciousness— temporarily slackened, allowing the boundary between the real and illusory worlds to be hazy, nebulous.

In the daytime, it was easy for humans to believe that ghosts didn't exist. But in a dream state, it just wasn't the same. Until they woke up, a human couldn't recognize they were dreaming. Night was the precarious time when the imaginary from the other world ran rampant, doing as they pleased.

But ever since the innovation of electric lights, humanity started sleeping fewer hours than in the days of the oil lamps. With advancements in science and technology in the digital age, the Curtain of Consciousness was already starting to become less rigid.

Gone were the days when people were assaulted by ogres at

night, when vampires and succubi slunk into bedrooms of humans, when humanity was haunted by the cries of banshees.

"…That said, the Curtain of Consciousness around the artificial island is in tatters and letting stuff leak out because of a certain idiot." Rintarou shrugged. "Which is why when night comes, these guys show up."

They were in a suburb in Area Two of Avalonia. It was one of the first areas that had been built on the man-made island, but it had been zoned for redevelopment and abandoned for the time being. They stood in an alleyway surrounded by tall bygone condominiums.

When they peered into the abyss's darkness, glinting pairs of eyes floated into view.

The beings that lurked in the shadows slowly approached Rintarou's group. Eventually, they were revealed to be a curiously small group of humanoids—small, bony, and old. They bared long fangs from gashed mouths, and their nails looked barbarically sharp. Their eyes were large and red as flames, glittering in the dark. Red hats with wide brims covered their heads. They shouldered hefty axes, disproportionate to their small frames.

These ominous, short humanoids appeared in a throng.

"Wh-what are those things, Rintarou…?"

"They're Redcaps. They're apparitions from Scotland and England," he answered as Luna's face twitched and she backed away. "They settle in ruins and attack and kill travelers who try to stop for the night… They were born from our fear of nighttime burglars and bandits in older eras when law and order were severely lacking."

It seemed those Redcaps had determined that Rintarou's group was their prey du jour.

The Redcaps appeared in droves, surrounding them quickly.

The apparitions were in front of them, behind them, and to the right and left. They had nowhere to escape.

Though they were small, these Redcaps were born from humanity's fear, which meant normal humans never would have stood a chance against them.

Key word: *normal* humans.

"*Hiss!*" The Redcaps vocalized in strange, shrill voices, raising their large axes as they made their move.

Some ran at full speed as though skimming along the ground; others leaped up high. There were groups that ran along the scaffolding of the building walls, and still others jumped from building to building. They were all coming for Rintarou's group.

They maneuvered quickly—as curious predators that were unimaginable from their petite frames.

"*Hisssss!*"

From all sides and above and below, the Redcaps' readied axes tore through the air as they closed in on the group, coming closer and closer—

"Heh!"

There was the flash of two swords. The glint of a crimson blade and a white blade mercilessly parted the dark night.

Rintarou slashed as he unsheathed his red and white, right and left swords, instantaneously switchbacked his blades, and cut through six of the Redcaps.

"Haaah!" Luna's silver blade flashed as it freely traced through the sky like a spinning bird. The sword whipped forward with the force of a whirlwind and bisected three of the apparitions.

"Hyaaah!" Sir Kay shouted, easily slaughtering two of them with a textbook example of swordsmanship.

"Hyuck?! Hyuck-hyuck?!"

The Redcaps' downfall was that their chosen prey was not a set of "normal humans." After seeing how easily the tables had turned on their own kind, they seemed to have finally realized these were people they did not want to mess with.

The Redcaps were confused, preparing to flee and turning their backs on the group. They quickly started running from the place, scattering like spider hatchlings.

"We won't let you escape!"

Felicia and Gawain were waiting and ready in front of them.

"Hah!" Felicia instantly shifted into action, elegantly jabbing thrice without a single wasted movement. Her rapier, which moved as though to deliver bolts of lightning, pierced through the hearts of three apparitions with peerless precision.

"RAAAH!" Sir Gawain used his strong swordsmanship to overpower the enemies. He had no need for another sword as he single-handedly moved with the rage of a fire. When he brought down his sword, Galatine, as if delivering a storm, he scattered four Redcaps.

"Noooo!"

Accompanied by trained vigor, the javelin flag of a sword swiftly and sharply sliced through the air. The figure swept sideways as though she had been in wait and cleared three of the Redcaps away. She used the recoil of the attack to rotate her hilt and use all the spring in her body to thrust straight on.

She cut through the air, and the tip of her sword jabbed into the throat of a Redcap dashing for her.

It was all Emma. She used both her hands to wield her elongated Excalibur that seemed unfitting for her slender and slight frame, but she controlled it like it was an extension of herself.

Her swordsmanship was impeccable. It was as though the idiom "better bend than break" had been specifically made for her.

Her agility and reflexes were on par with Luna's and Felicia's, but Emma's physical strength was inferior because of her small build. Even with *Mana Acceleration* to strengthen herself, Emma was still weak, which meant she had to be born with it.

But that was exactly why her swordsmanship was so nimble.

She would read her opponent's movements beforehand and use their momentum to guess their next attack sequence.

The crux of all her swordsmanship was to wreck the most damage with the minimum strength necessary by using reversals and reactionary moves.

On the other hand, Emma didn't just wait around. She kept her opponents in check by using the reach of her sword to attack. She had refined trapping skills using feints to bring her enemies down.

If a frustrated opponent was to attack after she toyed with them, she would immediately respond, leaving them prey to a counterattack.

Luna relied on her natural instincts when she swung her sword and practically ignored the logic of swordsmanship. Felicia focused on her speed and the economics of her attacks to force out her enemies, fussing over aesthetic elegance and beauty. Compared to the two, Emma's skills were two or three levels closer to perfection.

If they were limited to a sword battle, Emma was sure to be top class among all the Kings.

"Ugh... Th-that's ridiculous..."

"Emma Michelle, huh...? As far as candidates in the succession battle, she's a cut above the rest..."

Since they had learned swordsmanship, Luna and Felicia could understand each of the effortless moves employed by Emma—and the amount of sheer technical skill they required.

Luna and Felicia paled as they observed her.

"Hmm? Someone's been improving. Emma, you've done a brilliant job adapting my lessons." As he continued decapitating

Redcaps on the side, Rintarou smiled. "The idiots attempting to teach you were trying to show you the strength of the sword—even though it didn't suit your frame or your personality."

"...Which means you taught her the gentle side of the sword, Rintarou?"

"More or less. I'm not really into that stuff, but I knew the theory behind it." Rintarou yawned as if to say it was no biggie.

"Y-you know the theory...and you still managed to teach her all that?!"

"Yeah. Out of the knights of the Round Table, Perceval and Bedivere were the ones who used gentle sword techniques... They let me get a thorough look at their skills during the legendary era."

"A-all you did was get a look?! Wh-what do you think you're saying?!" Felicia's face spasmed.

"What? Everyone can copy any technique after seeing it once, right? Isn't that normal? You mean you can't do that?"

What are you talking about? Rintarou's expression seemed to say.

"It's no use talking to this guy. He's bonkers."

"...He's just got an annoying existence, huh?"

Luna and Felicia fixed glares on Rintarou.

"Hah!"

During this entire exchange, Emma continued to wave her sword without any wasted effort. She slashed, jabbed, and cleared the way—faced with her skilled and fast serial attacks, the Redcaps couldn't tell her actual attacks apart from her feints. She was taking out more and more of the apparitions, robbing them of the option to escape.

"Hiss! Hissss?!"

Some Redcaps put up their final resistance by jumping at Emma's back.

"Haaah!" Without even looking where her hand was going, she took careful aim and countered with a flash of her weapon.

Their heads scattered into the darkness between the buildings.

Then, the large heap of corpses surrounding her eventually turned into small light particles of mana and quietly vanished into the night.

Those from the illusory world existed as nothing but ideas. When they appeared in the real world, they were incarnations of mana, materializing their own bodies. That was why their bodies returned to mana, leaving nothing behind when they died.

"...Ah, well, it's over." Rintarou put away his red and white swords.

Emma ran over to Rintarou. "M-master! Master! How did I do? Did I do well?!"

She was acting like a puppy asking for a reward from its owner after accomplishing a great performance.

"Yeah. Good work. You're much stronger now! There, there."

"Th-thank you so much! ...Hee-hee..."

When Rintarou praised her and patted her head, Emma smiled happily.

"Grrr..." Luna ground her teeth as she stared at the two from a distance.

Clap-clap-clap... An applause echoed above their heads.

"What do you think of my King? ...Isn't she something?" someone asked.

Rintarou looked up.

A girl was perched on the railing of a veranda that faced the road. Her legs hung down, and her dainty mouth twisted into a sinister smile as she looked at him. Only her crimson eyes with their slightly dilated pupils glinted, burning and smoldering like a flame in the darkness.

"Heh. Just as I expected. Kicking back and watching the show, huh. Lucky you, Lamorak."

"Don't leave out the *sir*, Merlin… I mean, Rintarou Magami."

Rintarou and Sir Lamorak smiled and glared at each other, baring looks that made it clear they were snapping at each other's throats.

"Hmph, fine. Back to the topic at hand. It's odd for me to be saying this, but Emma still has a long way to go. She'll keep growing over time… *If* she has a good master by her side."

"……"

"In other words, I imagine Emma will be far superior to your current lord. You can mold her to your liking—unlike that shrew over there… Isn't that basically what men want?"

"……"

"I'm offering you a good deal… What do you say? Don't you think more use will come of you from being with Emma than Luna, Rintarou? …Heh-heh-heh…" Sir Lamorak tried to push her own King hard.

"Ugh… That girlish tramp… You haven't got a filter on your mouth…!" Veins rose on Luna's forehead in anger.

But there was something else that was making her angrier—

"……"

W-H-Y?! Why isn't he saying anything?!

No matter what anyone said to Rintarou, he remained silent as though he was considering something.

It was almost as though he was actually pitting Luna against Emma in his thoughts.

But you said you'd be my ally! You said you would make sure I'd win!

Ever since Emma had appeared, Luna had been irritated.

Sir Gawain chose to speak up at that moment—either to save

them from this dark mood or because he was oblivious to the dampened vibe.

"Hey, Sir Lamorak! We're still in a truce, and we're supposed to be helping one another! How 'bout you actually help with the fight, too?!" Sir Gawain looked up at her.

"Yeah, no thanks. If I fight, Emma won't seem as impressive."

Sir Lamorak brushed away her hair as she let Sir Gawain's reprimand wash over her, and she broke out into a smile that etched red into the darkness.

"And...are you sure, Sir Gawain? If I draw my sword... I just might accidentally slaughter you alongside the apparitions." She was smiling, but she wasn't actually smiling.

Sir Gawain was at the receiving end of her eerie little grin.

"Please enjoy your break, Sir Lamorak!" Sir Gawain turned blue and quickly retreated.

"Seriously. We don't have time for you to be blathering like an idiot," Rintarou said, and the mood returned to its original state.

"I can sense a Rift...down there in that abandoned building's underground parking lot. Hurry! Let's get going!"

Rintarou and the group accompanied one another as they made their way to the lot.

They went down the slope that continued underground and reached the parking lot. A dark space formed from concrete spread before them. There weren't really any cars. It was pretty deserted.

Rintarou and the others were cautious of their surroundings as they went in deeper.

...Eventually, the sound of their shoes suddenly stopped echoing.

In the very back of the wide underground parking lot was...a dully glowing summoning circle drawn on the ground. In the space above it was a black object like a chasm that had been artificially pried open.

"...That's a Rift for you... It's the biggest one so far," Sir Kay observed, knitting her eyebrows. "Compared to the other apparitions that we've encountered until this point...those Redcaps were a lot stronger... They most certainly must have come from this opening."

"...Right." With a nod, Rintarou scraped out letters with the tip of his sword over the magic circle.

Like usual, he was trying to *Undo* the fissure...when something happened.

"Oh, come on... All you do is cause me grief."

It had to be a girl. The comment rang through the parking lot.

Strangely, it was crystal clear, uncannily reverberating through the cramped space and echoing several times.

"Who's there?!"

They all turned at the same time.

A blackness even darker than the shadows lurked in the space behind them.

It turned into an inky mist and collected into the shape of a person, gaining mass and texture until it manifested itself into a girl.

"I worked so hard to create those Rifts... I can't stand having you coming in from the sidelines and plugging them up... Hee-hee-hee..."

Her black hood and robes billowed open, exposing her smooth skin that was scantily clad. Her features, half covered by lace, were creepy and beautiful enough to send shivers down a person's spine. Her shadows were ashy. She had appeared in front of them as though she had been born from darkness.

When her existence became definite in the real space, Luna, Felicia, and Emma felt something cold rushing up their spines.

The sensation was different from the mind-boggling fear or pressure or presence of the likes of Sir Lamorak, Sir Lancelot, or Rintarou in his *Fomorian Transformation*. The girl in black seemed to release a bottomless, sinister impression and eeriness as though looking into an abyss. It overwhelmed Luna and the others.

As they broke into an internal cold sweat, the girls became serious as they readied their swords at the person in front of them.

"You've finally decided to show up. I take it that you're the idiot who's been creating Rifts all over the island?" Rintarou shouldered his two swords and took a step forward. "I thought if we kept getting rid of 'em, you'd eventually turn up."

But contrary to his arrogant comments, Rintarou kept a cautious distance from the witch.

If he recklessly rushed into things, he'd be heading right into the jaws of death. Something about that witch made Rintarou, even as powerful as he was, wary.

"I don't know what you're scheming, but it doesn't matter. This is as far as you go."

But if he knew that rushing in would lead to his death, that just meant all he needed to do was fight carefully.

Rintarou didn't hesitate as he smiled.

Except he realized something with that bizarre witch in front of him...

"...Hmm? Have I...seen you somewhere before...?"

Something in Rintarou's head was triggered by a series of distant memories.

But...when? Where?

Was it at Camelot International? Or was it before I came to this artificial island called Avalon? Or was it during that ancient era?

"...What is this? Why do I feel this way? It's like I've met you somewhere before..."

But for some reason, he couldn't recall it or grasp her true identity.

As it slipped into his consciousness, the faint image in his mind had to be relevant information, but it was fragmentary. For some reason, he couldn't make the connection between it and the girl in front of his eyes.

He was sure that he knew this girl. He had met her before, but he didn't know who she was.

It was vexing and irritating.

Rintarou was overcome with dismay and an unpleasant mood as he gritted his teeth—which was incredibly unusual.

"It's useless, Merlin. Useless." The girl in black grinned.

Her smile was innocent, befitting a child who had found her favorite toy.

"It might have been a different story in Merlin's body, but your current inferior self just won't be able to comprehend who I am. You cannot break my *Identity Masking* magic. Anything you do is absolutely futile."

She shimmied out of her robe and spread her hands wide.

"Oh, what shame! Are you still the greatest sorcerer in the world, Merlin? Thee of the mighty Fomorian line?! Be sure to return to your former glory! You must cast away that clumsy human husk! Ah-ha-ha-ha-ha-ha-ha!"

"...*Tch*," Rintarou clucked his tongue from irritation and menacingly swiped his sword. "You've sure got a lot to say. Shut it. I don't care *who* you are... If you're going to interfere with the King Arthur Succession Battle and get in the way of my fun game, then I'll kill you right here," he snapped, irritated.

"W-wait a second, master!" Emma readied her sword and came forward.

Next, she turned straight to the witch and questioned her. "You there! Why are you creating openings in the Curtain of Consciousness?! Do you understand what you're doing?! If you keep it up, a dangerous apparition will eventually make its way to this world! If that happens—"

But she didn't get a chance to finish...

"Emma. Ah yes, Emma, the pathetic child..." The witch in black gave her a look of pity. "Oh, Emma, the busybody. Emma, the laughable puppet. Emma, the empty husk... For all this time, people have used you and forced you to dance for them. You're just a sad pawn, manipulated for your kindness."

"Wha...?!"

"Oh, what pity. Oh, how I feel for you. How long will you yield your mind and your life to someone else? What are you even living for? Heh-heh-heh..."

That just might have pierced through Emma's heart.

"'I don't want to do this anymore. Why am I fighting? Why am I trying to become a King?' Heh-heh-heh..."

"What are you saying?! D-don't underestimate me!" Though she was usually reserved, Emma had suddenly started to go into a wild rage. "Quiet, witch! We serve under the name of justice! For the people! Under God's grace and virtues, we punish those who wrong humankind! Prepare yourself!"

"Wait... Emma?! Calm down! What's gotten into you?!" yelled Luna.

"That's right! You can't let her cheap tricks provoke you!"

Luna and Felicia tried cautioning her, but they didn't reach Emma's ears.

"I won't forgive you! I'll never forgive you! How dare you call me a puppet...?!"

Her beautiful features were twisted with fury as she lunged at the witch. It had been impossible to imagine Emma in agitation and indignation until that moment.

"......" Only Rintarou watched Emma calmly with unconcerned eyes.

But the witch's malediction failed to cease.

"...You've had enough of being God's puppet doll. That's why you want your beloved master to take your strings and give you a dog collar, right? Heh... *Woof! Woof-woof!* Cute little puppy. ♪"

As though that were the finishing blow, the witch pivoted her head to the side, and a special, broken smile spread across her face, filled with first-class contempt and pity. She jabbed at Emma with no mercy whatsoever.

Then, that was Emma's melting point.

"SHUUUT UUUP!"

At the same time, Emma roared as she readied her sword as though she had snapped. She started to dash at the witch in black.

"You idiot?! If you get too close—"

"*Tch—*"

Luna and Rintarou followed after her.

"AHHHHHHH!" Emma closed in on the witch. She turned into a white flash as she approached.

Just as the tip of her sword was about to catch hold of the witch—

"Ah, this is too pathetic." The witch crossed her arms before Emma's eyes and spread them out lightly.

In that moment, in the space before the witch's eyes, a frighteningly large and black fissure opened its maw.

"Whaaat?!"

Emma couldn't stop her momentum. She had nowhere to go as the fissure in front of her eyes swallowed her, and she fell in.

"WHAT?! Emma…" Without thinking, Luna stopped, and Rintarou ran past her side.

"…*Tch*. What a pain."

It wasn't clear what was going through his mind, but Rintarou jumped right into that fissure of his own accord.

"Rintarou?!" Luna balked.

"You wait nice and patient on that side! I'll be right back!" he yelled from inside the dark abyss as Luna froze in place.

However, Luna immediately took stock of the situation around her, thinking about what was happening inside of the fissure.

"Hey! You're my vassal, which means you belong to me! I can't just leave you in there!"

Luna decided to let her body slip down into the depths of the abyss.

"Luna?! Rintarou?!" Sir Kay cried out, but it was already too late.

When the witch crossed her arms above her head, the fissure closed instantaneously without a trace.

"B-but… Luna, Mr. Magami, and Emma…"

"…They disappeared…? She made them vanish…?!"

Felicia, Sir Gawain, and Sir Kay froze from fright.

In front of the group, the witch in black started to sing. "Witless and mindless. Guess this is your last stop. You'll be enveloped in purgatory between worlds, drifting away. Good-bye…" The witch chortled elegantly.

"Now, it's time to deal with the rest of you…"

She slowly waved her arm at them in an inviting gesture.

A black aura coiled around her hand, and they felt something quickening as though she was cooking up some magic.

"I won't allow you!"

"I'll make you give back Luna and the others!"

Sir Gawain, Felicia, and Sir Kay readied their swords in opposition and came at the witch with the speed of a gale.

Except something unusual happened in that second.

When the three of them took a step forward, they felt like something at their feet had suddenly changed.

By the time they realized it, the hard concrete ground had turned into something like mud, like coal tar. It was a black viscous fluid.

"Whaaat?! Wh-what is this?!"

"M-my feet...?!"

Their feet sank into the morass, immersed by the liquid and preventing them from running. They were immediately rendered immobile.

On top of that, it seemed as though there was no bottom to the black swamp. They continued to sink deeper into it—from their ankles, their knees, their thighs... As they slowly went down, they became nauseated, and their hearts were eaten away by revulsion and fear.

"Ugh... Argh! Why you—*Wind Dancer*—" Felicia started to recite some sort of fey magic.

Zwoosh! A spray burst up around them.

They were bony hands, shooting out of the swamp and wrestling Felicia down.

The fingers were like withered branches, coiling around Felicia and approaching her mouth.

"E-eeeeeeeeek?!" Felicia screeched, overcome by the repulsiveness of it all.

Even as they were doing that, they were all being pulled into the black swamp by the hands, buried in it.

"Uh... Aaah...?!"

"Dammit! I—I can't believe this is happening now...!"

Sir Kay and Sir Gawain were already at their wit's end.

On her own, the witch floated above the black swamp, impervious to its weight as she looked down at them all and smiled ominously.

Then, it happened.

Thump! Accompanied by a loud noise, a gigantic cross stretched out of the middle of the black swamp.

It was Sir Lamorak's cruciform claymore.

Though the black swamp was on the verge of consuming everything whole, it suddenly shattered like glass, turning into tiny fragments and scattering through the air.

"Huh?!"

"...What?!"

By the time they realized it, the black swamp of their despair was nowhere to be seen. Felicia, Sir Gawain, and Sir Kay were panting hard and lying facedown on the hard concrete.

"A mirage...? A conjuring? What was that...? N-no way...?!" stammered Felicia in shock.

A girl who was composed—*too* composed—was next to Felicia.

"We don't need any of your dumb ploys."

That calm figure—Sir Lamorak—put her hand on the claymore stuck in the ground, pulled it out, and walked straight for the witch in black.

"Oh? Why, isn't it the famous Sir Lamorak...? I was actually being very serious just then."

Sir Lamorak didn't respond to the witch's words and readied her sword to strike hard with a *Zwoom!*

"...Give Emma back. Give back the lord of my affections. If you don't, I'll kill you."

Sir Lamorak's steady crimson eyes, which already tended to be dilated, were even larger than normal. In that moment, the temperature around them dropped to below freezing. She shrieked.

Though Sir Lamorak's anger was hot like scorching flames, the surroundings around Felicia and the others had been chilled to absolute zero. It was almost as though hell had frozen over.

"...Oh my. How scary...," muttered the witch. It was the first time she'd expressed anything other than composure—mixing with something curt. "But it's not as though I can give her back just because you told me to."

"Then die." Instantly, Sir Lamorak disappeared.

To be precise, she appeared to have disappeared because she was moving faster than the limits of what the human eye could perceive.

Sir Lamorak turned into a red comet and rushed at the witch—

......

"...Hey, Luna. Wake up. If you don't hurry and wake up, you'll be *absorbed*, dude."

"...Uh...hn?"

When she felt someone poking her side, Luna's consciousness, which had been wandering through the dark, slowly rose to the surface.

How long could she have been asleep? Luna had collapsed facedown on the ground, and she half-consciously shook her foggy head and got up.

"...Rin...tarou...?"

"You're finally awake, sleepyhead. Seriously, I told you to wait outside."

Luna blinked. When she looked up, Rintarou was standing next to her, looking down at her, exasperated.

"Right... We...fell into the hole that weird girl in black made..."

Luna looked at their surroundings, even though she wasn't totally conscious yet.

They were in someone's room somewhere. The walls and floors were made of wood.

It was probably a girl's room. There were cute patterned curtains and a rug. The desk was topped with trinkets and stuffed animals. It seemed a bit lonely, but the room didn't seem at all out of the ordinary.

But when something came into her vision, Luna opened her eyes wide.

"...What is that?!"

There were several windows in the room, but all of them had firm-looking iron bars on them.

Luna automatically turned to her back. When she did, she saw that the whole wall was made up of iron bars, and the door was restricted all around by chains. A stone corridor continued down the other side of it into eternal darkness.

The girl's room had looked typical at first glance, but it was actually incredibly bizarre. It was just wrong.

A birdcage. A dungeon... Those words were adequate descriptors.

"...It's a netherworld."

"This is a netherworld, too...?" Luna parroted Rintarou.

"Yeah. Our real world and the illusory one are firmly partitioned by the Curtain of Consciousness, but when it becomes more nebulous, it creates a Neverwhere... The witch in black did this."

"......"

"This netherworld is probably a reflection of the deep psyche of *someone* who was absorbed into the world."

"…Someone was…absorbed?" Luna checked her surroundings.

Now that he mentioned it, she didn't see any sign of the one other person who had fallen into the world.

"That's right. In this place, the boundary between the real world and the illusory one is iffy. You know what they say: 'If you stare into the abyss, the abyss stares back into you…' You keep on your toes, too, Luna. If you're careless, you'll be absorbed and become one with this netherworld."

Luna gulped beside Rintarou, who tilted his head.

"But…who *is* that girl? She made a netherworld that's close enough to the illusory world that it could even absorb a real person… Even a magic user from the legendary era would have a hard time making a netherworld that's this high level…" Rintarou's thoughts ran wild, trying to ascertain her identity.

Hic… Sniffle… Ugh… Hic… The sound of someone whimpering faintly reached their ears.

It seemed to be coming from the other side of the bars.

"…Who is it?" Luna asked.

"……" Rintarou stood in front of the iron bars of the door.

What are you planning on doing? Luna tried to ask, but in that moment, she saw two flashes of Rintarou's drawn swords. He had used his swords to cut through the iron bars and chains as though they were paper.

"Whaaa—?! Rintarou, you're a beast!"

"Heh. This is a netherworld that's close to the illusory one. The only thing that dictates what you can and can't do is your mind, Luna."

"I—I don't really get what you're saying…"

"I'm saying this place tests the strength of your mind rather than the strength of your brawn."

Leaving Luna in her puzzled state, Rintarou headed toward the other side of the iron bars.

It seemed he intended to go toward the crying voice.

"Oh...w-wait for me!"

Luna ran after Rintarou's back in a fluster.

They left the room of iron bars.

For a while, Rintarou and Luna walked down the stone corridor until their vision suddenly opened up.

They were in a forest, though the trees were sparse. The sun poured over them, and there was a gentle wind that rushed through the branches. They saw a carpet of leaves.

There seemed to be a town in the distance. They spied something that looked like an old castle wall and a small city.

"...I'm getting less and less certain about where we are." Luna scowled.

"...It's central France—we're in the Centre Loire region on the outskirts of the city of Orleans... It's the premises of the Religious Order of Saint Joan," Rintarou said plainly.

"I'm sorry, what? Looks like someone's an expert."

"......" Rintarou silently kept going into the back of the forest.

"What's with you...?" With a sigh, Luna could only continue after him.

The two of them entered the quiet, sunny forest. They relied on the sound of the sniffling girl to move deeper.

The area around them became thicker and darker as they left civilization farther behind.

Eventually, they came upon a clearing in the woods and found an old monastery towering over them.

In the clearing in front of the monastery, they saw a strange and repulsive scene before them. Priests in religious garb were surrounding a girl in a robe, and angels were flying above the girl's head. None of them had faces, except for...

"Emma?! No, wait. That's not her... That's weird. She seems young...?" Luna observed.

"That's Emma... She got absorbed."

"...What does that mean?" Luna asked Rintarou, who was trying to hint at something.

"*Hic... Sniffle...* Ah... Oooh..."

On the other side of things, the young Emma in her religious garb was bawling as the priests and angels surrounded her.

She had a collar around her neck and shackles around her arms and legs...from which stretched long chains.

Those chains extended out to the surrounding priests' and angels' hands, which firmly grasped them.

She was already in a state where she was immobile and unable to escape.

"Oh, Emma! Oh, Emma! Servant to the great Lord! This is pathetic!"

"You cannot even manage this, my girl?!"

"Aren't you going to save the world?! Aren't you going to become La Pucelle?!"

The faceless priests and angels were crowding Emma as she cried, saying all they wanted to her.

"I'm so sorry... I'm so sorry...! I'll try harder... I'll keep trying harder...! Please don't leave me, our Lord Jesus... Please don't abandon me...!" Young Emma was crying.

With Excalibur sticking up before her eyes, Emma could only break down in tears.

"As a protector of the great Christian religion, King Arthur was the hero of faith. You are a girl who persists his line of holy blood. You will save the world. Your mission and destiny is to lead the people."

"Now, Emma. Hear the voices of the people that call for salvation! Hear the anticipation in their voices!"

Hordes of people rose up around Emma, and the place fell to pandemonium. The great number of people, who had materialized out of nothing, had surrounded Emma at some point.

""""""Our savior! Our savior! Our hero!""""""

""""""La Pucelle! La Pucelle!""""""

""""""AAAAAAAAH!""""""

"A-ahhh...?!" The force of the angry roar made Emma's face twist in fright. She froze in place.

A sonorous hymn flowed in from nowhere, and new chains materialized out of nothing, stretching toward Emma, binding and tightening around her.

"Gah! Ah... I—I can't breathe... It's too heavy...! Ahhh..."

"It is God's will for you to fight! It is the request of the innocent masses, who plead for salvation!"

"Now, Emma. Take the sword! Plow down the enemies of God...for justice!"

Then, something as large as a mountain appeared in front of Emma's eyes, making her look up.

It was...inexpressible in one word.

It was a group of terrifying monsters, of heaping corpses, of a darkness even blacker than the void and mixed with blood. It seemed to seethe—it was something born from turmoil. It looked like a devil, though it could have been a god or even a monster. Or it was something more terrifying and repulsive. In that abyssal chaos that swallowed all possible light lurked a particularly concentrated darkness. The simplest despairs—death and fear—seemed to spread all around it. It was a hell that plundered anything warm in the world.

"Ugh... Wh-what...is that...?!"

Gulp. When Luna looked straight at the thing, she turned blue. She felt sick. Her head was spinning, and she felt like she was going to throw up. Just looking at it, her heart pounded against her chest, and a heavy sweat broke out all over her body. She was being robbed of her five senses.

A feeling welled up from deep within the back of her mind. It was like a poison could no longer be construed as anything else.

I'm scared. I'm scared of that black mess. I can't bear looking at it directly.

Faced with chaos, her despair was deeper than the darkest depths of the ocean.

"Ah—haaah…! *Wheeze…* Hrk…!"

Luna felt almost like she was hyperventilating. She gulped and went to her knees right where she was.

"Hey, hey, don't push yourself… That's the mental depiction of the world's annihilation and destruction." Rintarou sounded bored as he watched the black turmoil.

"The *what*…?! Wh-what even is that…?!"

"The apocalypse exists as a shared concept among all of humanity in their collective unconsciousness. Fear and despair exist in the same way… That's Emma's mental image of it given form. The only ones who can face this image with composure are people with a few screws loose."

Rintarou was calm. He shrugged, like he was enjoying things.

"That thing's a mental image?! Really?! Just looking at an image is enough to cause enough fear and despair to bring me to my knees?! I couldn't help but feel like killing myself earlier!"

"This is the netherworld…the spirit world, so to speak. If you let yourself get mired in the common sense of the real world, you'll get tripped up."

As Rintarou and Luna were having that exchange, the miasma released by that black turmoil enveloped the group of people, who were instantaneously mummified.

But even that did not stop the ivory bones from begging Emma to save them.

The sonorous hymn echoed and warped. It was maddening. It turned discordant as it reverberated around them.

The scene became repulsive to the eye. From how it looked, it might as well have come from the very pits of hell.

"Now, you must fight, Emma!"

"You must save the world! You must save the people! For the will of God! For justice!"

"That was the role you have been given! There is no other value to your life!"

"Ah… AAAH… *Sniffle*… No…!"

The mummified priests and angels yanked on her chains, and Emma's shaking hand gripped the Excalibur at her feet. While dragging the heavy chains and shaking uncontrollably, she tottered toward the monster.

However, her steps would not take her to the monster of turmoil.

"No… I don't want to anymore… Someone help me… Please save me…!"

Emma didn't even make a single attempt to strike at the monster of turmoil and let her sword drop. She had given up… She fell to her knees as though she could no longer withstand the weight of her own body… She moaned and burst into tears.

Even as Emma was in that state, those surrounding her assailed her by saying all they wanted to her.

"Save us! Help us, please! Our savior!"

"Why won't you fight for us?! Are you not going to save us?!"

Every one of them overlooked Emma's feelings and almost seemed to be one-sidedly praying to her. They were marauders indulging in their weaknesses.

"What is this...?! This is so horrible...!" Luna urged her trembling body to stand up using the rage that flared in her body.

"You've got to be kidding...! What do you think you're doing...?! You just pushed everything onto one person...and burdened her with it all...! Who do you think you are?!"

"...Calm down." Rintarou grabbed Luna's shoulder and stopped her at the moment she unsheathed her sword, about to run in.

"Like I told you, this is a netherworld that's a projection of Emma's mindscape. Those people, those messengers of God, that monster of destruction are all just figments of Emma's mind... There's no reason to take this seriously."

"B-but!" Luna glanced at Emma.

Emma was crying, unable to stand the weight of the chains, the fear, and the despair. She was bawling.

"We can't just leave her like that!" Luna yelled.

"!"

She brushed aside Rintarou's hand and kicked at the ground.

"AAAAAAAAAH!" She brought up her sword, shouldering it, and dashed at death and destruction with incredible speed.

"Oh?" Rintarou's mouth twisted wryly as he watched Luna from behind.

The momentum of Luna's dash was such that no one could stop her anymore.

But...

"Aaaaaaaah—*uh*?!"

Ba-dum. As she took a step and then another toward the black turmoil, the concentrated fear overran the inside of Luna's mind. *Ba-dum.* It crushed her. *Ba-dum.* It washed all over her.

Thump. Thump. Thump-thump—

Even then, the despair rising in her heart made it feel as though it were on the verge of rupturing as it worked her up.

"Aaah! AAAH...?!"

As her oxygen-deprived lungs clouded her thoughts, her arms and legs rapidly weakened, and the speed of her charge wavered. The extreme pressure of the despair that pushed on her body made her feel as though she was about to collapse right in place.

Why in the world was she standing up against this dreadful thing?

That despairing doubt ruled over Luna's mind.

But it'll all be fine if I die. That destructive impulse maddened Luna's heart.

The grim reaper was playing a sweet invitation in Luna's ears—but...

"RAAAH! AaaaaaAAAAAH!"

Luna pushed aside all those sweet, dark impulses, yelling loud enough to almost burst her vocal cords.

She gritted her teeth. In that moment, her eyes and soul burned as she focused a sharp gaze on the monster of turmoil.

Once again, she devoted the strength of her whole being and soul into her legs and kicked hard at the earth—and closed in on the monster.

"Like I'd let you defeat me!"

Using all her power, she brought her sword down on the monster of turmoil.

Fwisht. Luna's Excalibur bit into it.

"What the—?!"

But she felt no resistance.

The deathly turmoil had swallowed up Luna's blade and—that was it.

"Da...mmit! Uuugh!" Luna panicked and tried to pull her sword away, but it did not so much as give an inch.

For some reason, the sword was glued to her hand, and she could no longer let go of it.

Shloop. Shloop... Shloop-shloop... The sword was swallowed deeper into the turmoil, and Luna was pulled along with it. Luna's mind was immediately overcome with an acute sense of helplessness.

Rintarou said...this place tests the strength of your mind rather than the strength of your brawn! Luna ground her teeth.

This is an image... It's just an image! It's not the end of the real world or anything! In that case, if my heart is strong, I can win! I should be able to win...! But then why...why can't I win?! Is it because I'm not the right person?!

Luna desperately tried to pull out her sword, but everything she did was in vain. She could not resist it.

If I can't win...does that mean I've lost in this psychological battle?! Does that mean I've given in to the fear of the world's destruction...?! Is that it...?!

Luna lamented her own weakness and cowardliness.

"Hey! Hey! I told you not to do anything unreasonable." Rintarou slowly walked over to her. "...*You* can't do it."

That last comment made Luna feel as though a sharp knife had gouged her chest.

Not with your current capabilities..., he seemed to be implying.

"Ack... Th-then, Rintarou, th-this is an order! Do something!" she shouted.

"A'ight." Rintarou grinned and made his move.

"Ha-ha! Heh-ha-ha-ha-ha-HA-HA!" As he laughed loudly, he pulled out his sword and ran around the place.

He wasn't headed toward the black turmoil of destruction—but toward those who were surrounding Emma and connected to her by the chains...the *people*.

"...What?" Standing in shock, Luna bore witness to a grisly massacre.

Rintarou ran like a gale. He swung his right sword, then his left, then the pair together, unleashing enough impact to dispel a rough whirlwind.

With a mere swing of his sword, groups of people turned to bits of flesh and bone, blown away and scattering into the air.

The people who clung to Emma like vengeful ghosts were cut, sliced, chopped, and mowed down.

He circled around them and killed all the people surrounding Emma. He slaughtered and murdered until there was not a single one left—then he leaped high into the air.

"Oh, this is horrible! It's a devil! Leave—"

"Learn the wrath of our Lord—"

His pair of swords flashed at the necks of the priests holding Emma's chains and made them all fly—he brought the angels down to earth.

As soon as he did that, the chains binding Emma clattered as they fell and broke to pieces.

"HA-HA-HA-HA-HA-HA-HA!"

As blood poured like a heavy rain and splattered on him, Rintarou just laughed.

"You don't do anything for yourselves! All you do is want! All you do is pray! You're worthless pieces of shit with no reason for living! Just die! HA-HA-HA-HA-HA-HA-HA!"

"......" Luna could only be in shock as Rintarou acted like the devil itself.

"......Master." The young Emma was fully showered in blood as she looked up at Rintarou.

"Master... Master..."

She grinned.

While among the bone-chilling heaps of corpses and a river of blood, Emma smiled in bliss.

"…Ngh?!"

Shudder. Emma's smile caused a chill to go down Luna's spine—even more than Rintarou's rampaging devilishness.

How is she smiling…? At a time like this…? How can she smile like that…?

Then, in the next moment, Luna was struck by another blow.

"…It's okay, Emma. I'm here for you." Of all things, Rintarou hugged Emma from the front, smoothing her with kindness.

"…What?" Luna could only watch on in shock.

"…Master…"

"You've worked hard this whole time. You've been trying all on your own to save the world. It must have been difficult and lonely… I'll be watching you from now on. I'll be by your side. I'll protect you. So… There's no need for you to worry. You're not alone anymore."

With a clatter, Emma grabbed the single remaining chain on her own neck and wordlessly offered it to Rintarou. She was looking at Rintarou with eyes clouded by affection and love deeper than the ocean.

Those eyes were the same as those of the people waiting and hoping for a savior.

"……"

For a while, Rintarou looked down at that chain…and eventually he firmly grasped it.

In the same moment, Emma beamed with joy.

With a gentle expression, Rintarou patted Emma's head.

"R-Rintarou…" Luna was in pain as she watched.

Relieved that Rintarou had taken the chain, Emma moved away from him as though she had made up her mind…and took up her sword.

Slowly but firmly, she fixed her eyes on the black turmoil of destruction, and she walked.

"Y-you idiot! You can't come over here! Run awa—," Luna yelled in a fluster to stop her, remembering how she'd been sucked in herself.

But…the young Emma slowly brought up her sword…

Not the slightest hint of her earlier weakness was in Emma's eyes or her expression.

Slowly, she approached the monster of turmoil…coming close enough to it to use her sword.

Then, after taking a breath, she brought her sword down straight on.

In that moment, something unbelievable happened.

She cut that powerful black void down the middle.

It let out a mysterious death wail that seemed like it was concentrated with the intermingling screams of all of the world's humanity rising up, and the chaos that had been parted in half immediately vaporized like black mist and rapidly dispersed.

Before Luna realized it, the black turmoil had disappeared without a trace.

"A-amazing…" Luna was dumbfounded as she watched the young Emma.

She hadn't been able to lay a hand or a foot on it at all…but Emma had easily defeated the mirage of death and destruction.

Was this proof of the foundational difference in abilities between her and Emma?

"Ah, well. Luna versus Emma… This was the showdown… Well, I already knew it from the start," Rintarou muttered, which reached Luna's ears.

What in the world did that mean? …Luna was too scared to

ask, chained to an indescribable emptiness and sense of defeat in a daze...

"Hey, Luna? What's wrong?"

At some point, Rintarou had accompanied the young Emma, guiding her in front of Luna.

...He was leading the young Emma by the chain that stretched from her neck.

"That's the worst thing I've ever seen!" Luna spat as she came to her senses. She was seriously grossed out by this whole thing. "I knew you were horrible, but this just crosses the line! Let her go!" Luna tried to take the chain that connected Emma from Rintarou.

"—Ngh!" The young Emma roughly slapped away Luna's hand.

"Ow?! What're you doing?!"

"Raaah! Mrrr!" growled the young Emma, glaring at Luna with eyes filled with intense enmity. She clung to Rintarou.

"You know... Luna, I don't think I need to say this, but this isn't actually Emma. This is the mental image Emma created of herself... It's like her psyche."

"I—I know that! But what about your *morals*? That's my main concern!"

"Okay, okay." Rintarou easily brushed Luna aside and pulled on Emma's chain as he started walking.

"...Where do you think you're going?"

"Where else? We've found the core of Emma's mind...so we're gonna hurry up and bust out of this world," he said.

With Rintarou at the head, they all stepped foot into the monastery.

"I think the cardinal point at the core of the formation of this netherworld is around here. In which case, the exit must be around..."

When they went into the monastery, they were immediately met with the worship area at the front. In the very back of the worship area, they found the girl they had been searching for.

"Emma?!"

It was another Emma. This one wasn't as young. She wore white metal armor, a magnificent crown, and a gorgeous white surcoat that almost looked bridal. Emma carried her Excalibur on a strange stone pedestal, leaning over as though offering prayers. Her eyes were closed, and she appeared softly asleep.

That was when chains tangled around her sleeping form, shackling her to the pedestal.

"...A King...? Is this her as a King...?" Luna muttered despite herself when she saw Emma's magnificent form.

"Yeah, that's the Emma that came with us into this side... That's her real self."

"R-Rintarou, what *is* that...?!" Luna exclaimed, noticing something.

Where she was sleeping and standing, Emma's hands and feet...were changing color.

Luna heard a cracking noise as Emma changed texture. Whatever was coming for her spread from the bottom up.

She was petrifying. Emma's body was gradually turning to stone.

With Emma in front of them, Rintarou let out a long breath. "That means she's becoming part of the netherworld. Seriously, that was a close one. If she had assimilated with this netherworld completely, we wouldn't have been able to bring her back. We still have time."

Rintarou pulled on the collar of the young Emma clinging beside him.

"Look, Emma. Go back to your real self. Go back where you belong."

"......"

"This world was made by you. It's a projection of your internal self. If you go back to your real self...if you wake up from the dream, it'll collapse. You can go back to reality."

For a while, the young Emma looked at Rintarou intently.

"...Hey, master...," she started with a lisp. "Will you stay with me fowever?"

"?!" Rintarou narrowed his eyes, and Luna opened hers wide.

"...*Sniff-sniff*... I... I...was always all by myself..." Emma started to snivel with Rintarou standing still beside her.

"No, that's not true... There were tons of people around me... but everyone prayed to me and revered me and praised me... I was alone... They asked me to save the world... And I was always by myself... All the time. Forever. All alone... Ever since I was born..."

"......"

"They said I had come to this world to become the King and save the world... They said that was the reason I was born... That was my reason for existing... Everyone—*everyone* said that... They said that an Emma who didn't save the world...an Emma who didn't become King...had no value... *Sniff*... Everyone kept me held down with chains and pulled me around by force..."

"......"

"But I... I love them all...and I want to save everyone... I had to become a saint... I have to save the world... I need to get better... I need to walk forward...but my body was too heavy from the chains, and I couldn't help anyone... I don't want to walk...but I need to go forth... If I don't walk...then I don't know what I'm living for...!"

The young Emma turned her eyes to Rintarou as though imploring him.

"I can't save everyone on my own... I can't save the world...!

Please...lead me along, my lord. To save everyone...to save the world...please pull my chains gently by my side. I'll do anything... I think I'll be able to walk then... I'll be able to become a great King... I'll save the world... *Hic... Sniff!* Please..."

"Emma..." Luna looked down at the crying child.

Emma must have led a brutal life; Luna couldn't even imagine it.

She had weakness in her heart, but she braced herself to be a saint and a King.

She was fundamentally different from Luna. She wasn't aiming to be King for her own self-interest.

She was weak. Certainly, Emma's heart was weak.

But why did that matter?

Even if she was a King, she was human. Normal people had weaknesses. They would want to rely on someone else. Even if someone was a King, there was no need to be strong and independent out of pride...just as King Arthur was with Sir Kay and Merlin.

Just like Luna was with her Excalibur, the Steel Sword of Camaraderie.

To compensate for weakness, they would rely on the support of others. That itself would become strength.

The most important thing was how they chose to respond to that truth.

And Emma had embraced her weakness and continued to face forward.

To save people, she was trying to fight. She embraced her pain and tried to walk.

She had to be the loftiest saint in the world and a person worthy of being King.

As though to corroborate Luna's thoughts, Rintarou continued...

"Right... You were trying your best this whole time... You're almost at a point where you can let go of the baggage on your shoulders." Rintarou was unusually gentle with Emma. "Don't worry. I'll *save* you."

In that moment, Luna felt as though everything in front of her eyes had gone black and she was pitching forward.

...*I lost*, Luna bitterly realized.

"...Thank you, master..." The young Emma grinned.

She dissolved into a mass of light particles. The particles that wandered through the air poured down into the quietly snoozing Emma.

The parts of Emma that had half petrified rapidly regained their normal texture... Eventually, the pedestal and the chains that bound her broke and clattered.

"......"

Just like that, Emma came to stand on the ground slowly, drifting like a bird, weightlessly.

She cracked open her eyes.

"...I'm sorry, master. I've caused you trouble."

"Not more than usual."

When Emma woke, fissures began to open up in the netherworld, and it started to collapse.

As that happened, Emma and Rintarou looked at each other.

"Um...s-so... Master..." He had a feeling she could remember what had transpired when she had been in the body of young Emma. Emma's face was red, likely from being embarrassed, and she tried to say something.

"...It's fine. You don't need to tell me."

"O-okay..."

Rintarou hugged Emma, and she entrusted him with the weight of her entire body.

"......" Luna watched the two in mute astonishment.

Eventually, the fissures in the air covered the area completely, and it started to slip away.

The whole place fell into darkness—

It was the boundary to hell. Its ruler was a dainty girl of carnage.

"AH-HA-HA-HA-HA-HA!" Sir Lamorak laughed loudly and swiveled her claymore around like a storm. She was mowing the place down.

In a single breath, she struck more times than they could count. She made an immeasurable number of charges.

With one attack, she'd form a vacuum that would warp the atmosphere. The rough and maddening pressure unleashed by her sword would seek a place to escape.

Without sparing her any mercy, Sir Lamorak struck the witch in black from every direction.

"—Ngh?!" The witch in black narrowly parried with a short sword—over and over again.

When she blocked the blows, the gruesome sound of the fighting swords rang out, and sparks scattered.

"Tch—" The witch clicked her tongue in annoyance and stopped a sideswipe from Sir Lamorak as she quickly retreated.

She raised up her left hand and tried to chant some sort of magic, but—

"Too laaaate!"

Almost instantaneously, Sir Lamorak appeared in front of the witch's eyes and showered her arched form with attacks that came down on her as bolts of lightning.

"Ugh— Hrrk?!"

She narrowly met the attack, but the impact made the witch buckle down to her knees despite herself.

Sir Lamorak struck back instantly.

The claymore whizzed and transitioned with extreme speed from her upright position to sideways. A flash fluttered from the side.

The witch flew up above Sir Lamorak's head and evaded the attack.

Sir Lamorak reacted and slashed upward and traced a crescent moon like a soaring dragon.

There was a loud reverberating sound as if the air were exploding. As she was still upside down, the witch was blasted away to the side like she had been hit with a bullet.

"I've still got more where that came from!" Sir Lamorak hounded the witch with the speed of a bullet.

Sir Lamorak was completely overpowering the witch in black...

"Th-this is too amazing..."

...And Felicia.

"I-I'm not sure what else I expected from Sir Lamorak..."

...And Sir Kay.

"Guess she's still going strong as one of the most powerful on the Round Table... (Wait a second. *That's* who's after me?)"

...And Sir Gawain.

They couldn't intercept Sir Lamorak's attacks, which seemed to house the power of a natural disaster. They simply stood in place in wonder and could only watch the fight unfold before their eyes.

At worst, if they got involved, they could get swept up in Sir Lamorak's aftermath and find themselves dead.

Naturally, that witch could also probably "bring it," too.

When that witch had pulled out her sword to meet Sir Lamorak's weapon, there had been self-confidence and composure in her expression. The witch seemed to be better at magic, but even with just that sword, she probably was powerful enough that she likely wouldn't have needed anything else even if Felicia, Sir Kay, and Sir Gawain attacked her at once.

But that witch was not calm in that moment.

Sir Lamorak was overpowering her in the sword fight. She must have wanted to cast some spells, but Sir Lamorak wouldn't give her a single moment to begin chanting.

On top of that, Sir Lamorak seemed like she had energy to spare.

This was the cream of the crop of the Round Table. They were totally beyond everyone else's league.

"Oh?! I wonder what's wrong?! Are you starting to regret this?!"

"_____?!"

Sir Lamorak and the witch were crossing swords.

Obvious impatience was starting to mix into the witch's expression.

"Now, give Emma back! I bet you're starting to think you should hand her over! If you don't comply, I might try taking one of your arms soon!"

"You insane knight…!"

As weapons collided and sent sparks flying, they heard the sound of breaking glass echoing through the place.

When they looked around, a large black rift opened in the air near the ceiling, and three shadows floated down from inside it.

"Y-you're all—," Felicia yelled with delight.

"Yo! Sorry for the wait!"

"We're back!"

"…I'm so sorry for causing so much trouble."

It was Rintarou, Luna, and Emma.

They had made their way back to the real world from the netherworld.

"Th-that's impossible…?!"

The witch couldn't hide her surprise at their comeback.

"H-how?! I'm certain I had locked you up in the boundaries!"

"Oh, dear. Looks like we forced our way back by our own strength," he said, chuckling.

"...In that case..." Sir Lamorak had a first-rate smile on as she brought up her sword. "I can go a little more all-out... Die already," she coldly muttered, and her bloodshot eyes opened wide.

The witch's head went flying.

"...N-no way...?" The witch wailed as her head was severed, staring at the composed Sir Lamorak, who whipped her blade downward in a flourish to get the blood off.

The witch hadn't seen the moment Sir Lamorak had stepped in to face her. When Sir Lamorak had swung the sword, she hadn't been able to react.

Her face was frozen with astonishment as it sailed through the air...

Eventually, the head dropped to the ground and rolled away. While they were all watching, the body decomposed into a misty black substance...and completely disappeared.

The witch who had been stirring up trouble for the succession battle on the artificial island was dead.

"*Cinis ut cinis, pulvis ut pulvis*... Ashes to ashes, dust to dust... Amen."

Sir Lamorak drew a cross with her sword and offered a moment of silence as she put away her blade.

Then, Rintarou and the rest turned around.

"Geez, guess it's finally over."

"It's because you were all whining."

Sir Lamorak saw her own lord snuggling up to Rintarou and suddenly noticed something.

"Oh? Emma... You..." Sir Lamorak broke into a happy smile at

Emma's cheerful state. "I have no idea what happened, but…it feels like you had a breakthrough or something."

"Huh?"

"You look really happy."

"Uh. Um… Y-you think so?"

"Yes, you look even cuter than usual, Emma."

"Y-you think I'm cute? …But…"

Emma glanced up at Rintarou from the side and then turned her face down, embarrassed.

On the other side of things, Luna was distant from Rintarou, appearing lonely… She avoided looking at him.

This indescribable vibe puzzled Felicia and the rest of them. They became silent.

"About that showdown. I think the results are settled," Sir Lamorak reminded them. "I, Sir Lamorak of Gales, was the one to decapitate the culprit creating the Rifts. I'd just like to say…a vassal's deed is their King's achievement."

Sir Lamorak turned to Rintarou. "What do you think? Rintarou Magami, what's your decision? Emma or Luna… Who will you join?"

Felicia, Sir Gawain, and Sir Kay held their breath as they stared at Rintarou.

"……" For a while, Rintarou remained in silence…

Clack. As he started walking, his footfalls echoed… He stood next to Emma and turned to them all.

"Well, this is it," he declared dispassionately.

"M-master…?!"

Felicia and Sir Gawain grew agitated.

"Mr. Magami…?! Are you serious…?!"

"You're…betraying your lord?!"

"What? Betraying her? Don't be stupid. For starters, I was just helping her out of my own goodwill, but I wasn't really Luna's vassal or anything. I'm free to volunteer wherever I want, aren't I?"

Rintarou wasn't bothered at all.

"That may be the case, but still...! L-Luna, what's gotten into you?! What in the world happened?! Are you fine with this?! Do you accept this?!" Sir Kay seemed to implore Luna with her eyes, even as Luna turned away from a distance.

"I didn't win Rintarou's favor...that's all," she muttered forlornly.

"Hee-hee-hee! Well, looks like everything's fallen into place. And that's the most important thing!" Sir Lamorak laughed. "Anyway, the truce was shorter than anticipated, but I guess it's over now. I wouldn't mind fighting right here."

"Sir Lamorak... Please stop with that boorish behavior at least for tonight," Emma scolded.

"I understand. But next time...things will go down." Sir Lamorak deflected by joking around.

"Luna... If you'll excuse us," Emma said.

"......"

"Please don't think ill of me. This is the difference in our capacities as Kings... That's all it is."

"......" Luna didn't respond. She didn't have anything to say back.

"Let's hurry and get home, Emma," Rintarou urged.

"Yes, master!" Emma happily clung to his arm.

Finally, Rintarou turned to Luna. "See you. Take care, Luna... I mean... *King.*"

"What? ...Rintarou?"

Luna's eyes opened wide, boring into him.

And then Rintarou, Emma, and Sir Lamorak left.

Luna could only watch Rintarou's back and see him leave in silence.

CHAPTER 5

True Intentions

Once humans obtained lighting from electricity, they no longer slept immediately when the sun went down. The night was no longer a time of lurking shadows when everything would forever be ruled by peace and quiet.

But of course, when the dead of night came, the town would be fast asleep.

It was already that time when most of the building lights would extinguish, the place would be deserted, and the streets would be devoid of cars.

"...Ha-ha-ha... Heh-heh-heh..."

In the slumbering stillness of the shadows, Luna grinned as she walked.

Her shoulders trembled as though she couldn't help herself. Whatever it was she was thinking of was just that hilarious... That was the mood she was in.

"...L-Luna...?" From behind her, Sir Kay tried to say something, but...she didn't know what to do and stopped at muttering Luna's name.

"W-w-wait, Sir Kay... Is Luna okay?"

"Y-yeah! Sh-she's been seeming weird since earlier!"

From a bit farther behind, Felicia and Sir Gawain were walking on eggshells around Luna and glancing at her back as they spoke to each other.

"I-it couldn't be…because of the shock from being ditched by Rintarou…?"

When Felicia pointed that out, a pained look crossed Sir Kay's face as she glanced at Luna from the side.

It really…might be from the shock…

Sir Kay knew that Rintarou Magami held a special place in Luna's heart.

At her core, Luna acted like a genius who didn't need the strength of others. People idolized her, but she could be very aloof and independent. There was one person who she was stubborn around, that she had her way with, that she depended on as far as Sir Kay knew. And that person was Rintarou.

Sir Kay had no idea why Luna was so insistent when it came to Rintarou Magami…but even if it wasn't much, she knew that Rintarou was someone who Luna trusted with her heart.

Regardless of that… Luna had been abandoned. She had been betrayed.

Of course, even Luna couldn't have helped the profound mental shock that would come from that.

Sir Kay sighed…

"Heh-heh-heh… Seriously. What is with that Rintarou…? You knew it all along… Oh, c'mon… That guy, I swear… Ah-ha… Ah-ha-ha-ha-ha-ha!"

Suddenly, Luna burst into cryptic laughter in front of Felicia and Sir Gawain, whose faces spasmed as they shied away.

"Uh, um…Luna…?" Sir Kay cautiously asked Luna. "Wh-what's gotten into you? You've been acting very strangely…"

"Ah-ha-ha-ha! What? Oh, no! Sorry! Sorry! I was thinking I really am the only one who's qualified to be Rintarou's master! That's just what was on my mind!" Luna replied as she laughed, as though something were incredibly funny.

This is no good. She's seriously depressed..., they all thought.

In that moment, Sir Kay, Felicia, and Sir Gawain each held their heads in their hands.

Their minds were fully in sync with one another.

"*Sniff...* Luna... I can't believe you had these feelings for Mr. Magami all along...? I won't forgive him... I can't ever forgive Mr. Magami...for treating my friend in this manner...!" Felicia was indignant as she held back tears in frustration.

"A knight! Nay! A man who would lead along a lady is a disgrace! I—man among men—shall vow to slay Rintarou Magami, Lady Luna!" Sir Gawain promised on his sword, righteous and indignant.

"Ugh. Urk. L-Lunaaaaa! *Hiccup!* It must have been so hard for you, and you must be so dejected after your abandonment by Rintarou... It's okay! It will all be fine! You've got me by your side! You've got your own older sister here with you! *Sniff!*" Sir Kay wailed and held Luna. "You must hurry and forget that terrible heretic! I'm sure there is a more suitable, handsome gentleman out there for you, Luna! As your sisterly figure, I *will* start a search for suitors to be your husband and— Ow?!"

Luna gripped Sir Kay's skull with her open hand when the knight came clinging to her. *Hiss!* Luna sneered like a threatening cat.

"Hey! I swear you all are imagining the absolute worst for me! Are you pitying me?! *Hey?!*"

"Well...but..."

"I mean..."

"Right there! You ragtag master-servant duo! Don't exchange those looks out in the open! Don't you dare sigh! You know what? It's not like I'm a sick stalker who can't forget a guy from my past! For starters, Rintarou didn't betray me! It's not like he'd ever betray me!"

"Luna...that's what a stalker would say."

"...She's really sick. She must have really been traumatized."

"AAAAAAH! UUUUGH!" Luna rapidly charged at Felicia and Sir Gawain and sent them flying with a dropkick when they looked at her in considerable pity.

"Anyway! I think the situation will work in our favor...starting *now*!"

"Ow! Yow-ow... You've gotten my nice clothes dirty... What do you mean?" Felicia blinked at Luna's sudden declaration.

"The situation will work in our favor? What...do you mean?"

"I'll explain later! Felicia, I have something I need to ask of you!"

Without knowing what Luna meant, Felicia was just in a stupor as Luna gave her a set of orders.

As for the contents of those instructions—

It had been a while since they had parted from Luna and the rest of the group.

"Well, I'm going to patrol the area around the hideout. You take it from here, Rintarou Magami... Oh, Emma, if anything happens, summon me immediately, all right?" Sir Lamorak left them suddenly and disappeared into the night alone.

"Hey! Hey! I know you can call her in an instant, but is it really wise to leave you with a past enemy? I mean, it's hardly been a day! Normally..." Rintarou trailed off, exasperated as he watched her back when she left.

"I'm sure…she was trying to be considerate for my sake."

"Hmm? What was that?"

"N-n-nothing! Well, i-it's over here!"

Even in that darkness, he could tell that Emma's face had reddened as she guided him, and they walked down the twilit streets together.

Eventually, the two made their way to Area Three on Avalonia and the seventh block in the City of Halos.

In the suburban area, homes were sparse, and skyscrapers were unheard of. On a lot littered with abandoned houses was a church that Emma was using as her base of operations.

"You live in a pretty weird place, huh?"

"…This is a property that we own—and by *we*, I mean the Religious Order of Saint Joan. It might look all creepy, but it has a magical perimeter around it. In terms of defense, it's really amazing." Emma smiled at Rintarou, who looked up at the church from the middle of the front garden.

"…But it looks like no one is here," Rintarou muttered after he'd searched the inside of the church for presences with his supernatural senses.

"Yes, Sir Lamorak and I are the only ones living in the church right now."

"…What? They don't think commoners would be useful for this battle or something…? Well, the Religious Order of Saint Joan, that was your first mistake."

"It's fine. Our Lord, who art in heaven, conferred me with this test—a trial I must overcome for myself. It's because becoming a King…and saving the world is my role." Emma grinned and smiled without worry.

"……"

"Now, master, please come inside. We've had so much happen

today that I'm sure you must be tired. Let's rest at the very least," she urged.

Rintarou silently stepped foot into the church.

An area of worship was immediately at the front entrance. The back of it continued into the residential area.

She led Rintarou along straight into the back, passing by a particular room.

"This is my room, master."

"Oh?"

"It's already late, but…would you mind talking with me for a little longer?"

"…Yeah, if that's what you want, I don't mind."

"Hee-hee, thank you… Oh… I guess I'll get some tea ready?" Emma flashed him a smile and left the room.

"……"

Rintarou looked around the room, not concerned if he was being rude. He recognized the room. There weren't any iron bars, but…it bore a strong resemblance to the room in Emma's netherworld that they had first encountered.

He could see the deep darkness of night outside the window. The dim lights of the distant city only registered as spots.

Then, Rintarou looked outside the window for a while without a word.

"Sorry for the wait." Emma came back with a tray in her hands. The tray had two teacups and a prepared teapot that was letting off warm steam.

They started their late-night tea party together.

Emma sat on her desk chair, and Rintarou plunked down on the bed.

The two of them sipped at their teacups and enjoyed trivial

topics for a while. Emma took the initiative for most of the conversation, switching from one topic to the next.

She talked about the previous year, back when Rintarou and Emma first met. They talked about how Rintarou had ended up beating the priests who were training Emma to a pulp and staying at the Religious Order for a while to help with Emma's training. Eventually, they veered into a conversation about the events that had happened when Rintarou had left Emma...

Emma continued to talk to Rintarou. She confessed all the things she had secretly kept locked in her chest. It was as though she was trying to fill the time that Rintarou had been absent.

"Heh... You seem to be enjoying yourself, Emma," Rintarou commented as he listened to her.

A smile played across her lips.

"What? Oh... Yes... Um, I'm just so happy that you're here with me, master." Emma's smile was as warm as sunshine.

However, in the next moment, Emma's expression seemed to cloud as though she had suddenly come back to herself.

"...I feel like... I've done something terrible to Luna..."

"......"

The room instantaneously went from a happy atmosphere to a heavy and suffocating one.

"Luna tried to sell you to protect herself. There was something about that I couldn't forgive. But I still stole you from her..."

"......"

"I'm sorry, master... I'll need to become the King to save the world... I need to become a saint, but...I'm such an incredibly bad and unpleasant girl...but I still... I still want to be with you, master—" As though Emma was overcome by emotion, she tried to desperately appeal to Rintarou.

"...Don't worry about it." Rintarou looked straight at Emma. "I told you, right? I said I'll *save* you.'"

"M-master...?"

"There's no need for you to suffer alone anymore. There's no need for you to carry that burden. You tried your best... You worked for so long... It's about time you were rewarded."

Then, with slightly dewy eyes, Emma looked at Rintarou...and said it.

"Thank you so much...master... I love you."

"......"

"Ever since we met, this whole time... This whole entire time, I've cared about you... I thought you were stronger and freer than anyone... I believed that if there was anyone who could free me... it was you..."

Emma stood from her seat and stepped toward the bed where Rintarou sat...and joined him. She moved next to him, inching toward his shoulder to lean on it.

"So don't leave me... Please stay with me forever..."

"......Emma."

For a while, Emma entrusted the weight of her body to Rintarou.

Then...eventually, she didn't know what he was thinking, but he made a move.

"...Master...? ...Uh..."

Rintarou gently grabbed Emma by the shoulders...

Thump. He slowly pushed Emma's slender body onto the bed.

Her dainty limbs splayed out. Rintarou pinned her and looked down.

When Rintarou snapped his fingers, the lights in the room disappeared of their own accord until only moonlight illuminated the inside of the room, and the space was filled with shadows.

"Wait—mas...ter...?!" Emma's heart beat rapidly at that unexpected situation.

Emma wasn't so naive that she didn't understand this situation.

"...Wha...? What...?!"

At the same time, Emma's face became hot as though she were burning up, and her body went limp. The sound of her beating heart became terribly loud. It was almost unnecessary. Next, her breath started to heat up like fire. The inside of her head went white, and it was almost as though her mind were melting into mush from being exposed to the delirious heat. She didn't feel like she could string together a coherent thought.

"...Emma."

Rintarou was looking at Emma so closely that they could feel the warmth of each other's breaths.

His eyes were sincere and serious...alluring and captivating.

His gaze pierced through her. Her heart and body felt as though they were being bound by something...that she was held captive by Rintarou.

"...We...we...c-can't...do...this...," Emma muttered softly over her breathy sighs, which never seemed to stop, even though it felt like she had exhaled all the sighs in the world.

As though it were her final act of resistance, Emma stirred and tried to get back up, but...

"...Can I?" Rintarou whispered with a gentle smile. His sweet words obliterated the last bits of resistance that Emma had clung onto.

Rintarou gently pushed her body with his hand, causing her to sink deep into the soft bed.

"...Ah...ah... Ah..."

Eventually, Rintarou used his right hand to grip both of Emma's wrists and brought them above her head… He pushed her wrists into the top of the pillow. With both hands restricted, Emma could no longer move.

Well, if she wanted to resist, she could have.

However, there was no strength anywhere in her body anymore to hold out against him.

"……Ah…ah…" Tears started to form in the corners of her eyes.

But she knew those weren't tears from pain.

"Master…master… Rintarou…!" With rough breaths, she looked straight at Rintarou, who was holding her down… Emma had earnestly called his name.

Continuing to hold her hands hostage, he undid the ribbon on Emma's chest with his steady left hand…graciously opening one button on her blouse at a time.

"…Hah… Ah… Aaah…"

Eventually, Emma's skin was bare as her clothes audibly slipped to the ground.

The light of the moon filtered through the window, making her immaculate bra glow faintly white. As anyone would imagine from her petite frame, Emma's body drew a trim and gentle curve. It wasn't seductive or bewitching. It was as pure as fresh snow.

On the flip side, it felt absurdly holy and sacred.

At that point, Rintarou stopped for a while and stared down at her as though she was precious.

"…Uh… Um… Master…? Maaaaster…," she muttered, straining her words together. Overcome by bashfulness and passion, Emma was half-conscious.

"…Th-this…is…my first time…so, um…," she said in a delicate, quiet voice.

"…Will…you…*please*…take…it slow…?"

She couldn't even finish that last sentence.

However, it seemed that everything had been communicated to Emma's beloved master.

"It'll be fine. Don't worry about it... Leave everything up to me," he whispered.

And the last barrier in Emma's heart dissolved.

Her body was no longer tense.

When he saw this, Rintarou slowly reached his hand out to Emma's chest.

"...Master..." She was in a state of euphoria and felt as though everything in her body were being melted away by the heat.

In that moment, she abandoned her whole self over to Rintarou and quietly closed her eyes.

From the corners of her eyes, beautiful tears went down her cheeks.

Shrrk.

Something uprooted and dispelled Emma's euphoria.

Suddenly, she felt a sharp pain running through her chest, coursing through her nerves like lightning.

"...Ow?!" Emma automatically snapped open her eyes...and an unbelievable scene came to her vision.

On her chest...in the vicinity of her heart, Rintarou had carved letters in blood with his left finger.

"M-master?! What in the world are you doing?!"

"The *Blood Sorcery of Fomorians...* It's a *Carved Seal for Control.*"

"Wh-what...?! B-but doesn't that take away a person's freedom and allow you to use them according to your will...?"

"Don't worry. I don't want to make you my slave or anything.

I'm using this seal to have you do something in particular for me. Right—"

There was something cold and somewhat pitying in his face.

Rintarou spoke dispassionately. "I'm asking for the destruction of your Excalibur and Round Fragment. In other words, I'm having you decline the King Arthur Succession Battle... That's all."

"Wha...?" Emma was at a loss for words.

Even as they spoke, Rintarou continued to plug away at his work, carving the insignia dispassionately into Emma.

The magic must have already taken some effect, because Emma's body started to feel like stone, and she couldn't move.

"Why...are you...doing this...?"

"I told you, didn't I? I said 'I'll *save* you.' This is the only way to save you now," Rintarou said coldly. "You understood it a long time ago, right? *It's impossible for you.*"

Shrrk. Pain seemed to carve its way deep into the bottom of Emma's heart, jolting her entire body.

"It's impossible for you."

This sentence...had history, back when Rintarou had been training Emma.

"I'm going to save the world...," Emma had told him with glee.

But that had been how he'd responded... They had been the last words he had told her to end their relationship as teacher and student when he had been training her.

"I need to apologize to you... I'm sorry. This all happened because I had a lapse in judgment." It was unusual for Rintarou to give a laudable apology. "Back then, I didn't know that you were forcing yourself down such a cruel path. I didn't know about the King Arthur Succession Battle, either.

"That's why when I saw those infuriating priests picking on you, I wanted you to get revenge. I wanted to see those assholes in tears when they realized they couldn't use you. That was the only reason I taught you how to fight in the legendary era. It was partially for fun. I ended up opening up those abilities in you."

"......"

"Because of me, you couldn't turn back. You got caught up in this fight... This right now—I'm just taking responsibility."

"Please stop!" Emma shrieked. "Please don't steal my role as savior from me! I don't have anything else! If I lose even that...how will I be able to live?!"

"I'm sure you'll come up with something. You ended up in this mess because you lived the way others told you to and didn't think for yourself. I'm scum, too, but you reap what you sow."

"No! No! No, no, no! I'm going to save the world! That's what I wish from the bottom of my heart! Even if you're my master, I won't forgive you for robbing me of that! I'm going to become King! I'll become King, the savior, and then this world will—" Emma desperately begged him.

"You...*were smiling*," Rintarou mercilessly told her.

"...Huh?" A ragged voice escaped Emma's throat, and she tilted her head.

"That netherworld was a projection of your heart. When I was killing the people begging you to save them...you saw that and smiled...from the bottom of your heart."

"...Oh."

As though she had been hit by something, Emma's eyes opened wide.

"You can't lie to yourself in a netherworld. That's a reflection of you. I mean, of course you can't lie. It's a mirror reflecting your own heart. You were smiling. You get it, right? You *don't care* what the hell happens to the world or the people or anything. If anything, you detest them.

"Because that was the role given to you…because you got it in your head that this was the only thing that made you valuable… That was why you were just only *acting* like a King, a savior, a saint. Has there ever been a King as empty as you? What's the final destination of a King without self-confidence, without ideals? …The answer is *destruction*. Without exception. I mean, look at all the centuries and places in the world.

"A person who doesn't love people, like you, who saves the people and the world out of obligation, will always be unhappy.

"Eventually, you'll lament the world, lament yourself, and when all hope is lost, you'll curse the planet and everything in it. You'll resent it, miserably, pitifully, and die alone. That's your fate."

"Ah… Aaah… Ah…"

"On that point, Luna…and her capacity as a King…are *overwhelmingly* greater than you as a savior. During that showdown… there was a clear *victor*. She…actually fought against that image of the world's death and destruction of her own will."

"O-of her own will…?"

"That's right. That world was your world. What brought about the destruction was your own heart. That was why you're the only one who could have won against the mirage. But you didn't try to fight it…and Luna was the one to face it…*of her own will.*

"Do you get how amazing that actually is? She proved herself. Even if this world is on the verge of destruction, even if she's shaking with fear, she'd face it willingly… Now that's strength. Sometimes, I think she's just a stupid girl and all mouth, but…she really is my King."

"But, master?! I willingly defeated the destruction, too…," she started to say, but Emma got caught on her words.

What had she done back then?

She certainly had let Rintarou take the chains connecting her neck...and let him pull her...

In other words, did that really count as her fighting of her own will?

"You get it, right, Emma? You can't do it... It's impossible for you. You got a slight knack for fighting...but otherwise, you're just a normal girl."

"......"

"You're different from Luna, Felicia, or Kujou. They have their own clear will and their own way of achieving their goal to be King. You're not like the 'strong' ones... You're weak."

"......"

"Turn back. You still have time. You don't need to be on *this side*," Rintarou coldly spat, continuing with his indifferent work of carving the seal.

"...No...," Emma entreated him with her last bit of resistance. "No... No... Please stop...! Don't steal this kingly position from me...!"

"I can't hear you."

"Nooo!" Emma cried and yelled at Rintarou like a child, as he dragged his fingers across her skin.

"Sir Lamorak?! Help me! Please help! *My Aura, guide my knight. The fourth seat of the Round Table—*"

"That's useless. I've already secretly isolated this place with a boundary. Sir Lamorak can't answer your call."

"No! No, no, no! If I can't be King...if I'm not the savior anymore, then how will I live?! What am I supposed to do now?!"

"You'll have plenty of time to mull it over... Don't worry. I'm in the same position as you. We can think about it together..."

"Liar! You're unbelievable! There's no other way of life for me!

Everyone told me that! They said that was the reason I was born! That's why my only option is to become the King of salvation! If I don't, I have no value! Spare me! Please don't take away my reason to live! I don't want to be whipped anymore! I can't stand to be sealed away in a dark dungeon anymore! I will die if I'm shoved back in that strange iron cage, strung up to prevent me from moving! I don't want to be deprived of food until I'm on the verge of starvation or prodded awake for days to read the Bible! P-please, master! I'm begging you!" Emma cried out.

Rintarou was aghast.

"...Are you serious...? That's what the Religious Order of Saint Joan put you through...? Those bastards! I should have killed them all back then!"

They had completely brainwashed her—a "curse" binding Emma, the pitiful and weak girl.

The Religious Order of Saint Joan had ensnared the blood of King Arthur and touted world salvation as their dogma... How had they indoctrinated Emma? It made Rintarou, who was already heretical and self-aware of his broken code of ethics, enraged. He was nauseated.

"...You...really need saving. You need to be released. Even a villain like me believes that at the bottom of his heart."

"You traitor... I'll never forgive you...Rintarou Magami... I can promise you that...! If you take away my role... I'll never...ever...!" Emma cursed with resentment.

But Rintarou was unperturbed.

Of course, he was convinced that this was the only way to save Emma from the spell binding her.

Rintarou tried to complete the seal on Emma's skin—

Suddenly, the room tore in half lengthwise. The top half blasted away.

*　　*　　*

"Gah?!"

Rintarou smashed the window and leaped outside, rolling on the ground in the inner garden on the church grounds.

If he hadn't jumped, he would have been bisected in two, stippling the place with his entrails.

Using his momentum, Rintarou regained his balance to stand again and looked up behind him.

"I wonder what in the world could be going on here... Merlin."

At a ledge before the crumbling second floor stood a young girl shouldering a claymore and looking down at Rintarou with maddened eyes that glared.

"Lamorak, you—?!" Rintarou yelled, and the second floor fell behind him, collapsing loudly.

"You underestimated me. I had a bad feeling and came running home. And here we are, with my beloved lord in this state of disarray... This is going to be difficult to overlook."

Sir Lamorak beamed as though she had been waiting for this all along.

"Shit..." Rintarou ground his teeth, uncharacteristically discomposed.

Why?! Why is Lamorak here?! My secret boundary was perfect! Even a wizard from the legendary era couldn't break it, much less a knight like Lamorak! But then why is she here?! How did she break through?! Rintarou thought while gnashing his teeth.

"...Sir Lamorak...you...saved me..."

As she collected her clothes, Emma made her way over to Sir Lamorak...and nestled in next to her.

The *Carved Seal of Control* had disappeared. It must have been because their session was cut short.

"Oh, it must have been so scary, Emma... I'm sorry. This happened because I was careless..."

There was something shameless in Sir Lamorak's outward kindness.

"I thought that...I could leave Rintarou Magami to you. But...I couldn't have guessed this would happen. I never would have thought he would toy with your heart and betray you... I couldn't even imagine that! I'm really sorry, Emma... I'm a failure as a knight."

She voiced regret and atonement of her own blunder, but there was definitely something behind them.

But Emma didn't even notice that.

"...It's okay... I'm fine...so..." Wet with tears, her eyes steadily burned with extreme loathing and rage.

"My beloved lord, please give me an opportunity to atone for my sins. Allow me to use my weapon to fix my blunder. Now... what would you like me to do, Emma? What would you like me to do with that backstabber, that bottom-feeder, that vulgar boy?" Sir Lamorak asked.

"...Please...kill him..."

Fwoosh. Something ghostly and black rose up from Emma's body...

"Rintarou Magami! You betrayed me...! I won't forgive you... I'll never...! This is a royal order...! Kill that unsightly traitor... Slaughter Rintarou Magami! Murder Rintarou Magamiiii!" Emma shrieked, releasing her wrath.

"You got it, my beloved lord—ah-ha-ha-ha-ha-ha!" replied Sir Lamorak.

Overflowing with indescribable delight and divine euphoria, she headed toward Rintarou with a smile—degenerate, morbid, and insane.

It felt almost as though she had finally gotten her chance to fulfill a long-standing wish.

I see. There are still things I can't figure out, but…I'm starting to see behind this charade. Rintarou glanced at Emma next to Sir Lamorak.

The faint and strange aura that wrapped around Emma couldn't have been discerned without spiritual sight.

It was reddish black, as if concentrated down from human malice. It was nauseating.

…That's…a Curse of a Changed Heart…

A *Curse of a Changed Heart* was one of the evilest of curses, and it could chillingly sever irreplaceable bonds—between the platonic bonds of a King and a knight or the romantic ones between a man and a woman.

The curse was simple. The cursed would experience ten times the amount of hatred, disgust, and resentment if the designated party "betrayed" them.

But relationships without any betrayal or lies didn't exist in this world.

At times, there was a need to lie or conceal the truth for the sake of the other person. However, the *Curse of a Changed Heart* made those trivial things unforgivable.

This isn't the work of Lamorak. She's doesn't know the first thing about magic. I don't know who did it, but it looks like Emma was specifically selected for this purpose. Wasn't there a wicked witch during ancient times who used that curse to interfere with the Round Table and other countries…?

Now wasn't the time for him to take that into careful consideration.

Fwsht. In front of Rintarou, Sir Lamorak jumped down from the second floor in full armor.

"You heard her. Fight me, Merlin."

"Why you! …Was that your real aim all along?"

"Hmm? I have no idea what you could be talking about," Sir Lamorak said, a bald-faced lie… She unsheathed her claymore and calmly walked toward Rintarou.

Then, the Rothschild formed around her…

Ha-ha. This is bad… There's no way I can win! Rintarou couldn't help but laugh.

He took in Sir Lamorak's stance, spirit, aura…and he knew this was fact.

It was almost exactly the same as when he had squared off against Sir Lancelot and Kujou just the other day.

It was one thing if he were Merlin in his heyday, but as Rintarou Magami, this was far out of his reach.

Lamorak with the red shields, the Rothschild—Sir Lamorak of Gales.

Back in the day, she was the top brass and one among the strongest knights who gave the Round Table renown.

"C'mon… Hurry and show me that power from earlier…," said Sir Lamorak, closing in the distance on Rintarou.

By that, she must have meant his *Fomorian Transformation.*

"Merlin, you've got something special in you, haven't you? It seems you still can't use it to its fullest extent, but…that's okay. I'll be gentle while I teach you the basics, like it's your first time. Show me the most dynamic version of yourself you can… Okay?"

Dammit, what do I do? Rintarou desperately tried to think of a way to survive while savoring the adrenaline.

If he was going to fight Sir Lamorak, the *Fomorian Transformation* would be essential, but even then, he would be far from what he needed.

If he tried using the *Fomorian Transformation* to fight in this situation, he'd only get closer to a slow defeat.

...What do I do?

It just made no sense to fight here. It wasn't wide. He wanted to make a strategic retreat, but Sir Lamorak wouldn't let him escape that easily.

In that case, he needed to find an opportunity to get away from the fight, but he would need the *Fomorian Transformation* to do it. The only problem was that it would put an immense burden on Rintarou's body.

After all, he was still recovering from the reactionary damage from the fight with Kujou. If he activated his powers now, he wouldn't be able to continue on, even if he managed to escape.

"Hmm? You're not going to do it? Well, I don't really mind..."

She didn't even give Rintarou the chance to figure out what to do...

"...We're starting now."

Bam! There was the sound of an impact, as though the air exploded.

Sir Lamorak kicked the earth and readied her claymore as she launched herself at Rintarou.

He couldn't postpone it anymore.

Heh! Guess I've got no choice!

Preparing himself, Rintarou started to invoke his *Fomorian Transformation*—

Rustle! Rustle-rustle!

Suddenly, Rintarou was engulfed by a blizzard of scattered leaves.

"Whaaa—?!"

Rintarou, Sir Lamorak, and Emma were in shock.

A maelstrom of dancing leaves whirled before their eyes and obscured their vision.

However, Sir Lamorak didn't so much as flinch, and the hair-trigger flash of her claymore cut through in that moment.

It should have caught Rintarou, but—he had disappeared into mist, vanishing into the scattered leaves.

Sir Lamorak's claymore cleaved through the sky and blew away the entire fencing surrounding the church.

Some seconds of silence elapsed...

"...He escaped," Sir Lamorak spat out in annoyance. She sheathed her sword and drew back her Rothschild. "That was *Blood Sorcery of Elves. Secret Fey Road*, huh? It must be the work of that little nymph Felicia. Hmph... I thought she was a worthless lackey, but I might have underestimated her. I can't believe she pulled one over on me."

She had been robbed of her opportunity again before she could tear into her feast... Sir Lamorak's expression put her emotions on full display as she ground her teeth.

"...Sir Lamorak!" Emma carried her Excalibur in her hand as she came down. "We're going after him. The *Secret Fey Road* is a type of magic that brings the designated party to the magic user using a Guide Pixie, but...its range isn't that wide. She must be nearby. If we follow the traces of aura, we'll definitely find them."

"Oh, Emma. You're coming, too?"

"Yes. He deceived me tonight, and I'll make sure to punish him!"

When Sir Lamorak looked, Emma was crying—from grief, even though her eyes flashed with anger.

"I liked him, but...I loved him, but...! But Rintarou Magami rejected me...! He chose Luna...! I can't forgive him...! I'm much better than her! As a woman and as a King! Rintarou Magami should love me and be by my side, but…! But…! There's nothing I can forgive him for now!"

She loathed Rintarou with enough intensity to stoke the flames of hell.

At the same time, she had love deeper than an ocean for him.

The flames of love and hate scorched her from within. For the first time in her life, she felt a strong impulse.

It was ironic that this was the moment that Emma had clarity on her reason to fight amid her oscillating emotions.

"I don't care about saving the world anymore! I don't care about a world where he doesn't love me back! I don't care about a world where no one watches over me, where nobody is kind to me! And you know what? I'll break it… I'll destroy everything about Rintarou Magami and Luna…! I'll make him regret not choosing me while he's in the pits of hell…! That's the reason I'll become King! I'll become King in order to destroy their royal path!"

Sir Lamorak watched as Emma burned with dark and passionate hellfire.

"Aaah… Nice… Emma… I really like…this new you," Sir Lamorak muttered as though she were in rapture.

"Yes… That is why I risked my life to serve you, my supreme King…Emma Michelle. I dedicate my sword, my soul, my life, and my everything to you! Until death parts us, my body will be beside you! …Ah-ha…Ha-ha-ha-ha-ha-ha!" She vowed her absolute allegiance to Emma.

Sir Lamorak's roar of laughter overflowed with delight. It was almost an ode sung for the birth of a lord. It echoed with glee through the night.

CHAPTER 6

The Bloodied Saint & the Knight with the Red Shields

It had been some time after Emma had been awakened to her new royal path.

The group was somewhere within Area Three of the international city of Avalonia in a certain Western-style house with a drawing room filled with fine furniture.

"Seriously... Even if it was all a charade, I wish you could have been a bit more lenient on me," chided a girl shawled in a black robe.

She was the one who'd had her head sent flying off by Sir Lamorak in the basement parking lot. Against all odds, she was well and sound as she stood in the corner of the room.

"It was a close call. I mean, I almost actually died... Well, I guess we'd need to go to extremes to deceive the eyes of Rintarou Magami."

"Hey, Morgan... Do you know the best way to enjoy a drink?" Sir Lamorak said, sinking deep into a luxurious sofa and ignoring the girl's objections. She sipped her wine.

For a while, Sir Lamorak admired the dim light of the chandelier passing through the crimson liquid in her glass. Her sweet lips kissed it.

"...I don't understand what you're trying to say. Just what are you trying to suggest with that question?" asked the girl in black, called Morgan, with unimpressed eyes.

"Hee-hee... Chateau Latour 1950...I like this one," the knight whispered to herself.

Sir Lamorak picked up the wine bottle that had been set down on the low table with a glass top and looked at that label. "Okay, let's continue where we left off. The answer is *destruction*. That's when a person is the most beautiful and dearest in the world. To pair this destruction with a drink... Now that's the nectar of gods in heaven... That's the conclusion I've come to."

"...Is that why? Is that why you answered Emma Michelle's summons?" Morgan seemed exasperated.

Sir Lamorak grinned. "Yes. I know Emma's destruction will be magnificent, especially with all her motley set of disingenuous ideals. She's a kind girl who won't ever be able to accomplish her fake goals. Even a Jack this good can't save her. And I'm supporting her with everything in my arsenal. When she learns the truth, she'll be at a loss, breaking down in tears from disappointment, sorrow, and despair—unable to accept the facts. Just imagining the sweetness of those tears...deepens the flavor of this wine," Sir Lamorak said in rapture, tipping the glass to polish it off.

Gulp. Her seductive neck constricted.

"Aaah... Yes, because of that, Emma is the best King for me. It makes sense for me to gamble everything on her. I couldn't be present at King Arthur's destruction, though I put my whole soul on the line for him... 'This time, I will sear the vision of the King's destruction into my eyes...and watch it come to pass'... That's why I fight."

"Ha-ha-ha... You're out of your mind," Morgan said with both glee and contempt. "I'm astounded that you would be called a knight of the Round Table who protects faith when you lived a messed-up prodigal lifestyle. And that's saying something, seeing you're from the time of legend. Your twisted sense of allegiance. Your love for destruction. Aren't you supposed to be a Christian? Aren't you afraid of the wrath of your God, your Father?"

"Scared? Why would I be?" Sir Lamorak asked with puzzlement. "I am *loved by God—more than anyone in this world*," she said, as though it were fact. She spoke without any hesitation or doubt.

"I'm the strongest knight there is. I've never lost in a one-on-one battle. I mean, you must know this. A duel between two knights is a holy ceremony granted to us as the will of the almighty God. If God shunned me, if I were to receive divine punishment, I would have lost my place a long time ago. Isn't that right?"

"......"

"Yes, I know God loves me because I've accrued a thousand victories. Because God loves me, I am promised victory. Because I am victorious, God has forgiven my sins. God is affirming my twisted ways.

"Because of that, until my life is over, I will continue to prove God's love with my sword.

"Because I am who I am, I can't allow things to rest at peace and order. I love destruction and crave pleasure. I'll continue plunging forward, fighting one thousand battles, resulting in a mountain of corpses and a river of blood. That is chivalry for Lamorak of Gales," Sir Lamorak said without the slightest hesitation.

"Ha-ha-ha! Ha-ha-ha-ha... Rintarou Magami... I mean, *Merlin*, the peerless soldier and strongest wizard in the world. My dear sweetheart. My beloved. How I have yearned for you, but I could never find an opportunity to fight. If I defeat him, I can prove the love God has for me. For me to meet him in this era can only be

God's will! Aaah, it is wondrous! What a beautiful world! For me to overflow with my Lord's love, fulfilled. How radiant and sublime!"

Like a virtuous child, she smiled, drawing a cross on herself with her left hand and clasping her hands together as though in prayer.

"That's why you responded to my deal when I contacted you in secret," Morgan said, as though she was almost exasperated with her.

"*You* had me place a *Curse of a Changed Heart* on Emma to fan the flames of love... *You* were going to have Emma and Rintarou Magami break up so you would have the pretext to fight him to the death. *You* did it not to stray from the chivalric way of the knights. You did it to deeply destroy Emma."

"Yes, that's right."

"Aaah... I wonder if your reckless plan will really work. Based on how I see it, Emma sincerely loves Rintarou Magami. I wonder if she'll be able to hate him?"

"All will be well. I'm sure it will go to plan," Sir Lamorak declared with confidence. "Rintarou Magami will certainly reject Emma... Betrayed, Emma will struggle with love and hatred. Rintarou Magami will choose Luna Artur, the one who is like the reincarnation of Arthur. I have faith that there is no other King in his mind, but... the greatest reason of all"—she halted for a breath—"is because I am loved by God."

Sir Lamorak's words were filled with so much conviction, even Morgan could only sigh.

"I don't understand it. Don't you love Emma, your lord, from the bottom of your heart?"

"Yes, I love her. I would even give up my body, my soul—anything for her."

"Then why are you treating her with cruelty?"

"Because...this is the only way I can love someone."

In that moment, Sir Lamorak's tone dipped slightly lower.

"I must have been born deranged. I want to force my love to destroy. I want to destroy with them. I want for us to fall as low as we can go. But I've fancied another situation at times... If I was a person who loved normally with a support person who was the same... I've wondered what would happen," she said, as though it was unavoidable. Sir Lamorak smiled faintly, alone.

"Sir Lamorak, it seems that we won't see eye to eye."

"Yeah, I didn't expect you to be so unyieldingly persistent or noble," Sir Lamorak said, as if trying to get a rise out of Morgan.

For a moment, Morgan's eyebrows arched slightly.

"Oh? Did I touch a nerve? Ha-ha, sorry about that. It's a joke, Morgan."

"...You didn't. I have no idea what you mean."

"Right. Ha-ha-ha. As a witch, you've driven many men into madness as a peerless temptress... Well, let's leave the preliminary remarks at that...and get to work soon."

Sir Lamorak glanced at Morgan, who seemed displeased. She put down the glass and stood up.

"I think Rintarou Magami should be starting to make his move on Emma right about now. I'll stop them right in the middle of it."

"What a joke... Well, it's fine. Sir Lamorak, if you say that you'll fight Rintarou Magami, that's enough for me. Our interests align after all."

After that conversation, Sir Lamorak and Morgan started running through the darkness of the night, heading to the church where Rintarou and Emma would be.

After that, Rintarou betrayed Emma, and Sir Lamorak intervened before he could go through with his plan.

Emma was frenzied, and Sir Lamorak just barely saved her.

"What a sorry sight!"

That was the first thing Luna said to Rintarou when they reunited.

"...Shut up." Rintarou faced her with crossed arms. He sat cross-legged on the floor and sulked.

They were in an abandoned construction site in Area Three, surrounded by other buildings. Around them were crumbled debris, littered wood planks, support beams, and reinforcement bars piercing through the concrete.

Luna, Felicia, Sir Kay, and Sir Gawain surrounded the sulking Rintarou.

"Bwa-ha-ha! That is what happens when you go off on your own and try to settle a fight all by yourself! See what happens when you get carried away?!"

"Oh, shut up! Be quiet."

"You better be grateful to Felicia for sneaking a Guide Pixie into your pocket!"

"Yeah, I got the hint! Loud and clear! I was wrong! Thanks so much, Felicia! Is that good enough for you?! Dammit!" He ruffled his hair and scratched at his head. A small fairy had been flying above his head since earlier... Finally, it disappeared, melting into thin air.

"Seriously... You're so reckless," Felicia said in exasperation, politely sitting on a tarp that covered the building materials. "Mr. Magami... You never even considered going to Emma's side from the start, did you?"

"...Well," Rintarou confessed, as though the idea had occurred to him. "Emma and I had...bonded slightly in the past. Because of me, Emma got stuck fighting in a battle that she had no desire to be in. That's why I wanted to give her a quiet send-off.

"I understood what Luna was trying to do when she said she was trying to 'sell me' and why she accepted a challenge to 'decide their capacities as Kings,' too. That was your way of keeping me and Lamorak from fighting, right? Because Luna got that conversation going, Lamorak had to follow Emma's judgment and directions—because she's a loyal knight. It's just in her character. Lamorak's loyalty to her King runs deep."

"Yeah, that's right. Your *Fomorian Transformation*…isn't actually a good ability, right? It's the kind of power that eats away at the irreplaceable…like your life, or soul, or sanity."

As though trying to escape from Luna's sincere eyes, Rintarou turned away.

"…Well, anyway, I was thinking I could use this truce as a chance to get into Emma's head. Luckily, Emma was all over me. I was thinking that I might've been able to use that in some way."

""Oh, that just crosses the line."" Sir Gawain and Sir Kay both drew away from him.

"I'm not going to deny that. But Emma's stubborn, despite the way she looks. She's not the type to listen if I was to talk to her. Emma's different from Luna, Felicia, Kujou, or anyone who actually has the capacity to be a King. She's empty. Frankly, she's the worst type of person to become King.

"But even if I was on the receiving end of her grudges, she had to be stopped. Otherwise, she would experience worse. Emma feels like she has an obligation to the people who fed and sheltered her. She's different from an asshole like me. I don't want a nice girl heading toward her demise… This isn't the time to be picky about how we stop her."

Rintarou sighed out of annoyance. "But…I needed a little more time before I could have used the *Carved Seal of Control* to get Emma to drop out. Lamorak ended up getting in the way… Well, after all the stuff that's happened, I'm sure there's another person pulling the strings behind the scenes. They really got me... Shit."

Rintarou suddenly looked at Luna as though he had noticed something. "Actually, Luna...I didn't think you'd figure it out."

"Figure what out?"

"Well...that I didn't betray you. You saved me just in time because you did, I guess."

"Oh, that's what you're talking about. Isn't it simple?" Luna thrust her chest out and spoke with a grin that anyone would have wanted to smack off her face. "Because in the end, you never called Emma your *King* even once!"

"!"

"When we went our separate ways during our situation with Mr. Kujou, you said the same kind of thing. 'Good-bye. Have a good life, Your Highness... No, *Luna*.' But...just now when you left me, what did you say?"

"See you. Take care, Luna... I mean... King."

"That's how it clicked with me somehow. I didn't really get the reason, but I got that I won in the battle against Emma to see which of us was the most capable King. I knew you'd come back to me right away."

"......" Rintarou turned the other way, looking all bitter and gloomy... Luna went around and looked at his face from above as she grinned smugly.

"What? I guess this means you really like me. You want to serve as my vassal? Ah-ha-ha! Gosh! What am I going to do with you? You're so cagey!"

"Uuuuurg...! Shuddup..."

They had reached a point where he would end up embarrassed,

even if he tried to refute her. Rintarou's face turned red as he could only go silent.

"Aaah. Could you stop acting like a couple of fools already?" Felicia put a damper on things as though trying to say she'd had enough. "So what are we going to do? Emma's definitely going to hit us back."

"If we stay here, there's no way to avoid a clash... We've got to attack," Rintarou declared, getting up. "But this time, this whole thing is my personal problem and responsibility... I'll fix this up on my own, so you all hurry and get lost—"

"You're such an idiot! What kind of King abandons her vassal?!" Luna butted in.

"L-Luna...you...?"

"I bet you want me to come with you, Rintarou! Right? Don't you? You do, right? Gosh! I guess I can't refuse! Cleaning up after a vassal's mistakes is a King's duty anyway."

Rintarou was in shock as Luna happily poked him in the cheek.

"If Luna refuses to retreat and fights, then I, of course, will fight as well." Sir Kay nodded in response.

"Though our truce is temporary, it is unspeakable for a King to abandon an ally! I will also enter the fight! On top of that, I'm already *prepared* for it!" Felicia grandly declared. "W-well, Mr. Magami? I owe you for saving my life...but don't get the wrong idea! I'm not wielding my sword for your sake! I'm doing this for my friend, Luna! This is for Luna!"

"Hmph. And of course, my sword will join my liege's. To be frank, I have some baggage with Sir Lamorak, but as an unimportant knight of the Round Table...I'll show her some guts." Standing up in a fluster, Sir Gawain shot them a wide smile.

"...Y-you guys." Rintarou seemed slightly shocked as he looked at those surrounding him. They met his gaze.

Eventually, he snorted as though he couldn't care less and turned away.

"So, Rintarou? What's the plan, technically? We don't know anything about the abilities of Emma's Excalibur...and Sir Lamorak is stupid strong," said Luna.

"On top of that, Sir Lamorak's Rothschild means trouble... You said that it automatically goes into defense mode, and it has the same amount of strength as Sir Lamorak? How'd we end up playing this impossible game...?" Felicia trailed off.

"To be honest, I don't think we could beat Sir Lamorak even if the five of us ganged up on her! Ah-ha-ha!" Sir Gawain chuckled.

In that entirely hopeless situation, they all could only smile dryly.

"When it comes to Sir Lamorak, our best bet is to have our strongest one in battle face her from the firing line. That would be Rintarou. But...to be honest, I think the two of them are on a whole other level," Sir Kay added. "Even though we've got more in number, if Rintarou and Sir Lamorak were to start fighting, no one would be able to give Rintarou any meaningful aid."

"I mean, even that time we fought Sir Lancelot...the best we could manage was barely a standstill...," Felicia lamented.

"How about we leave Sir Lamorak up to Rintarou, and everyone else will crush Emma? Though, that seems cowardly, too," Luna admitted.

"You think Sir Lamorak would let that happen? She has the Rothschild. If she was to even give one shield over to Emma for protection, then we wouldn't be able to place a finger on her."

At Sir Gawain's remark, Luna was taken aback. "What?! Sh-she can do that?! Isn't that kind of unfair?!" Luna asked, shocked.

"Yes, she can. When Sir Lamorak shows her true worth...it's actually much more amazing than you'd ever think. She can protect someone else in battle," Sir Gawain shamefully answered.

"L-literally that's the only thing knightly about her... Anyway, we need to do something about Sir Lamorak's Rothschild..." Luna nodded in worry, and they all followed suit.

"I think there's a way to break through the Rothschild," Rintarou said nonchalantly.

"""...Excuse me?"""" Their beady eyes all gathered on Rintarou.

"Hey, hey! Gawain... Why are *you* acting so surprised? You've broken through Lamorak's Rothschild, right? On the road back from the Surluse tournament." Rintarou looked at Sir Gawain, tired.

"Well...but Sir Lamorak had just battled against dozens of exceptional knights. We launched a surprise attack on her while she was exhausted...and we pitted her four against one, too..."

"Ha-ha-ha! You're an idiot. There's no way your quack quartet could've faced and beat Sir Lamorak's Rothschild. It doesn't matter how tired she was," Rintarou pointed out, mercilessly.

"Rintarou Magami! You grate my every neeerve!" Sir Gawain's face flushed as he stamped his feet.

"So...what, Rintarou?"

"I have an idea about how we can defeat the Rothschild. But honestly, it's a risk. I've got no idea whether I'm right about this. Actually, no one's ever actually fought Lamorak fair and square and won. I even question whether Sir Lancelot could have done it."

Sir Lamorak versus Sir Lancelot. In the era of legends, the battle had never been realized. But it was a chilling thought.

Rintarou continued with caution. "But if we're trying to win against Emma, all we can do is bet on it."

"I'm in," Luna said without hesitation. "Because it's your analysis, Rintarou. A King has got to believe in her vassal."

"Well, there's no alternatives, I guess... I'm in, too," added Felicia.

"And? What are we actually doing?" Sir Gawain asked.

Everyone believed in Rintarou. They all nodded.

"Felicia...Gawain...you all..." Rintarou took in all their gazes and blinked back.

"Ha-ha, we're all...'friends' right now, after all," Felicia added, looking bashful.

He flashed them a nice smile. "Well, none of you need to do anything. If you did anything, it'd cause trouble."

"...Huh?" Felicia let out, not totally grasping the picture.

"I kind of feel bad for saying this after you've gotten all worked up and promised to help, but...you're all going to be in the way."

"WHAAAAT?! You led us on! You're telling us you're not letting us on the team?! Wh-wh-wh-wh-what's the meaning of this?!"

Felicia and Sir Gawain turned unwelcoming eyes to Rintarou.

"It's gonna be one against one."

"Huh?"

"Don't you get it? In Lamorak's battles...she's weirdly obsessed with having these duels. She considers her 'duels' sacred and inviolable. It's her pride as a knight. That's why—"

Rintarou smiled with an evil and villainous expression. In vindication, though it wasn't clear what he was feeling vindicated about.

"I'm going to hit her hard... And shatter her."

They were running. They were sprinting through the suburbs of Area Three of Avalonia. Emma and Sir Lamorak dashed at the speed of wind.

They flew through the air from rooftops of sporadic buildings. Occasionally, they jumped down into the road, sprinting through the streets, before soaring into the air again. They ran past the building walls and danced through the darkness.

"...They're close," Emma muttered as she followed the residual aura left by the Guide Pixie.

"Yes. But are you sure about this, Emma? Are you sure you want to let me take Merlin... I mean, Rintarou Magami?" Sir Lamorak blatantly asked as they raced through rooftops.

"I don't mind. The result is the same, whether I do it with my own hands or yours." Emma aimed for the next building, gliding through the air.

"But...you love Rintarou Magami, don't you?"

"It's specifically because I love him that...I can't forgive him... I detest him...!" Emma shouted, strained. Her eyes were clouded from the effects of the *Curse of a Changed Heart*.

God's in his heaven. All's right with the world. Sir Lamorak secretly chuckled to herself.

Eventually, the two of them soared through the night in the shadows.

That was when something happened.

The scenery almost seemed to become enshrouded in darkness as it distorted in place. Their vision was engulfed in deep shadows of the night, and the area around them transformed into a world *bathed with sunlight pouring down on them.*

"AHHHHHHHHHHHHHHHHHHHHHHHHHHHHHH!"

In the same moment, a loud cheer accosted their ears, and they were surrounded by wild enthusiasm.

"What is this?!"

At the sudden change in their situation, Sir Lamorak and Emma both stopped automatically.

They weren't in the international city of Avalonia anymore.

As far as the eye reached, there was a plain that continued to expand. The sun radiated and burned in the sky. Knights on horseback were standing around them in magnificent armor.

An audience area circled around them and the knights. Noblemen and women were gathered around them, and the cheers of the general public rose up in excitement and encouragement.

Heroic banners billowed in the air from several camps that had been built for the knights.

The sparks flying into the air seemed almost like they would never peter out.

"...What is this place? What in the world happened?" Emma looked cautiously at their surroundings.

"Ah! Oooh! ...Ahhh! This is...!"

Sir Lamorak was enraptured. She seemed nostalgic when she looked at that scene.

"Yo, how do you like it?"

"...Emma. You made it."

Rintarou and Luna appeared in front of the two.

"...Did you create this netherworld, Rintarou?" Emma asked, interrogating him.

Rintarou grinned. "Heh. I can't stand having a scary group targeting us. We're doing this without any cheap tricks... Let's settle this without anyone getting in the way."

"...Just us?"

"Yeah, that's right. Sir Kay won't make the cut when it comes to battle power. Felicia and Sir Gawain aren't involved in this case, because this has got nothing to do with them. It'd be better if Luna and I settled this whole thing with you and Sir Lamorak. That's got to be a relief to you guys, too, right? That's why I got this netherworld set up."

"Hmm... I don't know if I can believe that." Emma glared

at Rintarou with steady eyes. "You're a coward and a traitor. Felicia, Sir Kay, and Sir Gawain are probably somewhere in this netherworld... You must be hiding them so they can ambush us by surprise."

"They're not here. Those guys aren't anywhere in this world right now. You should know that, right? You're a King! Take a good look around...at this netherworld!" he promoted.

Emma used her sixth sense.

The Curtain of Consciousness that separated the real world and the illusory one had been made *temporarily ambiguous* at that moment. A *Netherworld Transformation* spell had been used to create the other world.

When it came to the creation of these plains, there was *World Fusion Grade*. This was an indicator of whether the netherworld had been created from the real world or the illusory one.

There were four stages: *Assiah* for matter, *Yetzirah* for the formation, *Beri'ah* for the creation, and *Atziluth* for the foundation. The netherworld could be closer to the illusory one and become stronger by ascending those steps in that order. If it was closer to reality, physical laws and materiality would dominate. If it was more like the illusory world, psychological elements and spirituality would become stronger.

In any event, the only person who could freely enter and exit a netherworld without penalty was the maker of the world. If the enchanter was defeated, the world would immediately disappear.

In addition, netherworlds couldn't be maintained indefinitely. The world wouldn't allow this major inconsistency to exist.

Those were the absolute rules.

"...What?!"

As she searched the netherworld, Emma was in shock. She compared the makings of the netherworld to the groundwork laid out.

"*Yetzirah?!* I shouldn't have expected less from you, master... I wouldn't have expected you to make a *Netherworld Transformation* at this level! Just making an *Assiah* requires a first-class wizard...!"

This *World Fusion Grade* made going into and out of the netherworld mostly impossible. Performing a *Knight Summons* was already impossible, even in an *Assiah* one.

In other words, the humans inside could not escape, and those outside couldn't trespass in.

Emma was the most surprised about something else.

"And...there's no one else here...? There's no one...except us...?!"

Though it looked as though the crowd of spectators and knights were there, they only appeared to have substance.

Because of that, the four of them—Rintarou, Luna, Emma, and Sir Lamorak—were the only ones in the netherworld.

"What do you think? We've burned all the bridges. This is how ready we are. Do you get it now?"

"You're really...intending to settle this with just the two of you...?"

"Yeah, exactly. Emma, I'm sorry, but Luna is going to face you one-on-one, and—" Rintarou unsheathed his pair of swords and turned to Sir Lamorak.

"I'm your opponent, Lamorak! It's a one-on-one duel—just like you wanted! This is the kind of place you'd want to settle our battle, being as pretentious as you are!"

"...I do like this." Sir Lamorak was clad in a dark void, and her deranged, flaming eyes deepened in hue.

Her entire body was possessed by a euphoria that would have even penetrated the heavens. It ran through her body like a bolt of lightning.

"I would never forget it! Like I would ever forget! This! This is it!

These are the grounds for the Surluse tournament! This was the peak of my glory when I was enveloped in God's love. This was where I was fatefully killed by the hand of Sir Gawain and his three cronies as I was on my way home!"

She had a special smile on, as though she had gone deranged. She was savage, threatening.

"That's right! This is it! This is the most suitable place for me to take everything back! I'll defeat Merlin and prove God's love for me anew! I'll take back my glory as the strongest! Ah-ha-ha-ha-ha! You have my gratitude, Merlin! I love you! I love you! I love you! I love you so much I can't stand it! I love you so much that I want to kill you! Aaah! Merlin! Your blood, your flesh, your hair, your organs, your bones, every last scrap of you is all—*all*—mine! Ha-ha-ha-ha-ha-ha-ha!"

As though she could no longer wait, Sir Lamorak took her cruciform claymore and stuck it upright in the ground like a holy insignia. She put her hands together and kneeled devoutly like a maiden offering a prayer.

"*Laudamus te. Benedicimus te. Adoramus te. Glorificamus te. Gratias agimus tibi propter magnam gloriam tuam. Cum Sancto spritu, in gloria dei patris...* Let us praise our Lord. Honor our Lord. Revere our Lord. Worship our Lord. Offer our gratitude to our Lord's great glory. To the Holy Spirit and God, our Father... Amen!"

Sir Lamorak got to her feet and unsheathed her weapon, readying herself.

Her pure eyes that passionately looked at Rintarou could have been of a maiden's for her first love.

"What devotion... Aren't you popular?"

"I wish somebody would trade places with me... I'm not even trying to cause trouble," Rintarou replied, looking fed up to Luna, who readied her sword.

"Well... Anyway, we're doing this, Luna!"

"Got it! Leave Emma to me!"

Rintarou invoked his *Fomorian Transformation*. Luna readied her Excalibur again and took a step forward.

"Hmph, that's what I was hoping for. I'll show you exactly how different we really are, Luna," quipped Emma.

"Right, Merlin. Even though you're the master of this netherworld, you better not scamper off when things get messy. Well, if you do that, I'll just send over Luna's head after you."

Emma and Sir Lamorak each faced their opponents.

"Luna!" Rintarou encouraged the girl next to him. "Emma is a better warrior than you! But you're definitely a better King! Overwhelmingly!"

"?!" Luna's eyes fluttered, and Emma scowled unhappily.

"I know for a fact you'll win! There's no way you'd lose! You better win!"

"Heh... You too."

They didn't even look at each other during this curt exchange.

And then, they kicked at the ground and raced forth.

Rintarou headed toward Sir Lamorak, Luna toward Emma.

They each took on their opponents and faced each other.

Sir Lamorak and Emma readied their swords before the big clash.

After all the strife, this moment ignited their final battle.

"*AHHHHHHHHHHHHHHH!*" The crowd screamed. The cheers rose. Rintarou and Sir Lamorak clashed and parried, slicing at each other in their battle to the death. The spectators went into a standing ovation to cheer them on.

"Uuuu-rah!"

"Ha-ha-ha-ha-ha-ha-ha-ha!"

In his *Fomorian Transformation*, Rintarou swung his right and left swords, bashing them into Sir Lamorak's claymore, which changed course in the air like a whirlwind.

When their blades met, the impact blew through like a storm and gouged into the area surrounding them, rampaging as it went.

"Phew."

There was an extremely quick flash. Sir Lamorak's strike from above was stopped by Rintarou's left and right swords.

But that had been the afterimage. They scorched the ground as they kicked at it at an acute angle and circled each other. Rintarou went around to Sir Lamorak's back.

"Tchhhh!"

If he couldn't get her head, the frosty sword would attack him. However, that horizontal slash that spread like a ripple—

"Ha-ha."

Gonnng! The atmosphere sounded as though it had warped. Bits of light flew into the air.

Sir Lamorak must have read his next move. She turned around with her claymore and stopped him.

"Tch." Rintarou clucked his tongue. In that moment, Sir Lamorak used the spring in her whole body to swing her claymore in front of her.

"Aaaaah?!" Her physical strength was unimaginable.

With that force, Rintarou flew horizontally back, blown over like he was a projectile in a slingshot.

Wherever Sir Lamorak's feet hit the ground, pillars of earth rose forth.

Sir Lamorak followed Rintarou as he was blown away. She rushed in like a bullet.

"Dammit?!"

Schwoof! Schwoof-schwoof. Rintarou rolled along the ground and barely righted himself.

"Ah-ha-ha-ha-ha-ha-ha-ha!" Sir Lamorak seemed to fly through the air to pursue him, bringing her claymore down without mercy.

Promptly kicking the ground, Rintarou flew to the right.

Alongside an explosion, columns of dirt burst up, and the claymore bore a gigantic crater into the earth.

But by then, Sir Lamorak had already started to pursue Rintarou again. Rintarou instantaneously rolled to the left.

With another blast, more clods were sent through the air as her weapon dug into the ground again.

And then Sir Lamorak hounded him.

"Guh." Unable to evade her in time, Rintarou crossed his two swords over his head to go on the defensive.

"Ah-ha-ha-ha-ha-ha-ha-ha!"

Her power was close to a nitrate explosion. Her claymore pushed through the defense of his swords and destroyed it.

And she cut Rintarou into pieces.

But as sinew sprayed around him, his flesh suddenly melted and disappeared into the air.

"Don't underestimate me."

She had only obliterated a *Silhouette*. Using that as a decoy, Rintarou quickly came down from above to desperately strike at Sir Lamorak's head.

But something in the air shifted—accompanied by a blast and bursts of sparks.

The Rothschild had been invoked above Sir Lamorak's head, stopping his sword.

"Tch… Dammit! Hah…! Hah…!"

Sir Lamorak nimbly jumped away and took her distance from Rintarou.

Not much time had passed since the beginning of the battle, but Rintarou's breath was already getting ragged.

"Good... You're good," purred Sir Lamorak, stroking the blade of her sword with composure and leisure.

"That was excellent, Rintarou. Your attacks are getting stronger with each attempt... My body is getting hotter and hotter... I'd say we're highly compatible." She gazed at him with passion, seductively bringing her lips to touch the blade of her claymore.

"But...I think you could be better. Much better."

"......"

"You're acting like a flustered kid, like it's your first time. But that's not right. If you go all-out, I'm sure you could get me more excited... I'm sure you could make me feel pleasure like never before... Isn't that right?" Sir Lamorak grinned kindly.

"It's fine. It's fine, you know. Don't be nervous. Until you get the hang of it...until you can display more of your power...I'll be gentle with you. Ha-ha-ha..."

"I'm...thankful for that... *Cough...*" Rintarou steadied his breathing as he readied his swords.

"To be honest, I can't believe I haven't been able to draw out Merlin's power yet... If you're going to wait for me, that's fine by me... But don't cry about it later."

Suddenly, Rintarou's whole body was swelling with a black aura as he disappeared into mist.

And then he came striking from the right side. He brought his swords down on Sir Lamorak—leaping ten yards between the two of them in a split second.

But Sir Lamorak invoked her Rothschild on her right side, and her claymore met that instantaneous attack that had surpassed the boundary of human reflexes.

"…That's better." Sir Lamorak smiled in satisfaction and looked at Rintarou from above their crossed swords.

"Ha-ha, good! Good. Yes, that's the way to do it—"

"SHUT! UUUUP!" Rintarou drew back his sword and pounced, using every spring in his body to cut at her with his stormy attacks.

Made up of dozens of flashes of his sword, the whirlwind went berserk as though to pulverize Sir Lamorak. If his opponent had been a normal person, his prison of blades would have reduced them to mincemeat within a second.

"Yes! Yes! There! Harder! That's it! That's the spot! Oooh! Yes! …Uumph. Nice. ♪" Sir Lamorak had a composed smile as he continued to fend him off.

When their swords attacked, clashed, or crossed, the audience let out an earsplitting cheer. The place continued to be run by enthusiasm.

"Haaaaaaah!"

"Hmph!"

Luna and Emma were readying their swords as they closed in.

"Hyaaah!" Luna was the first to make a move. The flash of silver traced a circle and blew by.

Her blade swished from above, fending off attacks at her torso, and spun around to mow down Emma's feet.

The passionate dance of her sword was unconventional—flawless. She left everything to natural talent.

"Hah!" Emma had her sword readied at the middle—parrying everything with the most minimal movements possible, regardless of whether the attack was above, below, or aimed directly at her.

Her swordsmanship was beyond magnificent. It was almost an art form.

"Ugh?!"

Konk! Emma took on Luna's final attack with the body of her sword. Using its momentum, she beautifully returned the tip of the sword, turning the butt of her hilt right around at Luna.

Bam! At the same time, she took a sharp step forward.

Emma left an afterimage of her small body as she pounced and sank the butt of the hilt into Luna's stomach.

"Hurk!" Luna's body was blown backward, taking on the brunt of Emma's counterattack.

She rolled clumsily onto the ground.

"…Ugh! I hate that sword!"

"Hmph… I don't want to hear that from you, Luna. All you do is flail around with your sword."

As Luna crawled along the ground and cursed, Emma looked down at her with chilled eyes. "My moves were taught to me by my master himself. It's not as though you could put up any resistance to them."

"Shut your trap!"

Once again, Luna jumped to her feet and resolutely attacked Emma.

Their battle had been progressing only as this repetitive exchange: Luna tried to dauntlessly attack, but Emma would handle every attempt with finesse. Then, she would use a merciless reversal on the last attack.

Luna reacted to the crossing maneuvers by using her animal-like instinct to avoid any fatal wounds, but it wasn't as though she was escaping without a scratch. She just continued to collect more bruises.

"Aaack?!" Again, she was pushed over by another counterattack, thrown back.

"…How many times will it take for you to get it? You're a real dunce, Luna." Emma looked at her with contempt as she prepared for the next attack.

"I'm not—" Like a one-trick pony, Luna jumped up and sped toward Emma.

It didn't matter how often Luna did this; it was impossible. Emma waited with her sword readied.

"Hah!"

They were both taking a step forward, swinging—

This time, things developed differently. As Luna stepped forward, she used her foot to scrape at the ground and vigorously kicked up a cloud of dust at Emma.

"Cough?!" As she tried to protect her eyes from the rising debris, Emma turned her head slightly to the left.

"Got ya!"

In that second, Luna had created a blind spot. She turned to the right, sharply driving her sword in.

Skkkkt! Metal against metal shrieked on impact.

Luna's sword floated by Emma's right side as a Rothschild defended her.

"That shield again?!"

Bwoosh! It was time for Emma's counterattack. There was a flash from the side, and Luna jumped back in a fluster.

Sure enough, it seemed Sir Lamorak had given Emma one of her Rothschilds.

When Luna occasionally took Emma by surprise, this shield would defend against her attack each time. The battle progressed to Luna's disadvantage.

"That's why I've told you that it's impossible. Even if, by chance, you find an opening, I have Sir Lamorak's Rothschild. There is no chance of you winning."

"Y-you're so annoying! What's with you? Acting high and mighty when you're just borrowing someone else's power!" Luna howled with impatience.

"Do you hear yourself? A vassal's power is her master's strength... In other words, that is the difference in our abilities as Kings... Isn't that right?" Emma fixed a cool gaze on her. "...Is this all you amount to, Luna...?"

"...—Ngh?!"

"How...could Rintarou Magami choose you when you're obviously weak...?! There's something off about this entire situation... There's something absolutely wrong with that...!"

Emma gripped her sword tighter, as though she couldn't stand it anymore.

"I'm absolutely stronger than you! As a swordswoman! In our abilities as King! I should absolutely be better than you! But...but then why—?"

"...You don't know when to shut up. You're so annoying...," Luna barked back, using the back of her hand to rub away the blood that trickled from the corners of her mouth. "If that's true, hurry up and prove it by beating me... I dare you to try. I'm still here, you know. I've gotten the brunt of your sword, but I'm still alive and kicking! Have you ever considered that you're the one who doesn't amount to much?! I mean, that's all you can muster after getting all that training from Rintarou? Come *on*!"

"Wha...?!"

"Aaaaaah! Seeeriously! If you didn't have that Rothschild, I would obviously be winning! Well, Rintarou will do something soon, right?! I mean, my vassal is amazing, after all!" Luna provoked, readying her sword high above her head.

She was already battered. Be that as it may, she was in high spirits. It was almost like she didn't believe that she would be defeated by Emma—or that she was inferior in the slightest.

"Okay. C'mon. When you lose that Rothschild's protection, that's when you'll fall."

"…You're all bark and no bite!" Emma steadied her weapon again, fed up by the harassment. She let the battle flag on her hilt billow and readied it at a low position.

"Okay… Now I'm going to make sure you acknowledge your defeat! In fact, that's all I want! I won't stop until you've declared you've been defeated and kneel to me of your own will!"

"What in the…?" Luna answered, mocking her—

Suddenly, the thick and heavy aura rose from Emma's entire body. At the same time, her sword flared, coiling with crimson flames. The flames swelled, and heat prickled Luna's skin. Luna scowled.

And then, Emma declared: "Royal Road."

"And that was how King Lot had been defeated at the end of the intense battle.

"The eleven rivaling kings of Britain were defeated by King Arthur's army.

"The ten surviving kings captured by King Arthur cried out in sorrow.

"King Arthur is terribly angry. It was as though we were battling in a horrific fight against a demonic deity. It was as harrowing as the pits of hell.

"'Aaah. We who opposed King Arthur will most certainly be slayed, and none shall remain.'

"'We will die just as that fearless man of valor—King Lot.'

"Oh, how we have been fools.'
"However, King Arthur, in his magnanimity and greatness, called the ten remaining kings to him and said unto them, 'I will forgive you.'"

John Sheep,

LAST ROUND ARTHUR, THIRD VOLUME, ELEVENTH CHAPTER

"My Excalibur—the Steel Sword of Compassionate Guidance!" Emma boomed, thrusting out her sword.

The tip released a crimson flash that pierced the center of Luna's chest.

There was something abnormal about what happened. Luna was sure she had jumped to the side fast enough to evade that flying flash of red, but she had still been pierced by the sword.

"Uuuuurgh?!"

With no the time to question anything, Luna was sent flying back by that impact, and she rolled along the ground.

"…Don't worry. My sword isn't meant to kill anyone." Emma turned her blade around and readied it again.

"My Excalibur is a guiding one. It is stern to those who are wicked and hostile. At times, it is severe, as though burning you at the stake, but if you repent and submit, it will subside. My sword is the embodiment of King Arthur's compassion—and the importance and depth of it when he added people to his following… Though releasing a single attack with its true inscription won't take your life, *there is never a way to avoid a strike from it.*"

"Ugh! Gah…! *Cough…!*" Luna held her chest, which had been shot through by the crimson flash, crouching as she broke into a cold sweat.

"But it's only nonfatal until the tenth strike. At the eleventh, death will most certainly visit you. *It is fatal—and there is no way to defend against it.*" Emma's mouth twisted into a grin. "...It's a merciful sword, isn't it? As long as you choose to surrender to me, request my forgiveness, vow allegiance, and submit before the eleventh strike, your life will be spared."

"Hah... That's stupid... That's more boring than I expected!" Luna used her sword as a cane as she stood up. "I just...need to defeat you before you hit me eleven times, right?!"

"Yes, that's true, but—" Emma tried to say something...when it happened.

Roooar! With that auditory hallucination, a raging fire blazed up in Luna's pierced chest.

"Ugh! Aaaaaaaaah!"

It burned! It inflicted a horrific pain. It was distressing—and she couldn't breathe.

At the spot of contact, Luna suddenly felt as though she were being burned alive in hell. Despite herself, Luna dropped the sword in her hand. She almost felt as though she were being burned at the stake as punishment.

"Ah! Gaaaar! Uuuugh! Wh-what is this...? Ah! Aaah...?!"

It wasn't a real flame. Her clothes hadn't caught fire, and she didn't have a single burn on her. This was all a hallucination.

Then why did she feel as though her whole body was being tortured?

In the next instant, Luna's whole body was soaked in a cold sweat, and she screamed in anguish.

"Do you understand now? With each strike, hellish torture will increase. And once you've received that pain, it will never disappear."

"...What?" Luna's face twisted in despair.

"A person with a weak will would be crippled from pain with just one strike. Luna... Knowing you, I'm sure you'll fight through it, huh. But will you actually be able to battle properly?"

When Emma saw Luna's despair, she faintly—but clearly—*smiled*.

An Excalibur was a mirror that projected the true face of a King. Luna wanted companionship, Felicia valued pride and glory, Kujou believed righteousness was overpowering others by conquest... An Excalibur would reflect the state of one's heart through its form and ability.

In which case, what did that say about Emma's torturous ability? What did it mean that her power seemed to be embracing deep compassion but was oddly twisted?

...Her mind is seriously effed up...! Luna endured the acute agony assailing her body and ground her teeth as she fixed a stare on Emma.

"Now, then. It's time for your counseling, Luna." Emma flashed another saintly smile at Luna. "Declare that you do not have the capacity to be a ruler and reject being a King. Acknowledge that I am superior to you. You must beg me for forgiveness. If you do that, I will release you from that pain—and spare your life."

"...You've got to be kidding me," Luna spat when Emma boasted as though she had already triumphed. She got to her feet and readied her sword. "Like anyone would acknowledge a 'weak' child like you!"

"Ah... Oh, well. I didn't think you were this stupid," Emma muttered in pity as though she was looking down on Luna.

"Royal Road—"

Once again, she tried to release Excalibur's ability.

"AAAAAAAAAAAAAAAH!" With unimaginable speed, Luna pounced on Emma's chest.

This was the only way out. If her opponent was going to release an unavoidable attack, the sole choice was to defeat Emma before getting hit. Luna's only option was to move first and defeat Emma.

But because that was her only means of opposition...

"I see what you're doing." Emma easily repelled Luna's sword, assaulting her with a precise counterattack.

"AAAGH?!"

Emma's sword cut into Luna's side before she calmly took her distance from Luna, who had collapsed on the ground.

"The Steel Sword of Compassionate Guidance—Excalibur!"

Once again, a flash of red released from the tip of the sword, aimed directly at Luna. When it was released, the strike was already hitting Luna's left shoulder. That was the truth.

It really did always hit its mark. Even a heroine or peerless soldier would never have been able to evade the strike.

"Aghhhhh?!" When the infernal torment flared up in her left shoulder, Luna couldn't help but scream.

"Hee-hee. Nine strikes left."

Emma smiled. The way she did it was dark and sinister.

"RAAAAAAAR!" Rintarou roared. He burned his mana to its limits and converted it into aura.

Triggered by his call, a black aura swelled up from his whole body.

The patterns carved into his hands made a prickling noise as his soul was starting to erode.

At the same time, Rintarou was surging with a new power.

Wheeze! Haaah! Haaah! Rintarou struggled to catch his breath.

This change progressed further as he called more of his ancestors.

A Fomorian soul was trying to devour Rintarou's soul.

The phenomenon wouldn't normally arise from simply invoking a *Fomorian Transformation*.

He was crossing swords with the strongest knight of the legendary era—Sir Lamorak—and their savage fight was building up quickly. In the interval between life and death, he was forced to awaken his power as Merlin as quickly as possible. Those effects were only happening because he was striving to master its energy.

"...This is amazing. Absolutely stellar," Sir Lamorak muttered as though intoxicated, like a girl perplexed by her first love, as she watched him awaken a power that was leagues beyond his strength before.

"You're positively marvelous... No way... I'll fall head over heels for you..."

"GAAAAAAH!"

With an uncontrollable energy expanding from his whole body, Rintarou danced with Sir Lamorak.

His blade tore through the very foundation of the atmosphere.

But the Rothschild stopped his heroic attack.

Rintarou's two swords had been firmly stopped by the shields.

"Ha-ha. I'm not going anywhere. You don't need to be so greedy..." She looked lovingly at him, protected by her defensive powers.

He ground his teeth, and she swung up her claymore—and fiercely hit back.

"AAAARGH?!" His body made an arc as he was blown back.

"Don't stop! I bet you can still come!" Pursuing him, Sir Lamorak carved up the ground as she raced toward him. "More! Come on! Collect your power! Make me euphoric! Let's go together!"

She whizzed toward Rintarou, who had crashed, jumped up, and steadied his weapon again.

Sir Lamorak hit him with her claymore—and Rintarou stopped it.

Honestly...this is close. What's going to happen to me after this fight...?

Sir Lamorak cut at Rintarou with a stormy attack as he was thinking.

His soul was grating, creaking under the pressure. He had wielded too much power in too short of a time. He had progressed too quickly.

Whether he won or lost, he probably wouldn't come out unscathed.

He might lose his power as Merlin. Rintarou faced this premonition.

"Like I can...lose...!"

"—Huh?!"

It was all or nothing. Rintarou used his swords to push back at Sir Lamorak.

"She's...depending on me...! She's believing in me, after all!"

The Jack briefly backed off to get back in a standing position, and Rintarou flew at her.

"This isn't bad...! Yeah, this...doesn't feel too bad!" Rintarou yelled.

"AAAAAAH!" Luna's scream echoed through the battlefield.

The hallucinatory flames flared up on Luna's left knee and her right shoulder.

"The Royal Road of this Excalibur," Emma started, twirling her sword as she sauntered out of range after Luna had been on the receiving end of yet another attack.

From over the fluttering flag, Emma had some choice words for her.

"We're already at a total of nine strikes... What's wrong, Luna? You'll die after two more. Are you a little closer to yielding to me? How are you feeling?"

"Ah... Gah... AAAAAAH?!" The agonizing flames lapped up Luna's body.

She barely balanced on her feet by propping her sword as a cane. In that moment, she was in excruciating pain. She thought she would go mad.

She couldn't even breathe properly. Maintaining consciousness without going insane was getting increasingly difficult.

"Guh...! Uuuurgh! Errgh... Ack..."

But even then, Luna gritted her teeth and stood.

"How...am I doing...? Ha-ha... Ah-ha-ha... Not...bad..."

"...What? Not bad? Have you finally lost your mind?"

"...Not really? Unlike a certain girl with a one-track mind... who selfishly...does things only for herself...and pushes her responsibility on other people... You could never understand...!" Luna spat and took on her fighting stance.

"You *still* want to keep going? I guess you really won't understand until I give you the tenth strike. You'll understand the true difference between us...and our capacities as Kings."

That was when Emma saw a fireball tracing a curving path, flying straight for her like a dodgeball. Using magic, Luna had released a generic *Fireball*.

Emma immediately leaped away.

It smashed onto the ground—just where she had been standing—and raised a fiery storm before exploding.

"Gah?! You're doing this all in vain...!"

Emma was distracted by the *Fireball*. In the moment, she turned away from Luna...

"Ahhh!" Luna brought up her sword at Emma's back, then sliced down.

Gonnng! But her desperate hand was deflected by the Rothschild.

"Ugh?! A-again... Seriously, what's he doing...? Hurry up and do something about this already..." Luna scrunched her face in frustration and slight glee as her sword was repelled during direct combat.

"Like I said, it's all in vain."

Emma kicked Luna hard with the back of her foot and sent Luna flying.

"The Steel Sword of Compassionate Guidance—Excalibur!"

Another flash aimed at Luna in midair, raining down on her.

"Gah! Ah?! AAAH!"

The tenth strike mercilessly caught Luna on her right arm. She felt shooting pain go through her brain as though she were being burned to ashes. The pain had accelerated.

But Luna gritted her teeth, endured it, and twisted her body to land. She immediately kicked hard at the ground and jumped at Emma's chest.

"Haaaaaaaaah!" She used her left leg to pivot and roundhouse kicked Emma from up high with her right foot, using every ounce of her strength.

She no longer had any clever ploys to use. Her attack was desperate and clumsy.

In fact, the move was pitiful enough for Emma to let the Rothschild defend her and decided any counterattack would be idiotic. She just shrugged.

Rintarou versus Sir Lamorak.

Luna versus Emma.

Each fight had a clear victor at the moment.

Even if Rintarou heightened his powers by letting the *Fomorian Transformation* erode him, Sir Lamorak would destroy him, knock him down, and hold him down.

Nimble sword in hand, Emma continued to toy with Luna.

On top of it all, they were dealing with the Rothschild, which protected both Sir Lamorak and Emma.

Anyone watching from the sidelines would pity Rintarou and Luna during those one-sided developments.

The battle had already been decided.

If there had been real spectators, they would have collectively made this observation. The only problem was that they were just figments of illusions, which made them incapable to formulate thoughts.

Emma's side was victorious. Defeat loomed over Luna's team.

The outcome had already been set.

Luna and Rintarou were barely hanging on, but the fight was already over.

And then—

"...Hmm?"

In that battle where she had an obvious advantage, Sir Lamorak suddenly realized something.

While they had passionately battled, she had chased Rintarou, been pursued, and been hot on Rintarou's heels. In the span of that time, their battlefield had, at some point, shifted away from the tournament grounds of Surluse.

A dense forest was on either side of a single road.

They were far from the tumult of the grounds—instead, on a lonely high road dominated by silence.

"This place is...?"

That scene brought forth old and bitter memories.

She couldn't forget it.

This place was her path home that day after Sir Lamorak had won dozens of matches as the undefeated victor.

The next day, she would have had her decisive battle to

determine who was strongest with Sir Lancelot, who had also won every round. It was supposed to have been the peak of Sir Lamorak's glory, but that honor had never reached her hands—because everything had gone down on that fateful day.

As she had been heading home by horseback on that road, Sir Lamorak had suddenly been attacked.

The four of them—Sir Gawain, Sir Agravain, Sir Gaheris, and Sir Mordred—had assaulted her.

She had certainly been careless. That was the only explanation for it. She knew the brothers had felt enmity toward her for being the daughter of Pellinore, the enemy of their father—Lot—and held a grudge against her for being the lover of Morgause, their own mother, but…she never would have guessed they would bare their teeth at her.

All four of their weapons skewered Sir Lamorak. Even though she had been called the strongest and fought with glory, she had come to an abrupt end.

"Aaah… I've recalled something very unpleasant."

The netherworld couldn't have been made in any worse taste. She couldn't have imagined that he would go through with reproducing this place.

As she clucked her tongue, Sir Lamorak looked down the high road in annoyance. Farther down, Rintarou was battered and covered in blood, barely standing as he used his swords in place of canes.

"*Wheeze… Hah…*"

Rintarou was already as good as dead. He was slumped over, facing down. If she hadn't heard his rough breathing that mixed with bloody vomit, she wouldn't have thought he was still alive.

Sir Lamorak faced Rintarou, walking toward him.

It no longer mattered that her glory had been taken from her in the past. She would start anew here. She would get the better of Merlin in this holy duel and seize her glory once more.

The curtain would rise on her new adventure, another trial for God's love.

The best thing about this battle was that Rintarou's powers from his past life were coming back.

...She would soon be able to devour him.

"Now, Merlin... Have you had enough of a break?"

She would carry on the battle—the passionate affair.

She was intoxicated and enraptured from the fight. When Sir Lamorak leaped at Rintarou, she readied her claymore at her hip and gathered her strength in her legs—

"Sorry this is so sudden, but—"

Rintarou suddenly grinned... The corner of his mouth lifted up horribly.

"—you know how I said I'd duel with you? ...Sorry—that was a lie."

"...What?"

"Heh! Like anyone would face a monster alone! Duuuuummy!"

Sir Lamorak was caught off guard for a moment...which was when something happened.

"I've had enough physical therapy! Now! Do it!"

Suddenly, three fissures cracked open to the right, left, and rear of the Jack.

"Sir Lamoraaaaak!"

"Haaaaaah!"

"Prepare yourself!"

Sir Gawain, Felicia, and Sir Kay jumped out from the cracks.

Just like that other time, they struck at Sir Lamorak in an unanticipated surprise attack.

"Whaaat?!"

Even Sir Lamorak was shocked and swiveled around the claymore in a fluster. She drove away Sir Gawain's sword, but Felicia thrust from the side. Sir Kay slashed from the back. They hit their marks, piercing her from the side and cutting into her back.

"Gaaaah! AAAAH?!"

Because she had wrenched herself around, she had avoided a fatal wound, but it by no means was a trivial injury.

"No...?! Why...?! Wh-why are *you* here...?!"

Her face twisted in surprise, looking at the people who shouldn't have been able to enter the inside of the netherworld.

Bwoosh! Sir Lamorak swung her weapon in a wide range and chased the three of them away. However, blood was seeping out of the corner of her sweet mouth, and as she weakened, she slumped to her knees despite herself. It seemed the blade had caught her in a vital spot.

"Huh? I actually hit Sir Lamorak with my sword...?" muttered Felicia.

"...W-we actually got her...? She didn't invoke the Rothschild...?"

From the distance, the three were shocked by this development.

"Heh-heh-heh. It looks like we've actually got a second chance at this... Well, good work! You guys did great!"

In the midst of all their surprise, Rintarou grinned smugly like a know-it-all.

"You're one hell of an idiot. I can't believe you'd actually trust an enemy."

"MERLIIIIIN!" Sir Lamorak howled. Her eyes were practically red as she roared in wrath and rage.

Her howl made the skin of those around her crawl.

"I won't forgive you... I'll never forgive you! Merlin...you intend to sully this sacred duel?! How...atrocious...!"

"Heh! How long are you gonna pretend you're on the high road,

you crazy psycho-sadist? Checkmate. Now we've got you." With a dauntless expression, Rintarou turned his sword at Sir Lamorak, who was fuming with rage. "Your prided Rothschild is invalid now! Yeah, this is what happens when you end up in a one-versus-four situation!"

"Huh?!" Sir Lamorak's expression twisted out of disgrace.

"The Rothschild is a holy relic of a Celtic Christian saint! Three shields for the Father, the Son, and the Holy Spirit—the Trinity. That's the sacred representation of *Gunimo, Philiotaio,* and *Ramheid*! A fourth puts that harmony in disorder. It's an ominous, unlucky number in Celtic tradition, but I bet you already know!"

"Y-you couldn't have?!"

"That's right. The protection from the invincible Rothschild is only taken away when you're facing *four enemies*—no more, no less! It can't be three or five! It *has* to be four! That's how Gawain's four-person hack team won against you!"

"Rintarou Magami, you're reeeaaally getting on my nerves!" Sir Gawain screeched.

Rintarou continued. "Heh... It was a big risk, whether I guessed correctly, but...looks like that is how it works, and the bet paid off, Lamorak..."

Gnash... Sir Lamorak wiped away her own trickling blood and ground her teeth.

"Th-this is unfathomable..." Her shoulders shook with fury.

"This netherworld is a *Yetzirah*—a formative stage...! No one should be able to get in from the outside unless they came with you from the start...! How...?!"

Then...

"*Whaaat?* When did I say *I* made this netherworld?" Rintarou feigned ignorance, provoking her.

"What?! Y-you couldn't have…?!" Sir Lamorak shifted her eyes to the side.

In front of Sir Lamorak's eyes, Felicia stood resolutely with her sword at the ready.

"Yes, I'm the one who made this netherworld. I'm its master. Weren't expecting that, huh? I'll have you know…despite my looks, I consider magic my great pride."

"Whaaa…? Wha…?!"

"That's right. Only the enchantress who made the world can enter and exit on their own accord… In other words, Felicia can bring as many people as she wants with her!"

"How… How idiotic…?! To say a little girl did this…?!"

Sir Lamorak was only at a loss for words. She was dumbfounded. She would have expected it from Merlin, but she couldn't have believed that Felicia had enough skill with magic to invoke a *Yet-zirah* world… Sir Lamorak realized that she and Emma had been duped.

"After that, we just needed to wait for the perfect timing! You want to know why we had to time it for right now?! That's 'cause if we launched a four-person surprise attack on you in this place—well, we knew you'd be ridiculously angry! Mwa-ha-ha-ha-ha-ha-ha-ha-ha!"

Rintarou's loud laughter echoed sinisterly.

I can't believe that he would strategize to specifically rub salt in her wound after her terrible trauma…, thought Sir Kay.

I already knew it, but he's the absolute worst person ever…, noted Felicia.

…Merlin is terrifying, observed Sir Gawain with a shiver.

All three of them shied away, their faces pale and eyes disgusted.

"Merli… Rintarou Magamiiiii?!" Sir Lamorak raged, causing the air around her to become electrified. "You think you ants have accomplished anything just because you can group together and give me a mere wound?!"

She swung up her sword and leaped at them all at once.

Thud.

Sir Lamorak opened her eyes wide and took a knee when her body suddenly felt heavy.

"Wh-what is this...? I suddenly feel slow...?!"

"...Hey, Lamorak, make sure you don't underestimate us too much."

Sir Lamorak looked around.

"Royal Road! Excalibur—the Radiant Steel Sword of Glory. Pardon me, Sir Lamorak."

Felicia had lifted up her rapier, already invoking her order.

A blinding light radiated out from Felicia's Excalibur and dampened Sir Lamorak's power.

"Okay, Sun's Blessing is invoked, my liege." Which meant Sir Gawain was three times more powerful than usual.

"Gah... Wh-why you...?!" For the first time, Sir Lamorak looked uneasy, as it seeped onto her expression.

"Heh... If you were in your normal state, and if I did my *Fomorian Transformation*, Felicia used her debuff, Sir Gawain was three times his power...and Sir Kay...uhhh...Sir Kay?"

"It's fine! You don't have to force yourself to include me!"

Sir Kay was in tears.

"Well, anyway. Even if we did a ton of stuff, we wouldn't have won against you. You're just that overpowered."

But Rintarou dauntlessly smiled. "Now that you've let me get in a ton of practice, my powers are about on par with yours! On top of that, you've lost your Rothschild, and you're fatally wounded... Now then, I wonder which way the scales will tip?"

Sir Lamorak gritted her teeth with hate.

"In order to... In order to manufacture this situation, you tricked me into a duel...?! You did this because you knew that I would train you in a one-on-one fight?!"

"Ha! Of course! All you knights think battles are sacred and fair—to defeat your opponent at full power... I mean, you do that because you're all dumb!" The bite in Rintarou's mocking cackle was merciless.

And that infuriated Sir Lamorak.

"Fine... You asshole...! If you're willing to go that far to die a gruesome death...then I'll plaaaaaay!" she hollered.

Sir Lamorak brought up her claymore and lunged at Rintarou and the others.

"Ahhhhhhhhh?!"

At that moment, Emma felt a powerful impact that jarred her head and sent her rolling along the ground, crying bloody murder.

It had been caused by Luna's last-ditch roundhouse kick.

Emma had tried to take the attack with the Rothschild, but of course, something went awry.

The Rothschild that protected her...had suddenly lost its materiality and melted into thin air.

The end results were that Emma got a full taste of Luna's kick to the side of her head, knocked away.

"Hmm, look at that. I guess I finally got a point in?"

As Luna slowly brought down her leg from its position held high over her head, she smiled without fear.

"Wh-why did the Rothschild do that?! S-Sir Lamorak...?!" Shaking her head, Emma got up and looked around her but couldn't find her Jack.

It seemed that because she was so absorbed in battle, they had been separated at some point.

As a King, Emma had a spiritual line of connection with her Jack. Based on their connection, she didn't sense that Sir Lamorak had been defeated, but...that was all she got. They seemed to be in a peculiar situation.

"Ha-ha... Now that annoying shield is finally done-zo... In other words, Rintarou did good... Well, I knew that from the start! All according to plan!"

"Wha...what in the world did you do...?!"

"Well, well. More importantly, how're you feeling? You just got the hood pulled over your eyes by your 'inferior'! Who's looking down on who now?!"

"Aaah! This is absurd...!" Emma used her sword to support her weight as she forced herself to stand.

"I don't know what happened, but your attack only landed because of Rintarou Magami! It's not like I lost to *you*!"

"Erm? What're you talking about? A vassal's power is her lord's power, right? That's the difference in our abilities as Kings? Does that ring a bell?" Luna retorted.

"Ack?!" Emma could only grind her teeth.

"Well, anyway...this battle...starts now...!"

Even though Luna's whole body was tattered as a rag, she readied her sword.

When faced with Luna's incomprehensible and tenacious spirit, Emma was overawed momentarily and backed away.

"...I-it's useless. Even if I don't have the Rothschild, I'm stronger than you, Luna. This doesn't change how the battle ends."

"I wonder...if that's true...!" Luna declared, even though her consciousness was getting hazy.

"...Don't you get the situation you're in? Or have you lost your senses to the point you can't even make that judgment?" Emma looked at Luna, who staggered and was in a hopeless state.

The younger girl took back her composure in exasperation. "You've already gotten ten strikes of my Excalibur. In other words, in just one more strike, you'll be visited by decisive, unavoidable death. The battle is already over."

She saw the ten phantom crimson flames burning all over Luna's body. Luna was covered in figurative fire.

"I'm amazed you held out for this long, but...why don't you give up already? Think over the words that you'll use to beg forgiveness—"

"Shut up, you idiot! I'll say this as many times as I need!" Luna declared, swinging her sword. *Bwoosh!*

"As a King, I'm superior to you!" she shouted. "Plus, you've lost the protection of the Rothschild, and my swordsmanship is better than yours! You don't have a chance of winning anymore! You're the one who should hurry up and surrender already!"

"...Aaah. I guess there's no saving you." Emma chillingly narrowed her eyes and readied her sword. "It's fine now. My compassion as a King is at its limit. Luna, please die—like the eleventh king who died opposing King Arthur, refusing to accept his compassion until the bitter end. Meet your maker like Lot."

"—Ngh?!"

Then...

"Royal Road..." Emma tried to release the final order, but...

"RAAAAAH!" Luna leaped at Emma's chest with indiscernible speed.

How could she move this quickly in her state?

Emma could only be internally stunned by Luna's tenaciousness.

"Like I said, it's useless!" Emma's sword lightly swiveled.

She had trained to fend off attacks and deliver blows. It was like muscle memory at this point. She apprehended Luna's swift sword, sweeping it to the side, and at the same time, she pierced it deep into Luna's chest.

With this, it was over.

—Or it should have been.

However…

"AAAAAAAAH!"

"*What?!*"

Luna's thought process was incomprehensible, but she stepped forward, even as she took on Emma's sword. Because of that, Emma missed. Though Luna's wound was severe, it wasn't fatal.

Gong! She head-butted Emma's skull, even though Luna was bleeding.

"Argh?!"

In that moment, Emma's vision flickered. Unable to withstand the attack, she bent back and jumped away.

It was the first time Emma had ever retreated purposefully since the fight had started.

"Heh-heh… How's that? *Wheeze…* So this is all you amount to when you haven't got the Rothschild?"

Hacking up blood and in pain, Luna grinned smugly.

"Huh…? Wh-what are you saying…?"

As she held her smarting head, Emma wondered whether Luna had finally gone insane.

Luna proudly said she had gotten a hit on Emma, but…the younger girl had sustained just one head-butt. On the flip side, Luna had acquired nontrivial sword wounds.

In that match, the obvious winner was clearer than ever, but—

"*Wheeze… Hah…* Ugh…what's wrong? You couldn't be sacred, right? *Cough!*" Luna asked, but her eyes were obviously declaring something else.

She was saying: *I win.*

"Wh-why you…!"

Even though she had been hopelessly driven into a corner,

Luna believed in her victory, without bending and without yielding. She had come to the battle to win. Emma felt nauseated by that.

"Okay! In that case, we'll see how long you can keep this up with my own hands!" Emma tried once again to ready her sword and release Royal Road.

"AAAAAAAAH!"

And of course, Luna had no choice but to leap at Emma's chest again.

"I knew that's what you were going to do!" Emma easily drove back Luna's sword.

"I'm coooooooooooooooooooming!"

But Luna didn't stop, even though she had sustained a major injury, ramming her head into Emma's. The younger girl's mind was shaken and went completely white for a second.

"Ah! Gah?! Wh-why?! *Why?!*" Unable to endure the shooting pain, Emma took her distance, but—

"I'm not done yet! I'm not even close to being done!"

Luna mercilessly pursued Emma—without end, without fail.

Rintarou had advanced his *Fomorian Transformation*; Felicia had wielded her Excalibur; Sir Gawain had activated his Sun's Blessing; the surprise attack had been successful in landing a powerful blow. They had managed to force out the Rothschild.

Even with all those conditions in place...

"RAAAAAAAGH."

...Sir Lamorak possessed power that was beyond their leagues.

With raging ferocity, she swung her claymore at Rintarou, Felicia, Sir Gawain, and Sir Kay as they assaulted her from all directions. Her attacks bowled them over, sent them flying, threw them down, and shook them off.

If Felicia hadn't cast *Spring Wind of Abundance* on all of

them—which had the everlasting fey magic to continually heal their accumulating injuries—they would have already been six feet under by now.

"I'm the best! I'm the strongest knight in this place! All you little shits can do is gang up on me! I can't lose to yoooou!"

However—

"HAAAAAAAH!" Rintarou's swords had picked up pace, coming at her faster and stronger. It was nothing like the beginning of the fight.

"UUUUH-RAH!" Sir Gawain's sword came to his aid.

"Ack! Gah?!"

They had started to carve more than trivial damage into Sir Lamorak.

"Y-you bastards…! You little shiiiits!"

To win, this Jack had to break out of this disadvantageous setup of one against four and switch her focus to making counterattacks. But because of Felicia's *Spring Wind of Abundance*, any superficial wounds would immediately be healed, and Sir Lamorak couldn't get anything to stick.

"You're so persistent! Are you all zombies or something?!"

In that case, she had to reap their lives with one attack.

Once she determined that, Sir Lamorak followed through with a momentary opportunity that she saw in Rintarou, who had grown more fatigued in the long battle. She used her entire soul, amassing all the aura in her body and collecting her strength to desperately swing once.

"*DIE!* Rintarouuuuuu!"

Oh crap, what'd I do wrong?! In that second, Rintarou was prepared for his own death, but—

"Rintarou Magami!"

Blood sprayed through the air.

It was none other than Sir Gawain who had intervened between them. He had come to stop that fatal swing of the claymore with his Galatine. But her attack had been too savage. He had been unable to stop it, and the claymore violently split through his armor, carving deep into his flesh.

At long last, one person had fallen.

It wasn't just Sir Lamorak who had believed that, but everyone there, Rintarou included.

"Why…?!" Sir Lamorak snared. "Sir Gawain… Why aren't you dead…?!"

Her strike should have had enough power to murder any normal being, even though she had suppressed her strength. It had certainly been fatal.

It was a fact that even Rintarou would have died in his current form.

And yet, Sir Gawain was still alive, standing on his own two feet. Moreover, he was holding back Sir Lamorak's claymore with his own body.

"Ah…I can't…get the sword out…?! Let go…! Let *go*…!"

"I'm sorry, but…I'm proud of my strength and resilience…" Sir Gawain smiled as if he'd tricked her, blood trickling from the corners of his mouth.

"I think it might be because I'm part of the family line of Danann. If I focus my aura on defense, I'm hard to kill," he barked.

Come to think of it, Rintarou recalled.

He was thinking back on Mordred's rebellion in their past lives. It was the last fight between Gawain and Lancelot. Over the course of a few days, Gawain had continued to fight to the brink of death, even after being beaten to a pulp by Lancelot.

Sir Gawain. He was a step behind when it came to the sword or spear, but he had the greatest tenacity at the Round Table.

Sir Gawain had caused the collapse of the Round Table. Frankly, Rintarou thought he was the most infuriating person in the entire world. After all, he was Merlin. But…at that moment, in that situation, Sir Gawain had Rintarou's trust.

"It's go time! You've got to do it, Rintarou Magami!" Sir Gawain yelled.

"HYAAAAH!" Rintarou moved in a flash, brandishing his two swords to draw two metallic crescents through the air.

"AAACK! URK—!"

Fwoosh! The paired weapons closed in on her sides, causing a spray of blood to spurt up from Sir Lamorak.

The wound was deep, in the shape of a cross. It was almost fatal—a severe injury.

"Hurk?! Wh-why youuuuuuuu!" Sir Lamorak used all her might to kick at Sir Gawain, drawing back her sword and springing away to take her distance from Rintarou.

Drenched in blood, Sir Lamorak readied her claymore.

Rintarou was sticky with sinew, too, facing Sir Lamorak and darting at her at top speed.

He was close to his limit.

Well, he had already gone past his limit.

If he didn't finish her with this next blow, they would lose.

Resolutely aware of that premonition, he sprinted as fast as his legs would take him.

He dredged up the last of his strength and released the final stroke of his sword.

"LAMORAAAAAAAAAAAAK!"

"RINTAROUUUUUUUUUUU?!"

Rintarou and Sir Lamorak headed for their final clash, closing in on each other.

And then—

*   *   *

"Why is this happening?!"

Finally, Emma started crying.

"Why...? Why? Why-why-why-why?! Why can't I beat you?! Why won't you give uuup?!" Emma couldn't piece together the situation anymore.

In tatters, Luna stood before Emma. Well, it would be an insult to beaten rags to call her that.

She had already received the ten strikes of Emma's Excalibur, receiving the brunt of her sword countless times. She was soaked in blood and wiped out—a lost cause. In fact, she seemed close to death even in that moment.

And Emma wanted her to die.

Emma had only sustained damage in the form of head-butts— and not even ten, at that.

Out of a survey of a hundred, it was obvious that everyone would say Emma was the victor here.

And yet...

Regardless of this whole situation...

"*Cough! Koff!* What? Is it over alrea—? *Cough!*" Luna smiled with menace.

...The one who was overwhelming the place, the one who was dominating, wasn't Emma.

It was unmistakably Luna.

"*Wheeze...* Aaaah... Come to think of it, I'm actually in a bad place, too... I'll die at this rate...," Luna said, vomiting blood.

"Th-that's right! If you keep it up, you'll die! You're going to perish! Hurry up and acknowledge defeat and surrender to me—"

"...I won't!"

Why?! Emma was ready to bawl, regardless of how it would have looked to others.

"Well... I've bided my time long enough. Now, I present to you...my Royal Road," Luna started to suddenly say. "After this... it's over...!"

"Oh..."

Suddenly, Emma's expression twisted in fear.

I see... That was the plan all along! Her Royal Road! She has that ace up her sleeve. That's why she hasn't lost hope and kept up with her stubborn act... Gah!

The Kings who entered the succession battle had a trump card—that was their Excalibur's Royal Road.

At the sign that Luna would publicly exhibit hers, Emma's entire body tingled with nerves.

B-but...if she has a Royal Road that could completely reverse this desperate situation... What could it even be...?!

Immediately, Emma lost the composure her superior advantage afforded her. Her nerves were going haywire, making her breath go ragged.

No, it's fine. If she's been saving it until now, then it must be a deadly attack of Military Pursuit. Or maybe it's a Kingly Epiphany that gives her a boost... It can't be the most dangerous manifestation: a Royal Menace... In which case, I can still win, as long as I can keep predicting her attacks...! Emma readied herself and her sword.

"Okay, I'm up for it! Come at me anytime!"

"Yeah? Huh... Then, I'll take you up on it, and—"

Luna started to race forward.

In the eleventh hour, she turned to Emma all at once—with unbelievable speed and without hesitation. She brought up her sword, shouldering its weight.

"Royal Road!" Luna declared.

Emma chuckled to herself.

In that moment, Luna ran closer and closer within fighting distance.

I'm sure of it. She has the type that's all about Military Pursuit! And the type of ability that needs to be in close range!

In other words, it was possible she could more than handle it with her swordsmanship.

Emma had won.

Fwish!

But for some reason, Luna had suddenly thrown her sword to the side, right before Emma's eyes.

".........What?" Emma's mind drew a blank when she witnessed the unexpected.

What? Why? Did she just throw her sword down?! What kind of Royal Road is that?! Th-that couldn't be a Divine Revelation, right?! That's only been in rumors! N-no! It couldn't be...

Because if that was the case...

As Emma focused all her senses on the oncoming attack, she had left an opening for a very brief moment.

If just for one second.

But it still happened in that time.

"Royal Road! My Excalibur—the Steel Fists of Sheer Ol' Will!"

She pounced toward Emma's chest, *punching her with her bare hand.*

"Mm— *What?* What is that...?"

In a fluster, Emma leaped back, trying to swing her sword to intercept, but it was already too late.

Before Emma's sword could seize Luna, the straight punch from her right hand had made direct contact with Emma's left cheek.

Without mercy, Luna had swung her fist—striking a single

punch, charged by her imperceptible dash with her entire body weight behind it.

It blasted into Emma, shaking her off-balance and throwing her petite body back.

In that moment...

"Ah—"

...something broke in Emma.

It was what she had been protecting with the utmost devotion.

On impact, she felt like she was drifting—hazy, as her consciousness quickly flickered white.

Emma felt her own Excalibur slowly cracking.

"Why...am I...? Why did the Rothschild...? I couldn't...have been...beaten by you...?" Emma muttered to herself, as her consciousness and body floated through the air...

"Isn't that obvious? It's because our vassals are different," Luna answered plainly back.

"AAAAAAAAH!"

"WHOAAAAAA!"

In the battlefield, two screaming souls mixed together.

Rintarou and Sir Lamorak blended as one as they passed by each other.

Their swords swung in their full range.

"......"

"......"

The battlefield was unbelievably silent. It was serene, as though time itself had ground to a halt.

There was none of the thrill and adrenaline, none of those shrill whines of impacted weapons. It seemed far away—almost as though they had never existed at all.

Felicia, Sir Gawain, and Sir Kay gulped as they watched over them.

Rintarou and Sir Lamorak were still in the same position as they were when they had swung their swords. They only stood still with their backs to each other.

Eventually, the silence and stillness that seemed to stretch to eternity came to an end.

"...Did we...lose...?" Sir Lamorak had processed Emma's situation in its entirety, using their spiritual channels.

She opened her quivering mouth, turning up as though imploring heaven.

"...*Eli, eli, Lema Sabachthani*...? My God, my God, why have you forsaken me...?"

It was as though she couldn't know, that she just couldn't understand... Sir Lamorak questioned God...

"Isn't it obvious? Luna and Emma... They're so different—in terms of their abilities as Kings," Rintarou bluntly stated. He didn't even bother to turn around.

"Jesus...!" Sir Lamorak spat at the end, before her body turned to particles of light and started to disintegrate.

Her incarnation faded away, evaporating into a mist of mana. And she quietly and abruptly vanished into thin air.

And then—

Luna's and Rintarou's vision became scorching white—pure and bright.

Everything was as white as it could be.

The world had changed. And this fabricated one came to its end...

At the End of All Love and Hate

—Emma opened her eyes.

"...You're back with us?"

When she opened her heavy eyelids, the first thing in her line of sight was Rintarou. He held her up from where she had collapsed, peering into her face. He had already undone his transformative spell.

Then, she noticed Luna, Sir Kay, Felicia, and Sir Gawain looking down at her.

The night sky was a deep darkness, and the area around them was made up of the old and lonely vestiges of a construction zone.

"...How do you feel?"

"..." She said nothing, checking her constitution slowly.

She didn't hurt at all. All her injuries had been healed. But she felt leaden, weak.

It was almost as though she had confronted an empty loss that collapsed her chest, as if her soul had been ripped to shreds.

Even in her half-consciousness, she shifted her gaze and looked at the Excalibur in her hand.

The blade had broken cleanly in half.

"...I see... I lost..." Emma remembered everything, muttering as though in shock.

An Excalibur was a sword that reflected a King's way. It was a mirror that projected her heart.

And if her heart acknowledged defeat, then obviously it would break—just as it had for King Arthur when he had submitted to King Pellinore's unbearable strength.

"*Sniffle...* I—I...lost... I lost... *Hic*...and now...my involvement in the succession battle...is...over..." Emma cried softly, cradling her face in her hands. Warm tears fell from her eyes.

"We undid the *Curse of a Changed Heart* on you," Rintarou dispassionately told Emma.

"...A curse...?"

"It got to your head, right? ...That's why."

Now that he said it, Emma's head did feel particularly clear.

That was when she finally realized the abnormality of her thoughts, emotions, and actions up until now.

"You might not want to listen to me, but I think...the person who put the curse on you was—"

"No, I know... I already know..."

Emma had been with Sir Lamorak ever since she had arrived at the island.

There was no way someone could have placed this curse on her without catching the attention of a knight like Sir Lamorak.

In that case, the conversation was easy. The one who had placed the curse on her had to be Sir Lamorak...or it was an outsider helping her Jack.

Either way, Emma had been betrayed by her trusted knight.

"...Sir Lamorak..." Emma gently gripped the Round Fragment at her hip. It was now broken, too.

She had a feeling...that there was something twisted that

burdened Sir Lamorak. She knew she couldn't help. She had known...that Sir Lamorak had dealt with desires and worries that no normal person could comprehend.

But regardless of that, Sir Lamorak had been the one and only Jack who had answered Emma's summons... Emma didn't think her Jack had faked her allegiance, her kindness, her devotion to faith... She didn't want to believe that.

"...Why...?"

But the person who could answer her question was...gone.

Emma gripped the broken Round Fragment and wept in sorrow.

"...Wh...y... *Snigg*... Ugh... *Hic*... Urp..." She cried.

As Rintarou continued to hold her up, Emma didn't even care about how it looked to the others, sobbing uncontrollably.

No one could say a single word to her.

...After she had let out and dealt with her emotions herself, she regained her composure.

"...It's...fine now..." Emma got up and stood, rubbing her swollen eyes. "I...lost. The succession battle is over for me. But... I'm sure this is for the best."

She broke into a little smile. Though her lips were wet from tears, she looked brighter, as though she had shaken off a demon inside her.

"...In the end... I didn't have the capacity to be a King... I fought with Luna...and understand that now. I was...weak."

Then, Emma turned to Luna. "I'm so sorry...that I said you weren't suitable for my master because of your reputation and behavior... Of course you're amazing... My master is always right."

"Erm, it's not like... I chose Luna based on her skills." Rintarou had a complicated expression.

Emma smiled slightly at him.

"Master...and Luna...I hope you continue your hard work. I'm sure Luna is the true King who will get the better of this succession battle. And, master, please make sure you support Luna."

With that, Emma turned on her heel and left.

"What're you going to do now?" Rintarou called out to her.

"You mean...me? ...Right." She stopped in her tracks, gazing at the sky deep in thought for a while...

"I think I'll go home."

"!"

"I just transferred over here, but...since the battle is over for me, I don't have any reason to be here anymore. I was thinking I'd quit school and go back to Orleans, back home..."

Emma's home—the Religious Order of Saint Joan. For possessing King Arthur's blood in her veins, she had been forced into a grueling life, brainwashed and tortured. It was the lair of the inhumane.

"You're... But that's..."

"Yes, I know. I don't think any good will come out of going back to my hometown. Maybe they'll force me to get married to someone to protect King Arthur's bloodline? Or maybe they'll abandon me because I'm not useful anymore? ...But I don't have any parents or relatives. As someone without anyone else in the world, the only place I have to go home to...is there..."

"—Nh?!"

"...Good-bye, master... I'm really happy that I got to see you again..."

At the very end, Emma paid tribute to Rintarou with a soulful smile wet from tears.

Emma started to leave.

As he watched her lonely figure from behind, Rintarou was deep in thought.

She's been released from her cruel fate. She doesn't need to be the King of salvation. She never wanted to be that in the first place. I set her free. It was a drastic measure, but someone had to do it. I wasn't wrong. But she still hasn't been saved.

He should have stopped her. Leaving it at this would be irresponsible. It would mean he hadn't liberated her.

But I don't have the qualifications to do that. On top of destroying her support system, I've been progressively wandering away from living a virtuous life...

Rintarou didn't have the necessary traits. He didn't have anything he could say to her, either.

Any words he could offer would only save face. They wouldn't make a tangible difference.

But fortunately, there is someone here, isn't there? ...There's someone perfect in these situations. Rintarou's mouth secretly twisted up.

Someone had grabbed Emma's shoulder in a vise grip from behind.

"What? ...Just wait a sec, Emma. You thought I'd let you escape?"

It was Luna.

"...Mm? Uh. Um... *Luna?*"

"'I lost. Win in my place. Bye.' ...You really think you can just leave with that little flair of adolescent drama? EM-MA?" Luna smiled incredibly wickedly, and Emma immediately faltered.

"What? Uh... Th-that was... I did cause you a lot of trouble... and I'm very sorry about that, but..."

"Excuuuuse me?! If apologies solved anything, we wouldn't have police and postwar military trials! Now, let's see. What kind of debt should we collect from a failure of a King like you?! Hmm?!"

"E-eep!" Emma was in tears at Luna's mafia-esque menace.

"Right. How about we do this? My place is basically a mansion, and we don't have enough people to do chores… But it's not like we can hire on a normal person. So this is a royal order, Emma! I order you to be a maid at the Logres Manor!"

"Huh?! Whaaaaaaaaaaaaat?!" Emma raised a voice in disarray. "Wh-why would I do *that*?!"

"*What*?! What do you think you're saying? I won, and you lost! It's universal logic that the loser is absolutely obedient to the winner! I have a right over your life, and you're not allowed to deny me! Being the magnanimous King that I am, I forgive your insolent rebellion! In exchange, I'll graciously accept you as one of my followers! You haven't got anything better to do even if you go home, right?! In that case, I'll have you be my humble maid until you find yourself! And you've got to go to school! Got that?!"

"B-buuuut!"

Luna had created a big scene. From the corner of his eyes, Rintarou looked at their little scuffle.

Yeah… This is good. Her pushiness…is the right thing for this occasion.

Rintarou grinned and turned his back.

"Ah, well… Don't tell me this was your little scheme all along." Felicia planted a hand on her hip, grumbling in exasperation at Rintarou.

"Who knows? Well, when it comes to Luna, I had a feeling this is how it'd turn out," he admitted.

"I can't believe that Merlin would take on the hated role to save a girl… Did you hit your head or something?" Sir Gawain looked at Rintarou as though he were observing a strange creature.

"Shut up! God, leave me alone. Oh, by the way… There's something I wanted to say to you all."

Rintarou scratched his head in annoyance and cast a sharp look at Felicia.

"About that fight with Emma and Lamorak..."

Felicia and Sir Gawain steadied themselves, alarmed.

M-my liege, the way this is going..., her Jack thought.

...At this rate, he's going to give us an earful about disappointing him, Felicia finished.

From his behavior, the two sighed, as though they had resigned themselves to their fates.

When they thought back about it, the only one who had been able to directly fight against Sir Lamorak was Rintarou.

The rest of them were just flesh shields to achieve the right number of people.

The two of them readied themselves for Rintarou's scolding...

"...Uh...so about that..."

Unexpectedly, he had something else to say.

"...Felicia...uh, I'm glad you were here...I think. Honestly, if we hadn't had your magic and Excalibur, we would have been goners..."

"...What?"

"And, Gawain...you were also... Uh, I guess you kind of did a good job?"

"Huh."

"I didn't think you could have actually taken a hit from Lamorak and lived through it... You might be a rotten scoundrel, but you're still part of the Round Table, I guess? ...Hmph," Rintarou spat in a low tone.

"Well...it wasn't perfect, but you helped save Emma, too. Thanks... That's all I wanted to say." He snorted and turned his back to them.

"......"
"......"

For a while, Felicia and Sir Gawain let their eyes pop out of their heads, boring their gazes into Rintarou's back...

"You've really gone off the deep eeeend, huh?!"

"M-my liege?! I'm sure Rintarou got his head hit during the battle!"

"H-he must have! Of course! That's it! Just wait, Rintarou! I'll use *Healing* magic on your head right away—"

The pair roared, quickly surrounding Rintarou to apprehend him.

"SHUT IT, YOU TWOOOO!!" Rintarou boomed, forehead twitching in anger. He grabbed each of them with the palms of his hands.

""AAAAAAAAH?!""

He slammed them down on the ground.

The heightened anxiety of the battle must have finally worn out, because the three of them roughhoused each other.

Sir Kay was in front of them.

...Rintarou, Felicia, and Sir Gawain... Each had their own role in this battle... They possess such power...but I... She could only watch them with distant eyes.

Luna had no idea that this plagued her Jack. "Anyway! I just got a cute maid! You better be happy, Rintarou!"

Proudly, Luna gave them a thumbs-up and pulled along the dejected Emma, who looked as though she had submitted to her fate.

"Uh... I don't know the first thing about being a maid, but... I'm in your charge for a while, master..."

"I see, you've got rotten luck. Well, why not? It's way better than going home, right?"

"Th-that might be true…but are you sure you want me getting in your way…?"

"You heard the head of the household. Don't worry about it," Rintarou consoled, and she sighed in worry.

He noticed something else.

This is what you wanted, right? Gosh. You're a troublesome vassal, Rintarou. Luna moved her lips silently from behind Emma, grinning. He instantly read her lips.

"!" Rintarou looked at Luna's smug face and blinked.

…Ah, well, guess I'm no match for my King. In exasperation, he grinned wryly, shrugging in response.

"Hey! Mm! Hmm!" With a beam as bright as the midsummer sun, Luna lifted her right hand and jerked her chin. It seemed she was readying herself for a high five.

"…Okay, okay," Rintarou said as though he didn't have a choice, raising his right hand.

The two of them, neither of them being the initiator, stepped toward each other, and—

CLAP!

Passing by each other, their hands hit the other, echoing through the silent night over their heads.

The King Arthur Succession Battle had only just started.

From here on, they would be able to overcome any hardship in their way. This was what this fight had left them to think—and believe. This ringing sound seemed to reaffirm that.

The next day, they were back at Logres Manor.

"Yoo-hoo! My little maid! You master is home!"

Luna had come home later than usual—held up at a student council meeting at Camelot International. She kicked the front door open and barged through the entrance hall.

Behind Luna, Rintarou sighed and scratched his head. Nayuki Fuyuse peeked into the grounds, her eyes fluttering.

"We've brought an important guest from the student council today! Here, take her to the drawing room quickly and get some tea ready!"

"Waaah. Uhhhh, y-yes, master..." Emma greeted them in a maid uniform and teary eyes.

"Oh, what? I had no idea Emma lived here, too. But why is she wearing that...?"

"Ugh... Please don't ask, Nayuki..."

In the earlier Rintarou Pursual Battle, Nayuki had learned to recognize Emma's face. She tilted her head as Emma's shoulders drooped, avoiding any clear statements.

"Um... Luna? Why am *I* a maid, too?"

Next to Emma...in the same maid outfit, Sir Kay was also in tears.

Ignoring the pitiful duo, Luna turned to Nayuki. "Heh, Nayuki! What do you think? This is my castle! Isn't it grand?!"

"Y-yeah... I can't believe you have servants *and* live in this luxurious mansion... Luna, you're amazing. Of course, I suppose that's expected from a high-class English family... But why is Emma...?"

"Ha-ha. I know, right? Come on in! Relax! We're all going to start having a tea party—stat!"

"Um...Luna...?"

"You can't say anything to change my mind, Sir Kay... Hurry and prep the tea for our guest..."

Resigned to this new job, Emma and Sir Kay passed by Luna's crew.

"Hmm? Luna, you're back."

"Oh, welcome home, Luna."

Felicia and Sir Gawain appeared in the landing of the stairs.

Felicia was in her normal attire—a gothic dress. But Sir Gawain looked unusually casual in a tank top and military pants instead of his normal knightly attire.

"I'm home! Oh, Nayuki, I'll introduce you! That's Felicia. She's one of the Feralds, a distinguished noble family in northern Ireland, and that's her attendant, Gawain."

"A—a noblewoman and her attendant... N-nice to meet you! I'm the secretary from the student council! My name is Nayuki Fuyuse! Sorry for intruding into your space!" Nayuki was bashful after hearing about their titles.

"Hee-hee, it's my pleasure to meet you as well, Miss Nayuki." Pinching up the edge of her skirt, Felicia elegantly bowed.

Nayuki breathed out a sound of admiration.

"Felicia, we're going to have a tea party right now. Would you like to join?"

"Oh? Are you sure?"

"Of course!"

"I see. Then I'll be pleased to join you. Sir Gawain?"

"Yes! Of course, I will join you, my liege!"

Felicia and Sir Gawain continued to the drawing room.

"I—I remember you telling me all this, but...Rintarou, it seems like you're sharing a house with some amazing people... It's like they're from a whole other world..." Nayuki lowered her voice, cautiously speaking to Rintarou on their way over.

"Hmm, well, uh...it kind of like...fell into my lap..."

Rintarou had no choice but to be ambiguous.

"To tell you the truth, she bought this house with *my* money, so I don't know why Luna is acting like she owns the place..."

"Huh? What? Did you say something?"

"Nothing... Nothing at all," Rintarou deceived with a shrug.

"Really? ...Anyway...it feels fun and exciting here. It's nice."

"You think so? Seems noisy to me."

"I live alone in an apartment that used to be a boardinghouse... so maybe I'm just a little jealous that it's animated. It's the exact opposite of my home."

"Seriously? In that case, do you want to come here, too? We've got rooms to spare," he suggested jokingly.

"Ah-ha... Right. I might...take you up on that sometime."

Nayuki flashed him a slightly mischievous smile.

"Hey, Rintarou?" Nayuki gently asked. "How is your life with... Luna and everyone? Is it fun?"

"Hmm?"

There was something deeper to Nayuki's question. He could feel it.

Rintarou tilted his head.

"Well, I'm not bored," he answered bluntly.

But when she observed his profile, it seemed he wasn't altogether displeased...

"...Ha-ha, good." Nayuki looked at Rintarou, softly smiling.

On that day, they say the tea party was particularly fun—with Rintarou, Luna, Sir Kay, Felicia, Sir Gawain, Emma, and their guest of honor, Nayuki Fuyuse, all in attendance.

AFTERWORD

Hello! It's Taro Hitsuji.

We've managed to publish the second volume of *Last Round Arthurs*!

From the bottom of my heart, I am grateful for the editors, the people involved in its publication, and the readers who picked up this book. Thank you!

When you think about major characters other than Merlin and King Arthur in Arthurian legend, you might gravitate toward the famous ones: Sir Lancelot, Sir Gawain, and Sir Tristan, to name a few. But Thomas Malory's *The Legends of King Arthur* has a mob of many other charismatic characters.

In this volume, I wanted to place the spotlight on my favorite knight in Malory's tale—Sir Lamorak of Gales.

Sir Lamorak is a particular weirdo, a mass of pride with incredible arrogance. But his bravery makes him one of the cornerstones of the Round Table, among the strongest, next to Sir Lancelot and Sir Tristan.

(Well, according to Malory's version, Sir Gawain is technically a mid-level knight. He's pretty mediocre, and he's really missing that "wow" factor. Even if he had a supplementary power that increased his strength threefold, there are a whole gang of other knights who could have still beaten the living daylights out of him.)

Sir Lamorak's egotism is no joke. During one particular match after a bunch of successive battles, he was supposed to have another battle with Sir Tristan.

"Battling you in this fatigue state goes against the ways of chivalry," his opponent said. "Let us battle once more the next day."

He was a really considerate gentleman, you see.

"What?" Sir Lamorak barked back. "Are you trying to say that my tired state has no value to fight? Piss off."

And he ended up getting really upset. But his huge ego suited him, as Sir Lamorak was powerful as a knight.

Sir Lamorak is strong. He's desperately strong. In the original work, there isn't much mention of him losing a battle. He beat Sir Gawain and Sir Palamedes and other super-strong knights. In one match, he defeated five hundred knights. He was an unparalleled character alongside Sir Lancelot and equally matched by Sir Tristan. If we just look at fights on horseback, he's even won against Sir Tristan.

But in the modern day, it seems the seat of the strongest knight has been usurped by Sir Gawain for some reason. I'm willing to bet there are people who don't even know about the existence of Sir Lamorak.

That's probably because there was *that one thing* that Sir Gawain had done to Sir Lamorak. It might also be because Sir Gawain would end up in a small role if Sir Lamorak made his appearance.

There's even a theory that Cú Chulainn—that great Celtic hero—was used as a model for Sir Gawain. To bring Sir Gawain to the limelight, Sir Lamorak needed to be offed.

But that's got nothing to do with *Last Round Arthurs*! I made this weirdo even stranger in my interpretation of the texts—giving her a grand old entrance in this volume! I feel like I may have made a liiiiittle mistake in adapting her character, but I have no regrets!

(Also, Sir Lamorak is actually from England but uses Latin for...um, *reasons*. But it's kind of like when Japanese folks toss in some English when we're putting on airs. You get it, right?)

It would be great to keep expanding my own legends of King Arthur.

I have to extend a great deal of gratitude again to Kiyotaka Haimura, who is in charge of the illustrations. Thank you for the stunning illustrations for this volume. I cannot thank you enough for bringing this story to life with your gorgeous depictions.

And here's a small little announcement. It's been decided that *Last Round Arthurs* is going to become a comic in *Young Ace* magazine! I'm really looking forward to seeing how the world will take on a life of its own, even as the author!

I am so fortunate to have all of you cheer this series on.

I hope that will be the case in the future, too.

Taro Hitsuji